Chapter 1

L ady Rachel Denby faced the altar of the cold stone church trying her best to keep a straight face. The situation was hardly humorous. She kept telling herself that. But the dour, youthful curate, and the severe bridegroom beside her, were making the corners of her generous mouth twitch. The curate, obtained on short notice with her bridegroom's special licence, had just spent several minutes explaining the solemnity of the occasion. But still...

She took a deep breath, schooling her countenance, drawing her shoulders back and thrusting her chin up to better stare down her nose seriously at the fair-haired man clad in a white surplice before her. He had frowned at her twice when she had insisted on voicing her agreement to his statements. She could not help it. When Rachel came across individuals with an enhanced sense of their own status, taking them down a peg or two seemed the only right course of action. But apparently, the curate did not need confirmation from Rachel that God thought marriage was a holy covenant, or that it was to prevent fornication. It had quite put him off his recital of the marriage service.

She glimpsed Nellie out of the corner of her eye. Her loyal maid had offered nothing but service faced with her mistress' sudden marriage. Then there was Viscount Arleigh's valet Jeffries stood beside the maid. That made up the entire party.

She risked a glance at her bridegroom. His gaze was fixed ahead, his lips tightly pinched, with no intention of staring lovingly into his bride's eyes. The thought almost sent Rachel off into peals of laughter. She clamped down on the rebellious smile. Her bridegroom had not appreciated her humorous asides to the curate and she did not think he would enjoy her laughter during his repetition of the vows.

His expression, as cold as the air in the church that morning, was not exactly the expression a bride would hope for on her wedding day. But Rachel was not a bride of the common sort. She had been through this before. When she was sixteen, a suitable match had been selected for her, she had participated in the mandatory period of courting, and she had married with all the neighbourhood in attendance. None of that rigmarole was needed here. It was understood. A simple business transaction between herself and

A Dangerous Deal

Ladies of Worth Series

Philippa Jane Keyworth

Passalande Books

Works by Philippa Jane Keyworth

Historical Romance Novels

The Widow's Redeemer
The Unexpected Earl
Fool Me Twice
A Dangerous Deal

Fantasy Novels

The Edict

Historical Anthology

Castles, Customs, and Kings: True Tales by
English Historical Fiction Authors

Lord Arleigh. She needed Lord Arleigh just as he needed her. It was plain. It was simple. It was their deal.

"I require and charge you both..." The curate's crisp voice carried easily in the church. His grey eyes refused to catch Rachel's again. No more disruptions.

Good. She needed this alliance and the quicker they entered into it the better. Lord Arleigh had promised her security and independence. It was necessary, for she had been on the brink of throwing herself on her parents' mercy. Conditional mercy. That had always been the way. Do this, behave this way, marry that suitable gentleman. She would not be returning to the shelter of their roof. There was no need for such extremes—not now. She had no desire to be thrown into their power again, even now, when widowhood had overtaken her. Soon she would be a widow no more. Better than that, she would be indebted to no one, because her marriage to Arleigh was as much for his convenience as for her own.

Imagine if the curate knew the cynical nature of this wedding. Then again, this was how the ton operated. There was little room for love and affection where property and land were concerned. Those particular afflictions were a happy coincidence rather than a planned future and they happened to the few. Her first marriage had not been affected by such sentimentality. She had married where she had been bid, though—she noted with a quick upturn of her wide lips —she had not done so willingly. How she had screamed. The servants had mistaken the disturbances for someone dying and called the local doctor. But her father had always been relentless in his will, and though she had taken after him, there was only so much a woman could do, especially a young one. But she was no longer a young woman. Her position had changed and after this wedding, she would be mistress of her own fate. No master would be needed.

It had not been her intention to be widowed just yet. Not before she had provided an heir and secured her future at Godalming Hall. But nature was not always inclined to bend to the will of woman, no matter how desperate her desire. She pushed back the feelings that rose from some deep, dark place within her and focused.

She need only get through this marriage service and then she would be able to discard this stiff, uncomfortable gown that had already seen one wedding. She had not told the Viscount that. She doubted he would approve, but the speed of their wedding had necessitated the reuse of a gown. Of all the ones she owned, this one was, after all, the most appropriate. At least, she thought, as the curate droned interminably on, her dead husband's estate had backed onto a friend of Viscount Arleigh's. Otherwise she might never have met him and been given this opportunity for salvation. She had grabbed it with both hands, but then so had he. One must admit, Lord Arleigh's circumstances were less than normal. In fact, they were as peculiar, if not more so, than hers. It was the reason this deal had been struck.

After a respectable amount of time had passed, they would set up separate households and both their purposes would be served. Rachel would enjoy relative freedom, with a tidy sum for her independence. Lord Arleigh would have adhered to his father's oddly specific will, that his son marry by eight-and-twenty to receive his inheritance. To be perfectly honest, it was a very neat and tidy arrangement. Rachel was pleased with herself for thinking of such an excellent solution.

The curate was going on, rambling nervously so that Rachel lost interest. Fortunately she did not have to wait long for the important part.

"Wilt thou, Lord Julius James Andrew Arleigh, have this woman to thy wedded wife, to live together after God's ordinance in the holy estate of matrimony? Wilt thou love her, comfort her, honour, and keep her, in sickness and in health; and, forsaking all others, keep thee only unto her, so long as ye both shall live?"

"I will."

Fancy that. Without so much as a glance at her or a murmur of hesitation.

"And wilt thou, Lady Rachel Constance Denby, have this man to thy wedded husband, to live together after God's ordinance in the holy estate of matrimony? Wilt thou obey him, and serve him, love, honour, and keep him, in sickness and in health; and, forsaking all others, keep thee only unto him, so long as ye both shall live?"

"I will." That voice didn't sound like hers. All animation was lost in her pragmatic tone. "And if you could hurry a little, curate, my shivering limbs would be most obliged."

He jerked his head up and down, almost dropping his bible, and her betrothed, for the first time, turned towards her briefly.

She saw his glance rise from somewhere below her neck to her eyes, catching them with an unfathomable look, and then turning away. He offered a curt nod to the minister which the frightened young man took as his cue.

It was hardly her fault that they were getting married at eight o'clock in the morning when the temperature was well below acceptable levels in this draughty old building. Even the Puritan Cromwell would have cursed the cold. Apparently her outburst worked, for the curate tripped along with the next bit of the service and before she knew it, he was passing her hand to that of her bridegroom. She felt the cold of the jewelled gold ring as it was threaded along her finger. It matched the temperature of his hands. She wasn't the only one feeling the cold. Or perhaps they were nerves on his part. It was his first wedding after all.

"With this ring I thee wed, with my body I thee worship, and with all my worldly goods I thee endow: In the name of the Father, and of the Son, and of the Holy Ghost. Amen."

With his worldly goods. That part was music to her ears. When the hastily bought ring was installed on its rightful finger, they obeyed the curate and knelt for his prayer of blessing. He held their hands together and spoke those fateful words,

"Those whom God hath joined together let no man put asunder."

Rachel's brows rose a fraction and for a brief moment she could not look the man of God in the eye.

He made the pronouncement soon after and spoke several more blessings. Then it was over. They rose and walked towards a back room in which the register was laid out. A few dips in the ink pot, slashes across the page in clear, bold lettering, and they were married.

Lord Arleigh thanked the curate and then offered his new wife a courteous arm.

"I had best fetch Nellie. She has barely had a moment to understand these rapid proceedings."

"I can assure you Jeffries will not leave her behind."

He didn't speak with a peeved tone, nor

show a hint of frustration. He did not speak with any expression whatsoever.

Rachel did not budge.

"As you wish," he said when she did not respond. "I shall meet you at the doors, if convenient." He bowed her out.

Rachel strode from the room in the hopes that the quick movement might warm her chilled limbs.

"Well, I never," said Nellie the moment her mistress came upon her. She had dealt well with the shock of the sudden wedding, and Rachel was pleased to see a bright smile on her maid's face now. "Congratulations, my lady, Lady Arleigh. I only hope you do not catch a chill." Nellie's fine little hands grasped around at her large shawl pulling it tighter.

"So do I, Nellie. Come, we shall warm ourselves at his lordship's fires!"

Rachel hated to admit it, but for a brief moment her easy resolution had faltered when she had seen the ink dry on the register. Her talkative maid Nellie had been with her for years and she always had something to say which was calm and reassuring.

Feeling much more the thing, she took her gloves from Nellie's outstretched hands and marched with her maid in tow to the waiting man at the door. He dutifully took her on his arm for the few feet to the carriage and handed her up, while Nellie and Jeffries took the smaller vehicle behind.

"It is done then." He was turned away from her, his eyes on the rapidly retreating church outside the carriage window.

"Yes, and tolerably quickly—and you will be thankful to hear that will be the last time you need hold my hand." She refrained from adding, *and show me affection*, for even the thought of it caused her to start smiling. He could not have looked more coerced during the ceremony than if he'd had a loaded flintlock pressed against his spine.

Lord Arleigh did not respond. His lips pursed even further.

"Just think what Rebecca will say," she mused aloud. And what of her parents? That particular musing could wait at least a day.

"You speak of your sister?" He asked in a tone that did not invite a response. He was being polite, Rachel thought, as though it were an ingrained behaviour he could not shake even in this unusual situation. She found his eyes briefly but he failed to hold her gaze.

"I imagine," said Arleigh in pragmatic tones, "she will believe, like the rest of London, that we have taken leave of our senses."

"Oh, she already knows that of me. You, I suppose, will be a shock." Rachel threw her gloves into a corner of the carriage and slumped back. "Oh come, 'tis naught but a joke," she replied to his frown. "You must know I have a sense of humour if we are to be married."

"We *are* married," he corrected without pause. "Three months," he said, looking back out the window. "That should be sufficient time to satisfy the requirements of my father's will."

"Well, then you shall only have to laugh at my jokes for that long. I am sure you shall do tolerably well." She pulled out her hat pin which had been ill-placed that morning and removed the whole from her head. She sent it the same way as her gloves and sighed in relief at the loss of pressure from her head.

"A pretty ring," she said, admiring the emerald gem on her wedding finger. "I feel a fraud wearing it — perhaps you had better order a replica in paste."

"Madam," said her new husband curtly. "Your flippancy is hardly appreciated."

"Very well," said Rachel, straightening in her seat and looking very much the injured party. "But I don't see why you should be in such a foul mood. I have just become financially secure and you shall receive your inheritance. It is our wedding day after all!"

She caught him grimacing at her crass mention of money.

"It is no done deal—sordid though it is. My family must be deceived or the sham will be found out and I shall receive nothing."

"Sordid! I am not sordid and nor is the deal I proposed to you. It is as ingenious as it is clean. As good as any business deal. You should at least acknowledge our initial success." When his expression didn't change, she added, "If you continue with that face of yours, the wind will change, and you will stay like that forever." She raised her hands in surrender at the look he flashed in her direction. "Very well. I shall desist in my flippancy, but not my relief."

"Of course—you are to be a rich and independent woman when this is over."

"You make me sound the very caricature of a fortune hunter," she said, matching the sharpness in his tone. He clearly regretted his decision already. This marriage was off to a triumphant start. At least they only had to bear with each other's company for three months.

"You knew my circumstances when you agreed to this, as I knew yours." She spoke those first words with amiability but not the next. "I would ask that you kindly stop making a cake of yourself."

He unfolded his arms at that.

"I shall uphold my end of the bargain," said Rachel, "and perform beautifully for your family, but a word of advice—it is your acting that needs polish. Perhaps one small smile on your wedding day?"

As they pulled up outside Lord Arleigh's London home in Grosvenor Square, there had never been a married couple more at odds with each other so shortly after their wedding. Rachel shot a meaningful smile at her new husband as she was handed down from the carriage. It was not long before Lord Arleigh displayed one too, but Rachel thought it more akin to a snarl.

"I hope you are not tempting my wife with more fripperies, Lady Rebecca. You have spent quite enough of my wife's money—thank you."

Felton flicked up his cane and pushed a number of ribbons away from Caro Felton's large blue eyes. The draper holding them scowled at him.

"Oh pish!" Lady Rebecca Fairing flicked her fan shut and rapped Felton's cane thrice. "I have done no such thing, and besides, there is no harm in keeping one's eyes on the current fashions. My dear," she said, turning to address Caro. "This is why bringing your husband on such an outing is dreadfully ill-conceived. At least when we bring your brother, we manage to obtain such useful information as to the quality of the textiles we are handling."

"Very true." Caro linked arms with Rebecca and guided her from the shop onto one of London's busy streets. "There are benefits to having a brother in the cloth trade."

They stepped out beside carts and carriages and riders. Hawkers swelled the ranks of the passers-by. Ladies and gentlemen of every shape, size and age—all of the fashionable bent—milled and walked and talked and shopped.

"Excellent."

"What?" Rebecca called over her shoulder at Felton.

He followed behind them at a leisurely pace, unaffected by the jostling crowds.

"Don't humour him, Rebecca."

"Humour him?" She flashed her dark brown eyes over her shoulder and caught Felton's gaze fully intent on the figure of his wife.

"Is he…"

"… happy to walk behind us?" Caro finished for Rebecca. "He has recently taken it into his head that he much prefers the…" Caro blushed. "… the view if he walks at least five paces behind me."

"Scandalous!" Rebecca cried over her shoulder. "I should call you a scoundrel if Caro had not been your wife these last seven months."

Felton only laughed, and Caro did her best to ignore both the offended and the offender. It was enough to negotiate the swathe of people.

"Well," said Rebecca, before an uncharacteristic pause.

Caro knew what question was coming.

"Where is your brother? I have not seen him for several weeks."

"Now?" Caro responded mildly to the enquiry. "He should be halfway through his return trip across the Atlantic. He had hoped to stay in London until the outbreak of war in the colonies. It has been essential for him to continue fostering old and new trade associations during the upheaval."

"I suspect he is as irritated with those colonial upstarts as the King."

"Actually, I do believe he rather admires them. He said he has been reading Adam Smith's works and it has quite opened his eyes to an alternative form of trade."

"Well, I am sure I would like to hear about that when he is back."

"Would you?" asked Caro, a smile hovering about her lips.

"Oh." Rebecca rapped her fan across Caro's gloved fingers with little force. "Do not look at me so, you know how it vexes me."

"Very well—but don't say such silly things."

"Silly! How dare you. Perhaps a book on the economy is just the thing to keep me from buying fripperies. Wouldn't you agree, Felton?"

"Forgive me ladies, I'm afraid I was quite side-tracked." He came alongside them.

"Lady Rebecca was just saying she wished to look at some enlightened reading on the economy."

"James again?"

"I believe so."

The couple exchanged a conspiratorial grin.

"You two are working hand in glove with one another. I declare that ever since you married, I have been outgunned." She broke away from them. "Quite outgunned!"

"Oh come, Rebecca!" Caro's outstretched arm could not reach the rapidly striding woman, her efforts made all the more challenging by the fact she could not stop giggling.

Caro was so busy wiping tears of laughter from her eyes that she ran straight into the back of her friend. Recovering herself with her husband's help, she found Rebecca standing stockstill, staring after a black and yellow carriage as it dissolved into the London traffic.

"Rebecca? What is it?"

"My sister!" Rebecca's shocked face kept watching after the vehicle. "That was her in Lord Arleigh's carriage, I'm sure of it."

"But I thought you said she was still in mourning in Gloucestershire?"

"I did. I thought she was. What on earth is she doing with Lord Arleigh?"

Chapter 2

The wedding breakfast was a thoroughly awkward affair. It was hardly what a schoolroom miss would have dreamed of, but fortunately for Rachel, she was neither a schoolroom miss nor naïve enough to dream.

"Would my lady desire more?" asked the footman holding a silver dish of sweetmeats and creating a small mountain on Rachel's plate. He had already asked that question twice and her answers each time were in the affirmative.

"Well, yes, if there is to be only these as a sweet course, I shall have my fill."

"The arrangements were last minute," Lord Arleigh replied peevishly. "Had my cook had sufficient time to prepare, I'm sure he would have more than satisfied your desire for sweets."

"I doubt any cook could satisfy my sweet tooth." Rachel's full lips curled up into a smile and she popped another sugared almond onto her tongue. "An inheritance from my father— my husband never could abide it." She stopped abruptly, dropping the next sweetmeat onto her plate, making the porcelain clink. "Though I suppose you are my husband now." She spoke it so simply, the full realisation still bedding in. "What a funny thing it is—to be a widow in the morning and a married woman by midday."

"Are you feeling quite well?" asked her new husband, without the warmth of concern.

"I shall not have an attack of the vapours if that is what you fear." She resumed eating the candied nuts. "It has merely been a productive day, do you not think?"

"Productive?" Lord Arleigh dismissed the servants with an agitated flick of his fingers. He continued, "It occurs to me that since our agreeing to marry several days ago, time has moved quickly and… productively."

Rachel watched him lean back from the plate of food he had barely touched and draw the tips of his fingers slowly together.

"Yes," she said, realising that his green eyes would not break from hers until she acknowledged his statement.

"We are married, and you are now Viscountess Arleigh. As such…"

Rachel knew how this line of conversation went. Her first husband, Sir Denby, had used this dull, governess-like tone with her before, and it had meant only one thing. He was going to tell her to behave.

No matter the justifications or frustrations, Rachel had always been told to behave. In fact, she had been told so often that she was quite honestly sick of it. More than that, she was not going to be told again, especially by a man assuming more of his agreed role than he ought.

"There are certain expectations that come with assuming this title, and I have heard, as with the rest of Town, that your habits are less than conventional. I had assumed you would have realised your responsibility in this deal…"

"A deal, that is precisely it," Rachel cut in, all joviality gone. "We struck a deal that would see us both freed from financial troubles," she carried on despite the look of shock at her interruption. "I shall uphold my end as I have already promised, but if you think for one minute you will have me behaving like a meek little church mouse, then you are entirely wrong. We will live separately, as if we were merely brother and sister, or better yet, mild acquaintances—and I don't know what it is you have heard," she said, rising from her chair and swinging the wide skirts of her dress so that she could move around the table, "but you are in no position to complain. You needed to marry me quite as much as I needed to marry you."

Lord Arleigh stared at her in silence for several moments before rising from his own chair and, rather than answering, delving into the embroidered pocket of his coat and withdrawing a beautiful golden snuff box. He flipped the engraved lid and proceeded to take some, all the while, his eyes fast on Rachel.

But she would not be cowed. She had spent too long being commanded by the men in her life. First her father, marrying her off to Sir Denby. Then Sir Denby forever telling her how to dress her hair, what was wrong with her choice of dress and how her conversation on horseflesh and gruesome history was neither ladylike, nor becoming in a well-bred wife. She was not going to stand for that shabby treatment anymore.

For the first time in her life, she was going to be independent and able to set up her own establishment. She need only wait three months, but they needn't be three months of torture. She was as sensible to Lord Arleigh's position as her own. His part for her was largely completed, barring of course the little issue of the separation, but he needed her even more now and she knew it.

"It seems I have got into bed with a snake." Lord Arleigh snapped his snuff box shut and returned it to his pocket. "They told me you were unconventional—but such venom."

Was that humour?

"You have gotten into bed with no one, my lord," she responded airily.

"Husband, please."

He was funning with her! In fact, for the first time since she had met him a short while ago, he looked mildly amused.

"Husband," she returned, unconsciously relaxing. "And you shall certainly not be getting into my bed. We wished to be husband and wife in name alone, did we not?"

"I don't think anyone *wishes* for such a thing, dear wife," he replied sardonically.

"Whatever." Rachel waved a hand at him, ignoring the implication of his words. "But perhaps we should have a discussion of such matters," she said prosaically. "I am fully aware, having been a married woman, of a man's particular needs. Once Society has stopped ringing with the news of our hasty nuptials and we have our separate abodes established, I shall be deaf and blind to whatever goings-on you decide to undertake."

She saw her pragmatism catch him a little off guard.

"Madam, you continue to amaze me with your unorthodox manner. I fear I have married an eccentric."

"Fear all you want," replied Rachel placidly. "It shan't change the truth of the fact. I do not mean to embarrass you but..."

Lord Arleigh held up a carefully manicured finger. "I am hardly blushing, Lady... Arleigh, I was merely surprised at your candour."

"Why?" she asked, a brow arched and a challenging look in her eye. "Did you suppose I was married for five years without experiencing the marriage bed?"

She had hoped to ruffle him, something

she enjoyed doing to others, but she caught the surreptitious glance at her stomach.

She turned away from his gaze and the air became tense with unspoken questions. Then, quite suddenly, Rachel turned, all animation back in her face.

"I find myself quite worn out, my... husband. If it is agreeable to you, I shall go and rest for a while."

"Yes," he said, not waylaying her. "I have had the rooms adjoining mine made up for the servants' benefit. Your maid is no doubt available."

"I don't need, Nellie," replied Rachel, making for the door. "Just directions."

"The footman shall take you." He pulled the bell, his face puzzled by the continuing unconventional behaviour.

"Very well." She waited at the door for one to appear, her eyes averted from her recently acquired husband.

As she ascended the stairs of her new home, she took nothing in. It had been a bizarre day and she had no doubt tomorrow would be all the more confounding.

Lady Rebecca threw down a letter on the table

where Caro was pouring her husband's tea.

"There, you see!" Rebecca cried, no thought to splashed tea or rattling crockery.

"That awful Lady Goring has been so vile as to send me a congratulatory note. She says bravo to my sister for marrying twice so young— young is underlined as a snub to myself—and she is saying that Lord Arleigh has married my sister. My sister!" She was pacing and crying out, her hat and gloves not yet removed. "I have written to Rachel twice since I thought I saw her, expecting her to write to me and explain that my eyes were playing tricks on me. I thought she would tell me that she was safe in Godalming. Yet here it is in black and white! Only the Lord knows how that conniving Countess got wind of it. I swear she has half the servants in London on her pay. I cannot describe how shocked I am."

"Goodness!" said Caro when she finally got the chance. "But how can that be—I thought your sister in Surrey as you did? I have never heard you speak of her holding a tendre for Lord Arleigh. I don't recall him having set his cap at any woman yet."

Rebecca threw her hands in the air sending her fur muff sailing over Felton's head. It fell to the floor and rolled beneath a side table. "This is just like Rachel, to do something so outlandish, though she usually tells me—her own sister—at least a little of her plans. How could she be so heartless as to let me find out from that woman?

There was no tendre to speak of between her and Lord Arleigh as far as I was concerned! I've never even heard her mention him. I can't even think of when she would have met him. I have only seen him a few times in London myself."

"He's a peculiar one, is Arleigh," Felton offered, looking the most relaxed out of the three. "Can't trust a fellow who talks as little as him."

"I hardly think that is a reason to..." started Caro.

"But why didn't she tell me?"

"Oh Rebecca." Caro turned from husband to friend. "Perhaps they had to keep it a secret for some reason unknown to you."

"Well," Rebecca sniffed, "I cannot understand why I must be kept in the dark with the rest of Society. I am her sister after all."

"As I said." Felton's voice was as languid as ever in the face of such drama. "That Arleigh fellow is the silent sort. I am hardly surprised no one knew. Not even you."

Caro shot her husband a fiery look to which he replied with one of his irresistible winks. She pointedly ignored it and turned back to her friend.

"There must be a reasonable explanation."

"Reasonable? Well, my upset is not, for that isn't the whole of it." Rebecca swept an elegant hand over the discarded paper on the table. "Aunt Etheridge has already told me there are rumours circulating that the wedding was a rushed affair. There is talk of a special licence and not a relative in sight. Scandal is brewing!" The usual delight she took in such societal goings on had disappeared now she found herself in the middle of one. "I think my sister must have lost her mind."

"Perhaps it is love?" Caro suggested.

"I can't think of anything less likely. Her first husband has been dead less than a year and that marriage was not..." Rebecca trailed off in a most uncharacteristic manner. The swift, witty words that were wont to pour from her mouth had dried up at the source.

Felton straightened slightly in his chair, his quick green eyes pinging back and forth as the conversation unfolded between the two women.

"Could there have been a reason other than love?" asked Caro. "Perhaps a complication with her husband's estate that she would need to be married quickly? Perhaps Lord Arleigh was impatient?"

Rebecca suddenly fell to her knees before Caro, taking hold of her hands and pressing them hard.

"You don't understand. There is something not right. My dear, dear Caro, you must come with me. I must go at once to Lord Arleigh's and see her, but I... I fear I cannot face it alone."

"I would not wish to face that fellow

alone. Did you hear he's a crack shot at forty paces?"

"Darling, that is not providing comfort to poor Rebecca."

"Yes, *poor* Rebecca does not appreciate those kinds of facts at all!" Rebecca shot Felton a venomous glance. "And in repayment for exacerbating my nerves, you shall lend me your wife, you wretched man."

"I concede." Felton inclined his head and laid back in his chair again. "I am off to meet Avers at the club anyway. Have fun on your adventure." He kissed his wife on the lips without a thought to company. "Do not get into any coils, darling. I do not think my wound has fully healed from the last one yet." He touched a hand to his side and winked teasingly once again.

"Wicked man," Caro chided.

"And I command you to bring my wife back to me before long and without any lead holes." His voice was surprisingly firm, as were his green eyes, when he addressed Rebecca. She seemingly paid him no heed and he bowed to them both and left.

It did not take long to be ready and when they entered Rebecca's waiting carriage, Caro could see her friend's nerves had not lessened. She plucked irritably at her embroidered sleeves as if attempting to make out a tune.

"I swear, that husband of yours is enough to drive a woman to violence."

"I agree." Caro refused the chuckle that begged to be set free. Her friend was in a state of great agitation. It did not need to be made worse.

∞ ∞ ∞

The two women travelled rapidly through London's streets, only twice becoming stuck at crossings, firstly due to an ice cart manoeuvring, and secondly because an unfortunate wagon had overturned, spilling its produce hither and thither.

Before half an hour was up, they had drawn up outside an attractive Town house. It was situated upon a road of particularly distinguished looking dwellings hemmed in by railings and heavy doors. Caro descended from the carriage after her friend, but both of them hesitated before the steps of the house to which they wished to gain entrance.

When they regained the resolve that had briefly deserted them and went up to request entry, they found the door was opened by a fresh-faced, young man in livery. He politely bid them good morning and asked their purpose.

"Here," Rebecca replied tartly, handing the servant her calling card.

The man betrayed his youth by allowing

a questioning look to pass briefly over his countenance at the name he read in gilt.

"Yes," Rebecca said a little impatiently. "I am the sister of your new mistress and have only recently been informed this is her address. I have come to pay her a visit."

The footman's eyes lit up at the curt words and the flicker of a smile passed across his unschooled face.

"You are Lady Arleigh's sister, ma'am?"

"Of course I am. Lady Rebecca Fairing. Though I suppose you should hardly know."

"I will see if she is at home, Lady Rebecca."

"Yes, I don't doubt you will, and we shall wait in the hall rather than the street, I thank you." Before he could stop her, Rebecca had walked past him and pulled off her gloves. She handed them along with her hat to the footman. "I am certain she will be at home for me."

The footman looked less than certain but nodded all the same and went on his way, calling card in hand. Rebecca took a quick circuit of the entrance hall, her nose rising higher and higher until she came to a huffing stop before Caro.

"Well! It's dreadfully bare isn't it? One would expect at least a little more modish furniture in a viscount's home—that empty alcove is positively depressing—and not even a single flower, though they have only been married a few days. Where are the garlands?"

"I think it is a fine hall. Not everyone has a

liking for ornaments and things like that."

"Fashionable décor does not count as *things*, my dear. I would not demean it with such a nondescript title." The accompanying sauciness was not present in Rebecca's eyes in spite of her tone. "No, I cannot like it. It is hardly cosy."

"Since when do you think I care about cosy, Becky?"

Both visitors spun on their heels, eyes alighting on the statuesque woman who spoke from an open door at the end of the hall.

Caro had met Lady Rachel Denby née Fairing only once, shortly before her own wedding, on a brief visit Rebecca's sister had made to Town. She looked very much the same, if perhaps a little more imposing in this grand house. Rachel was taller than her younger sister, with a similarly Amazonian frame, and almost identical chocolate brown curls. That being said, Rachel's figure was hard to make out beneath the highly unusual outfit she was wearing, and her curling locks were rioting free of the weak ribbon that had perhaps once contained them. The unpowdered hair was a tumult of curls, tangled and wild, the blue-green ribbon clinging to a final lock by her right shoulder. Her entire frame was swathed in a gentleman's silk banyan, her feet bare on the cool wood floor, and a stiff muslin chemisette hiding her décolletage where the banyan's masculine cut was wont to reveal her feminine charms to the world. It was amazing that a woman wearing so strange an outfit could have such presence.

"Well, Becky? Are you here to insult my hallway or greet me?"

"Rachel!"

"Yes?" replied the older sister, her dark eyes sharp and bright.

"You are barely dressed! Is..." Rebecca looked away, a blush stealing up her usually immune cheeks. "Is that your husband's?" A judgemental finger pointed to the banyan.

"This?" Rachel replied calmly, a hand spreading over the silk drapery of her covering. "Goodness gracious no! It was Sir Denby's." She dropped her hand from her dress as if that settled the matter and turned to another subject. "Lord Arleigh said the announcement would be in today's papers. Do you want tea? Dear Caro, you are looking so delightfully beautiful. Marriage clearly agrees with you. Where is that dashing husband of yours?" She turned before hearing an answer, her presence commanding implicitly that the others follow her across the hall and through the open door from whence she had come.

Rebecca was not left speechless for long. She snatched up her skirts and marched after her sister. Caro followed them into a small drawing room painted in pale yellow and home to the morning sun. The mistress of the house was already beside the fireplace, pulling the bell rope when Rebecca cornered her.

"Rachel! In the papers. How could you not think to tell me? Goodness, I am honestly left to think you are touched in the head by the way you are acting. As if none of this is completely ridiculous—and that banyan—what are you thinking wearing that in your new husband's home? What can he think?"

"Oh, I have not seen him this morning," said Rachel with a wave of her hand, unperturbed by her sister's outburst and seemingly missing the point. "Please sit down." She took a seat herself on a chaise longue, her banyan draping attractively across her legs in plentiful folds. In this light, Caro had to own, the worn silk threads and oriental pattern that had seemed faded a moment ago, were brought out in breathtaking vibrancy.

"I certainly shall not—no, you will give me an explanation."

"Oh Becky, what more is there to it? I am married. There, you have it all."

"Do mama and papa know?" Rebecca continued to pace the room, every now and then throwing a glance of disbelief at her sister.

"They should receive my letter tomorrow."

Rebecca halted, her mouth hanging open. "You mean you didn't even tell papa before you married?"

"Becky," said her sister with a modicum of

gentleness. "I didn't have to. After Sir Denby died, I became independent, in a manner of speaking. Ah, Mrs Banshaw, lovely, thank you. Please set it down here."

A small, thin woman, whom Caro took to be the housekeeper, deposited the heavily laden silver tray on the table in the centre of the room.

"I'm assuming you still take inordinate amounts of sugar in yours, Becky. Caro, how do you take your tea?"

"Strong and with generous milk."

Rachel looked at her quizzically, a smile hovering around her full mouth. "The best of both worlds?" She laughed and poured the tea while Mrs Banshaw retreated.

The lull in conversation gave Caro and Rebecca the chance to shoot pregnant looks at each other. Caro's was one of concern for her friend. Rebecca simply looked furious. Still, she took her tea calmly enough from her sister and sat on the other side of the ornate table. Caro watched her take several sips of the steaming liquid. One might assume her silence was resignation to the situation. Caro knew better.

"And tell me, dear sister, how long have you known your husband?" Rebecca arched an attractive brow.

"Oh," Rachel's eyes wandered to the ornate plasterwork of the ceiling, "about a week."

Much to Rebecca's embarrassment, the tea she had just sipped came spewing out in a great amber plume, marking her deep cerise dress and half the lacquered table.

"Here." Rachel handed her a man's handkerchief she had squirrelled up one of her banyan sleeves. "I know this has been a shock, Becky, but Lord Arleigh and I had no desire to stand upon ceremony. There was no need for a frippery-filled wedding, as you well know I have already endured that, so being wed by special licence seemed just the thing to do. I understand you're upset I did not tell you." Rachel leant forward and spread several long fingers on the table, a gesture meant to bridge the gap, physical and emotional, between the two sisters. "Marriage is complex."

Her piece said, Rachel leant back on the cushions of the chaise longue like some kind of far eastern queen. The carefree look which had briefly left her face, overtook her features once more. Her final words had been spoken with such meaning, but now the connection between the two sisters was broken. "You may understand one day, my dear, but I pray that you won't."

Though Rachel immediately laughed the sombre words away, they affected Rebecca. Caro saw the quick movement Rachel made, bringing the cup of tea to her lips, to cover the shadow of something else there. Then it was gone, like magic from the eastern queen, and Caro was left to wonder at it, and Rebecca left to be frustrated by it.

"Caro, dear, tell me of that rascal husband of yours—is he well?"

"Yes, I thank you," Caro replied politely. "Though he is yet to realise he is no longer an adolescent." Her lips curled into a smile filled with secrets. The sort of smile that only a man and a woman in love would understand the true meaning of. "There is little hope that he ever will."

"Well, you married him, my dear," said Rachel, more than willing to play along. "He was always bound to cause a wife trouble. But I have not heard much of him since your rather talked-about marriage, so you must be doing something right."

Caro laughed. "That's exactly what Lady Felton said to me, but I assured her that if she thinks I have any power over her son, she is sorely mistaken."

Caro saw the shadowed look return. Again, it disappeared almost as soon as it had materialised.

"And now, my sister, are you recovered enough from the shock that you can tell me what beaus are parading through your life at present?"

"Beaus?" Rebecca's peeved tone showed that she was not recovered.

"Oh, do not keep at this dagger drawing, Becky, for heaven's sake. I am married. You would do better to congratulate me."

"Well, I..." said Rebecca, looking suddenly

sheepish.

"Never mind!" Rachel put down her tea cup and saucer with a clatter. "Perhaps a tour of my new home would be more interesting for your inquisitive mind? You shall be the first of the family to see it if you agree."

The trap was made, the bait laid, and Caro saw Rebecca take it up whole in her jaws.

"If you insist." Rebecca followed her sister from the room with more enthusiasm than her tone suggested. "Come Caro." She turned bright, suddenly happy eyes on her friend, and stretched out a hand to grasp Caro's. "There is nothing better than nosing through someone else's house for ideas of décor."

They were taken back into the entrance hall, but Rachel wasted no time on it, and Caro found it hard to keep up with her Amazonian strides.

"I have not quite found my way around myself yet, but I believe… ah, yes, this is the morning room. We were quite out of place in the back parlour, but I think it more… cosy." She shot a daring look at her sister and Rebecca replied by rolling her eyes.

"You see what I had to put up with growing up? She was an imp to the governesses."

"No such thing. Miss Randle thought me quite entertaining," Rachel replied.

"She did not!"

They had left the morning room by a

far door and, passing through a nondescript passage, had come into the library through a side entrance. The usual scent of leather-bound books and tobacco, so typical of a male domain, assailed them. Unlike many such rooms, this library was neatly arranged without a book or leaf out of place. The desk at the far end had papers, several ledgers with ribbons poking from their tops indicating important sections, and a pen laid exactly in the centre of the leather writing pad.

"Do you know, Rachel was insistent on performing a play and forced Miss Randle into the most odious part?" Rebecca said to Caro. "She made us perform before mama and papa and then poured a bucket of water over Miss Randle's head to show the rain in a particular scene. If it wasn't enough to soak the poor governess, Miss Randle was wont to wear an inordinate amount of rouge and the water sent it running down her face in the most spectacular fashion making her look like a fever patient. Very cruel."

Caro saw Rebecca struggling to maintain her look of disapproval, finally abandoning her attempt and giving in to the amusement by breaking into a grin.

"I wouldn't say cruel," said Rachel, pausing to wrap her banyan around herself again, her energetic stride having caused it to fall partially open.

Caro saw the flash of Rachel's chemise and

stays as the red sash drew the banyan closed again. The new bride was barely dressed beneath the silk gown.

"Perhaps too authentic for Miss Randle's taste in theatre," Rachel finished.

"It was revenge for Miss Randle telling mama and papa that you were not applying yourself to your needlework."

"Pestilential stuff!" Her clothing back in place, Rachel strode imperiously from the room as if it were filled to the rafters with embroidery projects. Caro had the distinct impression she would not like to be on the wrong side of this woman.

As if reading her thoughts, Rebecca leant close to her ear. "Don't let her worry you. She has always loved to scare people."

They had now come into a music room with a spinet and a harp positioned attractively at one end and several gilt chairs scattered in an anything but careless manner about the fireplace. Heavy brocade curtains hung beside the tall sash windows and half eclipsed by them were sweet, cushioned window seats in which Caro would have happily spent an afternoon curled up with a book.

They moved quickly through the chamber after a brief explanation from Rachel and were soon in a tapestry room.

"These are from Beauvais," she said, throwing a hand up thoughtlessly at the beautiful scenes surrounding them. "Mrs Banshaw, the housekeeper, has been wonderful in explaining the finer points of the house to me. They are supposed to depict the Loves of the Gods, though I must say it looks like a host of men having a jolly time at the expense of the ladies."

Caro saw a gaming table to the side of the room. Its sliding marquetry top would no doubt reveal cards and dice below ready to play. She felt a tingle at the tips of her fingers. It wasn't a feeling of desire, or excitement, but rather a memory. Her hands remembered the feel of the cards. She heard herself sigh and realised with contentment that she could look at that gaming table and in no way desire the thrills and the despair of her past life. She had been infamous once, played a dangerous game, and Felton had saved her honour when she had a losing hand. How long ago that all felt now.

"Then we come back to the hall. There is a ballroom through there, but it is hardly worth showing you, for it is as bare as anything without people in it. There are a number of fine paintings but I cannot see the merit in looking at a group of old men and severe looking women who clearly disapprove of you being so nosy as to peer up at them. Onwards and upwards!"

Rebecca and Caro scurried up the stairs after Rachel who bounded up them two at a time. When they had reached the top, Caro was suddenly overwhelmed with a feeling of discomfort. It was one thing to be shown the reception rooms of Lord Arleigh's house; it was quite another to be shown the private chambers without having met the man.

She remembered her desire for privacy when she had lived in her old Town house, barely a year ago. From Felton's description, Viscount Arleigh did not sound like a particularly conversational man. Though Caro was finding it difficult to discern the nature of Rachel's relationship with her new husband, something about the bride's behaviour and the unorthodox nature of the wedding led Caro to believe the Viscount would not appreciate strangers in the intimate sanctums of his house.

She certainly had no acquaintance with Lord Arleigh, even from her gaming days. That at least gave her hope for his character. She smiled, realising she was denigrating her husband's character by thinking such things. It was in such a haunt they had met. He would no doubt laugh if she told him her thoughts. Rebecca, however, couldn't be considered a stranger to Lord Arleigh. She was his sister-in-law now. Perhaps that made it acceptable.

Rachel showed them a series of large but modestly furnished rooms. The Town house would accommodate a sizable house party for some length of time. Caro wondered why Rachel had not told her family sooner of such an advantageous match.

"His mother's room is there—she has been in the country for the past few months. It will be quite a shock for her when she arrives in Town to find me."

Rachel carried on and finally they came to her room.

"There is nothing much personal in it. My things still haven't arrived from Godalming. It was all rather rushed, you see." She shot a provoking look at her sister.

The room was large and spacious, with an impressive four poster bed at its centre and a heavy sash window overlooking the square in which the house was located. There were some pretty pieces of furniture, not overly gaudy, but with a splash of gilt here and there, and carvings that spoke volumes about the cost of such commissions. Her bed had been freshly made and she sat on it with a thump, a whistle of air escaping the tightly made sheets.

"There you have it, are you satisfied?"

"It is large," replied Rebecca.

"Jealous?" Dimples appeared either side of Rachel's mouth forcing her sister to react.

Rebecca snatched up the fan that had been dangling from her wrist and reached out to rap her sister's hands with it.

"Ouch! Becky, you are too saucy for your own good. How are you to catch a husband with such a violent temper?"

That only made it worse and Caro decided

it was best to avoid the sibling fracas. She retired quietly to the window to observe the comings and goings in the square.

The view was beautiful, the well-kept area of green and trees giving the illusion they were somewhere in the South Downs. Carriages were coming and going, and fashionable couples were stepping out. One carriage in particular, a dashing yellow contraption just whipping around a corner towards the mews, caught Caro's eye.

Where had she seen it before? Was it yesterday? She placed it in her mind and dread shot through her. Swinging round, her mouth open and ready to give warning, she found it was too late. Viscount Arleigh stood in the doorway and he looked less than amused.

Chapter 3

"**I** appear to have stumbled into a fight," Lord Arleigh remarked, standing square and immovable in the doorway of Rachel's bedchamber.

His steady eyes took in his wife, thrown back upon the bed, another woman bearing a striking resemblance to the new Lady Arleigh towering over her. An arm was raised with a fan clasped in hand, ready to strike. Both women, caught in so compromising a position, had jerked round at his entrance and two pairs of dark brown eyes looked at him in surprise.

Caro was happy not to be in his line of sight. Or fire for that matter. Lord Arleigh was far taller than Caro's husband. His frame was fuller with what she did not doubt was well-earned muscle, for he looked the sporting type, and he held his nose high, looking down it at the scene before him.

"Perhaps you can enlighten me, Lady Arleigh, as to why you thought it necessary to... entertain in your own apartments. Was the morning room not to your satisfaction?"

He looked peeved. Caro could see the sharpness in his eyes and the white skin where his mouth was pinched shut. She watched him swallow the tension and keep his gaze steady.

"To be quite frank, it can be a little dull in there. The morning sun only reaches it for a little above an hour," Rachel replied, hardly perturbed by his unexpected appearance.

"Rachel!" Rebecca had intended to whisper it, but the whole room heard.

A flicker of irritation passed over Lord Arleigh's face. Caro looked back to her friend and saw the rigidity in Rebecca's frame crack away as she finally righted herself. Caro could not see her face, but Rebecca's exclamation was one of embarrassment and even from here she could see the tips of Rebecca's ears flushing red. She performed some quick, fraught movements, batting her skirt down and pushing her curls back into submission, hardly the actions of the usually confident Rebecca. But the heavy authority of the man in the doorway was enough to cow anyone.

"Lady Rebecca Fairing? You are my wife's sister." Lord Arleigh spoke with neither pleasure nor disdain. "We have met once or twice before, I believe. I wish we could be meeting in a more formal setting, but I fear my wife does not understand what such a setting is." He bowed stiffly.

Caro saw the expression on Rachel's face

darken and it sent anxiety shooting through her.

"Yes, well," said Rachel, sitting up. Her hair was even messier, a nest of starlings would no doubt have been at home upon the crown of her head, and the folds of her banyan were crumpled and caught up at awkward angles.

Lord Arleigh, who had clearly not been paying attention to his wife's dress up until this moment, could not hide a look of shock.

"You may look agog at me, Arleigh, but I hardly expected to see you back this morning."

"I suppose that is an acceptable reason for these less than agreeable circumstances," he said sharply, but refrained from going further. Even now, Caro could see manners prevailed over emotion.

"Ah, Mrs Felton," Rachel said, shooting a look of remembrance towards Caro and attempting an introduction, "My husband, Lord Arleigh."

Caro came forward from her unobserved position with more poise than she was feeling. He was only a man after all. She should be able to hold her own against his disapproving looks. She had borne far worse before.

"Another! Gracious, this is a veritable *salon* of my wife's friends. Perhaps, Lady Arleigh, we can move this meeting to one of this house's *many* reception rooms?"

Rachel nodded, not looking in the least admonished, and strode past him into the hall. She called over her shoulder for the two ladies to follow. Both had to cross the threshold on which the man of the house stood, and there he remained while they did so, immovable and thoroughly displeased.

"I shall not ask what you are wearing—though I do question how you can receive visitors in such a garb? It is hardly befitting a viscountess."

Rachel's sister and Mrs Felton had left shortly after the Viscount's return to the house, and it had been a rather awkward farewell. Rachel had felt his tension immediately and now they were alone he was baiting her just as he might a bear. She wished to bite his hand off, but she knew from past experience that it did no good. Whenever she had upset Sir Denby, which had been often and always unintentional, her sharp tongue had never been her friend.

"I was not expecting visitors," she said, regulating her tone. "I shall change."

She had already turned to leave when he spoke again.

"Are you in the habit of wearing men's clothing?"

She turned and felt the smallest stab of guilt. She brushed it away with a playful smile.

"If you are, can I not be?"

His straight brows rose a little at that, and she could have sworn, for the briefest of moments, that he was considering whether he wished to be amused or not.

"By all means, I suppose it should not matter to me, as long as you do not receive my family in a state of such dress."

"Family?"

He had decided not to be amused. At the mention of his family, she found her own pleasure temporarily dampened.

"Yes." He walked towards the chairs, which were artfully placed about the little parlour room, and saw the discarded tea things from earlier. Ringing the bell, he ordered the servant who appeared, to remove the spent porcelain and bring him a tankard of ale and a plate of meat and cheese. He requested no similar bacheloresque meal for Rachel and she did not ask for one. She had decided that it would perhaps be beneficial for them both to spend as little time as possible in each other's company before they separated.

After all, it was not essential, and she had experience of men who had spent too much time in her company. They would wear the look on their faces that Lord Arleigh had when he had found Rebecca and Caro in her bedchamber. Disdain. If it were a form of currency, Rachel would be rich. It did not matter that she cared naught for others' opinions, for they chose to give them to her anyway, whether by look or conversation. She had given up long ago any hope that another would ever understand her. After marrying Sir Denby he had removed her from Society and lost her the handful of friends she had. His age and determination to spend his days in the country seeing to that. And the men in her life had a propensity for tiring of her. They found her provocative temper too challenging, too exhausting. Try as she might, she knew from experience she could not tame it. So she did not try anymore. Unlike her uncertain younger self, she now allowed herself to be who she was, and everyone else could go hang for all she cared.

That being said, she had learned, in spite of her sense of injustice, that there were some battles not worth fighting. If she was only to be in the company of this man for three months, there was no use in fighting him, just in keeping out of his way.

She watched as her husband took a small silver box from his deep frock coat pockets. It was plain and unostentatious, much like him, and even the way he took snuff was without pomp or flourish.

"My mother has received my letter. She's a little disconcerted. I could tell by the way she formed her 'y's in the return she sent." That last part was evidently for himself, because when he realised he was conversing so freely, he stopped.

"Not that it signifies. She writes to say she wishes us to come up to Bath so that she may meet you."

"She knew your father's will?"

"Better than any other." Lord Arleigh sat comfortably in the chair that Rachel had used earlier. She realised that it fit him perfectly, that it was probably *his* chair.

"She has paraded a number of elegantly, well-schooled and well-bred females before me for the past six months."

"And you bought none of these fillies at auction?"

He frowned, looking at her for the first time. It really was obvious he was used to living alone with naught but servants to speak to. He wasn't used to being answered back.

"Until your proposition, I did not feel much inclined to marry."

"Am I to consider that a compliment?" She was jesting but his reply was in the same solemn accents.

"You understand the arrangement. You are not… naive. I had no wish to inflict a marriage of such a transactional nature on a girl barely out of the schoolroom."

"In that area you differ from every other man of your rank and age." Her brow puckered, and she looked up at the carvings projecting from the ceiling corners. "Is that why your father added the clause in his will—he did not feel you would subject a young miss to such a marriage?"

"He believed giving me a time limit to marry and making my inheritance dependent on it, might spur me along the path he took long before my age."

"He was not pleased with your bachelor-hood?"

"He was little pleased with anything." There was sharp bitterness in his voice. One of the few emotions he'd allowed to invade his speech. "My lack of marrying was a failing according to some." A muscle in the side of his jaw twitched. "I found it hard to reconcile myself to the idea of selecting a bride solely for the purpose of satisfying the requirement of my father's eccentric will. Marriages of such a transactional nature can be accepted by some, but hardly by the naive sort of female my mother was suggesting. She was adamant it was the way forward. She had accepted the same lot in her youth and so would my young bride."

"Hardly the love of Richardson's *Pamela*."

"Hardly."

He did not say anything further and Rachel did not push. She did not need to.

"I am a practical man, but I do not think myself cruel. When you approached me, however improperly, during my stay at Moreston's estate, you came with the same practical reasons that I held for future matrimony. I had no desire for a love match and needed a wife who expected none. There was no pretence. If we agree on nothing else, at least we seem to appreciate straightforward conversation."

"It is my favourite kind."

Arleigh sighed. She had noticed him do that every time she made some kind of inappropriate comment or humorous observation. Either that, or he was perpetually tired.

Jeffries, holding a tray complete with mountains of cold beef and cheese and a generous tankard of ale, arrived in the parlour. He placed it at his master's elbow and after bowing to leave, he paused and spoke with a temerity previously unseen by Rachel.

"Would Lady Arleigh be requiring any sustenance?"

A wide smile immediately lit her face and the retainer was hard-pressed not to respond in kind. Lord Arleigh, who was hovering over his tray like a bird of prey, looked up, a little surprised.

"That is most kind, Jeffries. I would be grateful for an apple, a little cheese and a glass of burgundy if it is not too much trouble?"

The retainer bowed, without a flicker of emotion at the unusual request, and left the room.

"You're hungry?"

"A little."

Lord Arleigh nodded, still looking a little ruffled, and then tucked into his plate of meat and cheese. It was as he was putting the first piece of cheese to his mouth that his confusion got the better of him and he addressed his wife again.

"You are having an apple and cheese? Will that fill you?"

Rachel looked up from the book she had started reading. "And a glass of burgundy."

"Yes, well…"

Before he could reprimand her, which she jolly well wasn't allowing, for she had been drinking wine ever since her coming out ball six years ago, she explained, "Apple, cheese and burgundy, are quite simply the best combination of food and drink stuffs I have come across thus far."

He looked less than convinced. "But no meat."

She laughed then, the sound deep and hearty, hardly the schoolgirl titter of other young women. "I do not see the need in every meal—though I am fully aware men do. Sir Denby could not sit down to a meal if he was not sure that some animal had come to its end in order to satisfy his stomach that day. I believe it was that and the port which finished him off—he never could rid himself of the gout that carried him away in the end."

"Sir Denby was a man of almost fifty even when I was a boy."

Rachel would not let him carry on. "Yes, but you spoke of visiting your mother?"

She didn't want to speak any more about her elderly first husband. He hadn't been an awful man, but it was similar to being married off to one's father, and she had been unhappy. She could speak of him in short bouts, but she knew what people always wanted to know, the sordid tittle-tattle that kept their minds curious about a couple with such a wide age difference. She did not wish to be interrogated on the matter.

"Yes, we will leave on Friday."

"Oh, shall we?" She didn't ask the question softly and the tone was not lost on Arleigh.

He took a long draught from his tankard before he deigned to reply, placing the half-empty vessel back on the tray carefully. Rachel wondered how many meals he had taken in this fashion. He was hardly a man of Society, one of the things people attributed his long bachelorhood to.

He leaned back in his chair, passing an unlaced handkerchief over his lips, and caught Rachel's eyes in a fixed stare.

"Yes, we will be. You are aware of the deal we struck. You promised to obey me in those marriage vows, and I will take that obedience now, and you will honour the deal with how you present yourself to my family."

Rachel's bristles rose with each word uttered. She willed herself to remain calm as she answered.

"Very well, but I would ask that we delay until Wednesday week. I wish to take leave of my sister and I have received a letter from my parents who have said they will call on us when they arrive in Town on Friday. I believe it my duty to see my mother and father before we leave for Bath, though I may be loath to fulfil the task."

He was exhaling audibly and making ready to leave the room, and the conversation.

"Very well," he said as he rose. "Wednesday week. I doubt my mother will be pleased." He opened the door of the room and disappeared through it without pause.

Left behind, Rachel walked a circuit of the room twice before she felt settled again. In her mind two things were clear. Firstly, she would attempt to steer clear of her husband as much as possible while they must remain together. And secondly, she had no intention of changing her dress today.

Chapter 4

C aro was slowly brushing her long, fair curls, the bristles making the locks shine like twists of gold. She sat at her dressing table, one which Felton had specially ordered for her, insisting that any purchases which were related to her beauty were not to be restricted by trifling things such as price limits.

She, of course, had swatted him for it and given him a set-down. Though to keep a straight face while she did so was near impossible.

Caro was sitting in quiet reflection, her eyes on the small tapestry of Mary Magdalene which hung beside the mirror of her dressing table, rather than her own countenance. Felton was currently in the adjacent room, bathing in the large copper tub which resided there. Since their marriage, they had lived in Felton's Town house and, rather than choosing bedrooms for themselves with adjoining doors, they had — quite against the norm — settled in a single room. When Caro thought of it, she was sure that she had intended to move to the room adjacent to her husband's. They had even discussed it. But as the days had drawn into weeks, and weeks into months, without them spending a night apart, separate bedrooms had simply fallen out of the equation.

Then, nearly six months after their marriage, Felton had, when drifting between reality and unconsciousness, settled the matter.

"I rather like you being here."

And that was that. The servants had not said a thing, but Caro could tell that Felton's sharp-faced valet found the presence of a woman in his master's previously male domain quite abominable.

In fact, when the dressing table had been moved in, along with a number of other female items, he had even ventured to question the positioning of some of them. His suggestions were mild, a turning of the angle, a move closer to the wall, but Caro was sure if he'd given voice to his full opinion, the objects in question would have found themselves much further away. In another bedroom, in fact. But like any faithful retainer, he had accepted the change, and to be quite frank, with Caro's housekeeper Libby staunchly defending the improvements, he had hardly been able to withstand the new matriarchal elements in the household.

Caro drew her shawl closer around her shoulders and poured the pot of coffee Libby had just brought in on a tray. She enjoyed these moments of solitude before the day began in earnest, when she was alone in the silence of the moment with her thoughts and the knowledge of the day ahead. It was in those times she considered the miracle of her salvation through Felton and the fact that she loved him more than she had loved anyone before. So much so, that sometimes it hurt.

She thought about her meeting with the new Lady Arleigh and the stern Viscount the day before. She wondered if they loved each other. Many did not. When it came to titles, land and wealth, the illogical occurrence of love was often passed over in favour of all too logical marriages. She shuddered when she remembered how close she had come to making that decision herself.

"Good morning, darling," Felton whispered huskily in her ear.

She jumped, but only a little, relaxing into a smile as he kissed her cheek.

"Good morning," she said. "You should not have left me abed. We are expecting James this morning, and what would he think if he came to find his sister undressed at midday?"

"That we are happily married, I dare say." Felton grinned at her as she turned towards him. She sighed, realising that she really ought to think about how she phrased sentences directed at her perpetually provocative husband.

"Which reminds me," he said, taking both

her hands and pulling her up into his arms, and she realised quite suddenly that he wore nothing beneath the banyan he had donned after his bath. "Coker is quite occupied with polishing my buckles this morning. Libby promises that stew of hers for your brother and is intent on getting it prepared early, so I suppose we do have a bit of time." He lowered his mouth to hers, pushing against her soft lips, his hands running up into her silky hair.

It was some time later that Caro sat up, her golden curls in disarray, clasping a bedsheet to herself.

"What are you doing?"

"Getting out of bed," she said simply, looking around for her discarded shawl.

Felton had thrown it somewhere without care, far too preoccupied with the delights of his wife to be worrying about clothing her later. In fact, Caro was sure that if he had his way she would never be clothed.

"No." His fingers traced a delicate pattern over the smooth white skin of her shoulder, tossing her thick hair out of the way. "Let's not. Getting up is so… overrated. I hear sleeping and resting up is quite the thing for one's health."

"I do not think," said Caro, turning and flashing her eyes at him, "that what we just did could constitute as resting."

"No," Felton sighed, staring up at the canopy above the bed. "I don't think it can," he conceded.

Just as Caro was about to slip from the bed and reach for the shawl she had spied, he grabbed at her waist, pulling her back again.

"But it is so amusing," he said, laughing, Caro feeling the sound deep in his chest as she lay her cheek to his body.

Knowing from previous experience that he would not let her go until he was ready, she relaxed against him, the sound of his heart beating beneath her ear, his arms about her. She traced the small indentation on his side. It was where the blade which had defended her honour had pierced his skin. Slowly her hand stilled and they were asleep, their breathing coinciding.

"You are looking quite flushed, miss," said Libby when Caro entered, drawn into the kitchen by the smell of tender beef and vegetables. Her maid called her as she always did. Libby had explained that seeing as she had known Caro since she was a babe, the maid should be allowed to call her 'miss' if she could not remember to call her Mrs Felton, and Caro had acquiesced without a fight.

"It smells wonderful," said Caro, ignoring the comment, but self-consciously raising her hands to her hot cheeks.

Libby never failed to pick up on her mistress' activities, though the maid feigned ignorance when she asked such pointed questions.

"That it does. Never fails me, this recipe. And the beef which Coker instructed to be brought up from Lord and Lady Felton's estate is quite the best I've cooked with. Fine cattle they must be, out of this London air, that's what it is. Makes the meat tender." Libby was stirring the stew steadily as she stood at the stove. Her round frame was clad in the new dress she had been able to buy since Caro had married.

"James said he would be with us in the morning—though how swiftly he must have travelled to get back from Derbyshire on the heels of the letter I received from him yesterday I do not know."

"Well, if he is tired, this stew will no doubt see him right. Whenever he was feeling under the weather as a boy I made him this."

Caro nodded with interest despite the fact that she knew these stories. After all, she had been there, next to James, being served the very same stew.

"If he has sold his shipment of cotton and obtained a regular order," said Caro, "I have no doubt he will be in good spirits."

James had been gone for more than three months. First he had travelled to the West Indies for trade, and then, when he had made port in

England, he had needed to travel north immediately to complete his business before he could return to London. Caro had missed him. The months they had spent together since the end of their estrangement had begun to make up for lost time. It had saddened her greatly when he had been required to travel again.

"Well, can you believe it? Mama and papa have arrived in London this very morning and are waiting on my sister and Lord Arleigh at this very moment!"

Rebecca's voice reverberated around the kitchen walls as she came bowling down the corridor which led in from the mews. When Caro had overcome her surprise, she asked what Rebecca was doing in her kitchen.

"Well, I have come to talk to you of course. My life is in crisis, Caro!" she said in exasperated tones, failing to see the point of Caro's question. "I say," she said, pausing for the first time, but still failing to see why her attendance in Caro's kitchen was so out of place. "You look very flushed, Caro dear. Is there something the matter with you?"

"As I said, Lady Rebecca, as I said," Libby spoke into the stew she was stirring.

Caro shot her a look of betrayal, knowing full well that Libby was aware of what had caused her mistress to be flushed.

"No, I am quite well, Rebecca," she said, turning back to her friend, "but perhaps we should go upstairs. Will you take tea?"

"Do not speak to me of food or drink! Oh, do not look so appalled at me, Caro." She glared at her friend. "Every time I come to call on you in the morning, you are down here with Libby. If I enter through the back, John always obliges me by undoing the latch, and then I can see you straight away instead of standing like a lemon upstairs. Oh, Maisy!" Rebecca suddenly turned around, snatching off her gloves and pointing them menacingly at her servant. "Do stop milling around in the shadows there. You are like a puppy without a kennel."

Her young maid, as scandalised as ever by her mistress' behaviour, came forward nervously. This was not the first time Rebecca had forced Maisy to show her the servants' entrance to one of Caro's houses.

"Did you hear what I said?" Rebecca's attention was now wholly back on Caro, who had suddenly paled considerably, despite the heat of the kitchen. Her skin was taking on the hue of the yellow silk dress she was wearing.

"Mama and papa have been driven to Town by Rachel's activities, and you know how the air affects mama's lungs. I expect papa will be furious when he sees my sister. Do you now see, there is something going on? Mama and papa, *never* come to Town, so they must know something isn't right. Dear?" Rebecca leapt forwards as Caro swayed. The mistress of the house put a thoughtless hand to the cooker on which Libby's stew boiled furiously away.

"Caro!"

But Rebecca was too late. Caro yelped, snatching her hand away from the scalding metal, and toppled backwards into some hanging copper pans causing a crescendo in the brick-walled kitchen.

"Miss!" Libby dropped the spoon in the forgotten stew and snatched up the rag tucked into the belt of her apron. She threw it in a pail of water standing by the door and drawing it up, wringing it a little, she rushed back to her mistress and wrapped her hand.

"Damnation!" Caro cursed as the cold cloth stung her hand.

"Is that the dulcet tones of my wife I hear?" Felton's jovial voice came ringing down the stairs. "Why must I perpetually find you below stairs, wife? Every time I lose you, you are having tea with Libby. I am beginning to think you prefer her company to mine…" As he rounded the foot of the stairs into the kitchen, he took in the scene before him with a rapidly changing countenance.

Maisy tried her hand at an explanation, but gave in as the stuttering became too much. Felton wouldn't have waited for her anyway. He strode straight over to where his wife now sat at the scrubbed kitchen work table.

"What have you done?" he chided, his

voice gentle as it would have been to a child.

"Oh, I touched the stove. I can't think why. I felt a little faint, that's all. What a goose I am—ouch!" She pulled her hand away from Felton's inquisitive fingers. "A curse on your careless hands."

"That is not what you were saying this morning," he whispered roguishly in her ear, trying to make her smile.

She pursed her lips, looking towards Rebecca and Libby, determined to pretend she didn't hear him.

"I said you did not look well when I came in," said Rebecca.

Felton turned upon her and said curtly, "What are you doing here, Rebecca?"

"It's my mother and father. They have arrived in Town."

"And you were giving us a bulletin?"

Caro touched Felton's arm gently with her uninjured hand. He looked down at her and she shook her head a little. His jaw clenched.

"Well, I..." Rebecca began on the back foot.

"Hallo! What's all this?"

All eyes in the room turned to the figure materialising from the corridor behind Rebecca.

"James!" cried Caro in delight, immediately rising from her chair. Ignoring Felton's stilling hands, she went to be embraced by her brother.

He laughed as she clung to him. "A wound

I see?" he said, drawing back and gingerly taking her cloth-wrapped hand.

"A burn—it's nothing. It is so good to see you!"

"And you, sister," he grinned, in a rare show of boyishness. Releasing her, he greeted Felton with a firm shake of the hand and turned to Rebecca last.

"Lady Rebecca."

"Mr Worth," said Rebecca, looking anything but happy to see him.

Caro watched the stricken look on Rebecca's face fail to pass away.

James smiled, a little shyly, and said with over-politeness, "I trust you are well, my lady?"

"I… yes… well, my sister…"

For the first time since Caro had known Rebecca, she seemed truly at a loss for words. The gathering stood in an awkward silence.

"Well," said Rebecca, making a clear effort to appear her usually animated self. Caro could see it cost her dearly. "My parents just this morning arrived in Town. I must be going. Caro, I'm sure I shall see you later."

"We shall have her hand seen first," said Felton.

Rebecca gave a small nod and was gone, Maisy following her with a rapid pitter-patter of steps behind.

"Felton, she's upset," said Caro quietly while James watched Rebecca go.

Felton made no answer, but Caro saw the muscle at his jaw clench again.

"Shall we reconvene upstairs?" Caro asked brightly, turning to her brother. "Otherwise I am fearful my redecoration of the morning room will never be appreciated."

Chapter 5

"They're here," Rachel announced.

Lord Arleigh was pleased to see his new wife had decided to dress with some sense of normality today. She had chosen a very becoming *robe à l'anglaise* which highlighted the curves of her figure pleasingly in rich turquoise silk. Arleigh was going to ask her whether she had ordered any lace caps, but reconsidered. He had already observed her tempestuous nature. There was no sense in poking an inquisitive finger at a beehive.

After her pronouncement, she came away from the window and he saw with some surprise that she was twisting a lace handkerchief between her fingers. She was unaware of being observed, beginning a circuit of the morning room before she caught his eyes. The change was instant. The anxiety which had been hinted at in the depth of her dark eyes was banished, and she stilled her hands, dropping one to her side in a bid to portray nonchalance.

"My mother and father will be with us in a moment."

The explanation was unneeded but he found it interesting nonetheless. Having spent a week in this woman's company, he had not seen anything unbalance her clear resolve of character. She may be an eccentric, in fact Arleigh had been concerned she might be touched in the head, but she had always appeared to have command over any weak emotions. Even in the face of his recriminations, which were enough to cow most young men of his acquaintance not to mention his younger siblings, she never seemed the least perturbed.

She tossed several curls, left loose from the high hairstyle she wore, over her shoulders. Raising her chin at him, she turned back and walked resolutely to one of the embroidered chairs. She seated herself with an air of confidence and stared at him frankly.

"Remember, we are to tell them it was a love affair and we could not wait to be wed."

Arleigh nodded. He had agreed to this some time ago. She was retreading old ground. She had made it clear this morning over breakfast that she did not wish her parents to know the straits in which she had been left after Sir Denby's death. He had put it down to her pride. It was a quality, Arleigh had concluded, that this woman had in abundance. She was more headstrong, obstinate and disconcertingly confident than any other woman he could remember meeting. Her stubbornness in this matter did not bother him though. If she were to act the part for his family, he would obey her wishes when it came to hers.

Before long, the door opened and the Earl and Countess Fairing were announced. Arleigh was surprised by the small, frail-looking woman who entered first. He could not quite believe that she claimed Rachel as her daughter. She was nothing like her. Countess Fairing shared neither her daughter's face nor figure. She was a fair-haired, slight little thing and without any of the commanding presence his wife possessed.

The appearance shortly after of Earl Fairing filled in any pieces of the puzzle that Lord Arleigh was missing. Earl Fairing was almost twice the height of his wife, broad shouldered, and clearly a sporting man. Arleigh had heard of Lord Fairing's riding prowess in his youth; Arleigh's own father had much admired him. Looking at the Earl now, Arleigh saw Lord Fairing possessed a face like thunder, one that no disobedient child would ever have liked facing.

"Mama, papa," Rachel said, coming forward, gracefully skirting the tables and taking her mother's hands gently in her own. She drew Lady Fairing forward, her father following behind.

"Father, may I present Lord Arleigh? Lord Arleigh, this is my father and mother, Lord and

Lady Fairing."

Arleigh bowed respectfully, his gaze catching his wife's hands around her mother's. "Will you both be seated? I must apologise," he carried on smoothly while his wife led Lady Fairing to a chair. "My marriage to your daughter must have been quite a shock to you both. I am afraid I am wholly to blame for this." He watched Rachel's attentiveness in placing a cushion behind her mother's back. "We met at a mutual acquaintance's near Godalming. I understood from Lady Arleigh that she held no desire for a large wedding, having been married before, and I have never been one for gatherings, so it suited us best to marry by special licence."

He had been determined to keep Earl Fairing's gaze throughout the entire explanation, but when he shifted it briefly, he caught a look of appreciation in Rachel's dark brown eyes. He showed no acknowledgement of this but carried on with a few particulars about the date of the wedding and which church it had taken place in.

Lady Fairing listened attentively, her eyes gentle and kind. Lord Fairing looked less pleased, but said nothing of his displeasure when he finally spoke.

"Well, I suppose congratulations are in order, my boy," said Lord Fairing, rising from his seat to take his new son-in-law by the hand. "Naturally we were shocked by the news, but we have become accustomed to it, and a fine match it is."

Each man resumed his seat and there was a pause in conversation.

"Has your aunt called upon you yet, child?"

"No. I confess I have not had a moment to tell her the news myself, but I am sure Rebecca has already let the cat out of the bag. She was quite scandalised by the, you know. You should have seen the fit it sent her into." Rachel was beginning to laugh when a look from her father quelled her.

"Well, I am sure she would appreciate a note sent round." Lady Fairing's voice was soft and sweet.

There was nothing in it that should cause offence. Yet, Arleigh found it grating on him.

"And what have you done with your hair, my child?" Lady Fairing asked. "It is looking positively wild."

Arleigh considered that his wife's hair looked more tame now than it had in the rest of the short time he'd known her. He saw her shift in her seat, and the sigh that moved her shoulders, but that she did not permit to become audible.

"I know, mama. If only papa had not given me his outrageous curls!"

Lord Fairing glared at his daughter for that. His powdered wig was smooth and well-ordered and for a split second, Arleigh imagined

Lord Fairing with his daughter's hair. He struggled to hold back a smile.

"Your aunt deserves to have been told by your own hand of your marriage, not by some second-hand tittle tattle from your sister." Lord Fairing huffed.

"Oh, you know aunt won't care a fiddle as long as she knows before her arch-nemesis the Countess of Goring, and the rest of Town for that matter." Rachel's face lit up with another smile and she squeezed her mother's hands affectionately. Lady Fairing suddenly looked uncomfortable. She withdrew her hands from her daughter's grasp and looked towards her husband for direction.

It was then that Arleigh realised what it was he disliked in the sweetness of Lady Fairing. She was weak. He could see it in the way Lord Fairing's actions and mood dominated her own tone and words.

There was another pause in conversation and this one did not show any signs of abating. Arleigh was just about to conjure up some sporting anecdote for the benefit of Earl Fairing and his glaring eyes when Lady Fairing spoke.

"Do you know," said Lady Fairing in her small, pretty voice, "that it was in the ballroom of this very house that Lord Fairing and I first danced together? I was the Honourable Constance Withinshaw then, and I came with my family to the first ball your mother and father threw together, Lord Arleigh. It was beautiful, was it not, Lord Fairing? Quite the most splendid of balls. I think it might have been the best of that Season, but then it was where we were first introduced, was it not, John?" Lady Fairing slipped into using his Christian name without intention. She had looked to him as she reminisced and Arleigh could see a sincere love in the nymph-like features of her face.

"Perhaps I can show you the ballroom, Lady Fairing? I understand it was one of the finest in London when it was first built. Maybe you would like to see it again?"

"That would be lovely, thank you, Lord Arleigh." The delicate Lady Fairing rose carefully to her feet and took the strong arm offered to her.

"Your mother has heard such wicked gossip from the Countess of Goring, Rachel," her father said in sharp accents as soon as the door clicked shut behind Arleigh and her mother.

"That woman is perpetually spreading wicked gossip, father. As aunt Etheridge says, one mustn't take too much notice of vulgar people." Rachel's calmly spoken words were ones she knew would rile her father, but she could see very well that he had been riled since he had first arrived and needed no help from her. He had been glaring at her abominably since entering the room in just the way he had when she had been too loud and boisterous as a child. Not content without a son, never mind a headstrong daughter, her father was determined to remain eternally dissatisfied. Whatever had ruffled his feathers this morning was just one in a long line of irritations she had caused him.

"Don't be trite, Rachel," he snapped, rising to his feet and clasping his hands behind his back.

She knew what this was. It was his lecturing pose. He was getting ready to pace before her as he delivered his sermon.

"Your mother has been most upset by this whole situation."

"Why? I have made a brilliant match, have I not?" she replied defiantly, refusing to stand up, remaining composed in her seat. "It is respectable and I am still not your problem anymore. I can hardly think what is so unsettling."

Lord Fairing was brought up short, his look turning even more thunderous at her words. "I have never understood your tendency towards caustic conversation, Rachel. You certainly did not gain it from your mother. And to speak to me so, when you know very well what it is that I have heard from the Countess of Goring."

"That woman does work quickly," Rachel

interjected with venom. "You have been in Town scarcely longer than twelve hours and already she is updating you on your own daughter. I thought, since I was married off, that my actions no longer concerned you. Was that not Sir Denby's role? To tame your wilful daughter. Quite the Shakespearean set of events."

"Stop it, Rachel! You know very well that Sir Denby gave you an advantageous match. He offered a handsome settlement and you were well situated for life."

"Oh yes," said she, her tone taking on that of a petulant child. She hated this. She hated what she felt reduced to before her father. "It worked very well. Tell an eighteen-year-old daughter what she must do and she hardly thinks she has a choice in it. Get rid of the troublesome daughter. Foist her on some grandparent for a husband. As long as she is no longer your problem, and you get your settlement."

It was one thing to be misunderstood by your parents as a child, but another never to escape it as an adult. Had she not married as they had ordered? She had turned off that handsome Mr Thayer who had been paying her court at the time. Even now, when all she had married for was the financial agreement Lord Arleigh had offered, could they not be happy with her brilliant match? She had inadvertently followed their guide and married for position with no thought to feelings. Could they not be proud?

"I honestly have no idea how you cannot be satisfied with my marriage to Lord Arleigh. He is from one of the finest families, and your anger at his haste is falsely directed towards me."

"An illicit wedding! That is what the Countess of Goring had such pleasure in relaying to your mother. There is talk of your behaviour and what actually provoked a wedding with a special licence when you had to know we would agree to the match. The Countess said many are expecting an heir to Arleigh's title within this half year."

At first, Rachel felt as though someone had grabbed hold of her heart within her chest and was squeezing it. The tightness was followed rapidly by a hardening and she set her jaw and projected a look of serenity onto her face. That hateful woman had clearly woven a brightly coloured story around the unusual, but nonetheless respectable, circumstances of their wedding.

"I dare not ask whether being married by special licence so soon after your first husband's death is founded on such an extreme reason." He looked pointedly at her stomach.

"Then do not ask," she snapped. How could her father possibly understand? How could anyone possibly understand unless they too had spent five years married without getting with child. Clearly motherhood was not in the divine plan for her life, but try as she might to make peace with it, the truth of it still stung.

When it stung, her temper was uncontrollable.

She smiled grimly, thinking that she had barely shared an evening with her new husband, let alone a bed. The expression did much to cover the deep, infected wound that ran beneath. It also happened to further rile her father.

"The worst of it is, I believe you capable of it." His flushed face was turned from her now.

She wanted to ask him if he knew the pain he was causing her in doubting her honour, her integrity, in such a manner. Yet, even as the words with their bile rose from the pit of her hurt, they halted in her throat. Why should she need to justify herself? It was pointless—a battle she knew from many years of waging that she had no way of winning. He would believe what he would of her, but for it to be so very insulting, was too much.

"Your behaviour has always left something to be desired, but to have fallen so low, to be so brazen. Did you have no thought to propriety? No doubt, you did it because it amused you! And to think of that look on Lady Goring's face when she told your mother. She positively revelled in it and your poor mother was stricken in her presence."

Rachel did feel guilty at this. She had never wanted to cause her mother pain. She was so frail. It was then that Rachel translated the fierce look on her father's face to concern for her mother. She would have pitied him if not for his next words.

"I am ashamed of you."

She inhaled sharply at the wounding words. "You will not even let me defend myself nor hear what I have to say. You assume that Lady Goring's lies are true."

Neither of the combatants had heard Lord Arleigh and Lady Fairing come back into the room, so when Lord Arleigh spoke, it shocked them both.

"My wife's honour is beyond reproach."

Rachel swung round to see him standing at the door, her mother still on his arm, his face unreadable. He had spoken the statement with such firmness it was bordering on severity, and he was looking at her father without flinching from the thunderous face. He gave Lord Fairing back stare for stare, not giving any ground.

"I believe my judgement is quite sound and I do not believe I would propose marriage to a woman in whose character I was not wholly trusting. I think, with respect, and without in the least meaning to be impolite, that you have upset my wife."

He drew Lady Fairing into the room and passed her hand to Lord Fairing, all the while maintaining a cool equanimity. He then walked purposely towards his own wife, coming alongside Rachel and taking her elbow with a firm, supportive grip.

"I think there has been much excitement—

all due to my hastiness in wishing to make this woman my wife—and as such, perhaps, everyone is overwrought. We are intending to retire to Bath for a month or so on Friday. I regret we will not be seeing you again, though Lady Fairing has already informed me that you are to set sail for the sunny climes of Greece in aid of her health. Therefore, I take it we would not be missing your company in London regardless."

Rachel stood in admiration of him and the way his certainty and underlying firmness kept her father mute. It had been enough that he had come to her rescue at all, let alone to do it with such gentlemanly kindness so as to spare her mother any embarrassment.

"I look forward to us meeting again when you are feeling restored, Lady Fairing." He bowed towards her but did not let go of Rachel, refusing to break their unified front. "Lord Fairing."

Her father looked from one to the other, his gaze finally resting on his daughter. There was no apology there, and she did not expect one, but he was silent for now.

Lord Fairing reluctantly took his leave of the newlyweds. Lady Fairing bid a lengthy farewell to her daughter, and all the time, Rachel could feel the warm hand of her husband on her elbow.

When the door of the morning room finally shut behind them, she could not smother a sigh of relief. Turning to Arleigh, her eyes were filled with gratefulness and a smile quickly spread over her tired face. "I am so thankful to you for saving me. That interview was not pleasant."

His eyes locked onto hers, an earnestness in them she was not expecting. "Had I known," said he, his face quite close to hers, "I would not have left the room."

"That is my father," she said matter-of-factly, shrugging her shoulders. She felt her composure returning and with it an acceptance. "I always know it will be so, but it is never..."

"Easy," he finished for her.

He was still holding her arm, their bodies so close it would only have taken a slight movement for them to embrace. She looked straight at him again, realising that they were almost the same height, he having only an inch on her. Something in his eyes shifted, and she found once again that she could not quite read the expression. Then his gaze moved slightly, resting on her lips. It only lingered there a moment. Then, as if a spell was broken, he came to himself, glancing at the hand that still held her arm.

"I apologise if I was overly forceful," he said, releasing her. "I am not used to my word being questioned by anyone."

There was such strength in his voice that she did not doubt it.

"I felt compelled to defend it, though I am sorry it was at the expense of your mother."

"I do not think either of them were much offended. Surprised maybe. You handled it admirably."

"A compliment?" he said mockingly, a very slight smile on his mouth.

Now she was looking at his lips. She hadn't noticed them before. They were broad and generous and curled in a pleasing way when he smiled.

"I think after that, we both deserve a glass of burgundy," he said, moving away from her and pulling the bell.

The conversation lulled a little as they waited for their refreshment, but when he spoke of the sporting anecdote he had wished to say to her father, they quickly and unintentionally descended into an animated conversation on horse-flesh. But they did not come near each other again. The closeness they had just experienced lay in a world of unspoken danger—one which was not part of their deal.

Chapter 6

"It is not that I do not understand your frustrations," said Caro, "but she needs me, Tobias. You cannot know how she supported me in my life before."

"I supported you in your life before," replied Felton in an irritated tone at odds with his character.

"She has had a blow dealt her by her sister's deception and she is now clearly worried about her mother. It did not help that James arrived so abruptly. Perhaps we should change our kitchen into the entrance hall. It seems destined to be where all our guests choose to enter our house." A gentle smile lit up Caro's blue eyes.

Felton had seemed distant since the fracas in the kitchen yesterday. Caro had let him be, but she could feel the tension of walking a tightrope between two people she loved dearly. She had found Felton's behaviour puzzling at the time, but now she understood it a little. Yet, her heart still ached for her friend who she knew was in pain. She only wished to explain to Felton why Rebecca needed support. And to explain to Rebecca that Felton was protective of her.

Caro could well understand Rebecca's sense of betrayal at her sister's actions. More than that, she had been suspicious of the newlyweds, telling Caro that not one look between the new man and wife had been filled with affection. Caro had endeavoured to explain to Rebecca that perhaps theirs was a marriage of convenience like so many others, but Rebecca had not been convinced.

"I cannot fathom why those two do not declare their love for each other," Felton said in frustrated tones. "It appears plain as day to everyone but themselves."

"I can hardly criticise James and Rebecca on that count." Caro hoped for a return smile at the allusion to their own love affair, but Felton was quick to pick up the thread of his conversation again.

"I know Lady Fairing is much occupying your thoughts, but you must have a care for yourself. You have been through a great deal in the last two years, Caro, this year especially. I know you dislike me telling you what to do, but you are still tired, and recovering. You are in no need of any more drama to exhaust you—yesterday made that clear." Felton raised his brows and looked pointedly at the bandages on her burnt hand.

"You can hardly blame Rebecca for that!"

"Can't I?" he said, gesticulating wildly and pacing the morning room. The cups of tea Caro had poured some time since were growing cold on the pretty little Chinese table. "I had no idea the woman was even in our house! She appears without so much as a card or announcement and suddenly my wife is lost to me for hours on end!"

Caro remained silent and after a time Felton stopped walking and cast rueful eyes towards her.

"Sometimes," he clenched his fists, trying desperately to communicate what he struggled to. "Sometimes I feel as though there are three in this marriage." He came to her then, kneeling before her and finding her hands. He squeezed the unburned hand and grinned lopsidedly. "I am a selfish man, Caro. Is that wrong?"

She sighed, a small gurgle of laughter escaping her, and pulled her good hand from his to touch his cheek. "Oh, you are the very devil himself, knowing I cannot resist those eyes."

This only widened his grin until all his white teeth were flashing at her. He turned then and sat on the floor, his back resting against her knees, his frock coat unbuttoned and his waistcoat open, revealing his white shirt. He kicked off his shoes and sighed while Caro ran a hand through the hair he had forgotten to tie back that morning.

"You know I cannot stop loving her, but I

shall balance my time better," said Caro.   Felton took his cup of tea from the table and drank it down in a single gulp despite its tepid temperature.

"I do think James feels very deeply for Rebecca, but Rebecca will not say anything to me. I have asked her, but she just goes quiet. That is never a good thing with her."

Felton chuckled, soothed by his wife's promise, and willing to be his usual self again.

"I do often feel tired," Caro said, finally admitting the truth in her husband's earlier words.

"What?" He turned round on the floor, facing her once again. "My argumentative wife is agreeing with me? I have been telling you that you need to rest these last six months!"

"I am hardly able to do so and you well know why."

"Well," said he, a wink flashing across his left eye and a playful smile on his mouth, "when a man has seen those legs, who can blame him?"

Caro thought she knew exactly where this was going until Felton's brows suddenly knitted and his green eyes lingered somewhere on her bodice. "You know, I've been thinking, though I am sure you will not wish to, with Rebecca upset as she is –"

"Tell me?"

"I have been wanting to take you to Bath. We never did get away for our honeymoon, but the time for showing Society that Angelica Worth is no longer in England and that you have made a respectable match has passed. Lady Etheridge has kept her ear to the ground and there seem to be no new rumours. They have moved onto that young chit who has become Duchess of Rochford and her husband's infamous behaviours. It could be the perfect time for us to slip away for a while.

"I can ask my mother to arrange for the house she has stayed in before to be engaged for us. You can be kept safe from any dramas, we can slow down, and if we feel so inclined, we can even leave the bedroom for a day or two."

"That sounds like a splendid idea."

"Really?"

"Oh yes," said Caro, her heart beating a little faster as she drew on her courage. "I should like to take the waters. I believe they will be very beneficial for my constitution, not to mention the baby's."

"Yes, well, that's what I've been thinking," said Felton, his gaze still on her stomacher while her words slowly filtered through his consciousness, until his eyes snapped up at her. "Baby's?"

Caro's full lips curved and her blue eyes started twinkling. "Why else would I be silly enough to faint and burn my hand?"

Felton took hold of her arms with a look of seriousness that did not sit well on his face at all, so Caro started to laugh.

"You're with child?"

"Yes," she said, giggling at the expression of awe on his face. Suddenly he pulled her up and kissed her before dropping to his knees and staring at her stomach. He put an ear to it, his hands spread around her sides.

"I don't believe the baby is big enough to talk yet," said Caro, the smile on her face irrepressible. She had been waiting to be sure before sharing the news.

He stood again, wrapping her in his arms and kissing her on both cheeks and then the mouth.

"You minx!" He laughed, kissing her again. "I am to be a father, and you a mother."

"Quite terrifying, I agree."

"And incredible."

He hugged her to him, burying his face in her hair and kissing every part of her shoulder he could find.

"Quite incredible," he whispered.

"That hat is too large for my carriage."

Rachel affected a scandalised look at her husband, a gloved hand touching the wide brim of the straw creation affectionately.

"Well, as you are riding, I thought I would take advantage of the extra space for my *beauti-*

ful hat." Her eyes were dancing and Arleigh knew she was challenging him.

She had formed a habit of doing it ever since they had spoken horseflesh together and he had agreed with the virtues of crossbreeding warmbloods and Irish draughts. Apparently she was under the impression she had won some sort of battle and ever since she had been provoking him. The problem was, he was beginning to find it amusing.

"I have no doubt it will take up the space of three other occupants. But it is not me you must negotiate with, rather, it is the door."

His wife turned to the carriage, her head cocking to the side, sizing up the door frame. He had thought his argument watertight, but apparently, she wished to test the gap, much like a farmyard cat would with its whiskers.

She ventured forward with her head at that odd, cocked angle and aimed for the door.

At that moment, Jeffries descended the steps of the Town house with one of Lord Arleigh's cases and, pausing beside his master, became quite as transfixed as the Viscount.

"She is attempting to fit through the door, Jeffries."

"So it appears, my lord."

The monotone reply, in light of his wife's actions, could not help but fan the spark of amusement in his lordship. He laughed.

"Should I ask Miss Nellie to pack Lady Arleigh's hat, my lord?"

"I doubt she will let you take it from her, Jeffries," replied Arleigh, turning towards the bemused look of his servant. "It is no matter. We shall merely have to leave her to discover the basics of measurements herself. Are we quite packed?"

It took a moment for the servant to recover. It had been some time since he had seen his master amused.

The Viscount listened to the list of duties, packed items and household notifications. Shortly after, his housekeeper came and told him the same but he found it hard to attend to what they said. He was considering the difference he had felt since the visit of his wife's parents. The dynamics between him and Rachel had changed. He didn't know how, but something *had* changed. It was one of the reasons he had decided to ride to Bath rather than sit in the carriage with Rachel. He enjoyed riding, it was true, but he could easily have foregone it for this long journey.

Her provocative comments. The dangerous tone she insisted on using. The intimacy it all implied. None of it was part of their deal and to be perfectly frank, Arleigh had not been prepared for it.

He had been used to living his life as he pleased for the past twenty-eight years. He had never done any serious courting. He had never been good at that sort of thing. Other men in his youth had possessed silken tongues and all the courtly platitudes which he had never been able to replicate. He had been a tall, broad and ungainly youth. He had not enjoyed the raucous behaviour of his peers and he hadn't cared much for their attitudes. Frivolous spending, wild antics and a rambunctious lifestyle had simply never made sense to him. And Arleigh liked sense.

He liked working hard on his estate, he enjoyed a good night's sleep and he appreciated intelligent conversation. Everything else simply felt like a waste of time. His mother, of course, had never understood. She had described the late Viscount Arleigh as quite the man about Town. He had been an excellent politician and together they had hosted some of the biggest balls of the Season.

Of course, the actions of the late Lord in the public sphere had never matched up with those in the private. His marriage of convenience had been one of oppression and control. But his mother would never admit that. Arleigh was not sure she would know how. To her the marriage had been a success. She had married well, given her authoritarian husband a son, and performed her Societal duties. She had conformed to all expected norms and so that was success, no matter the joy or happiness involved. But Arleigh had seen the silent suffering in his mother's eyes and he knew he could not cause such pain in another, no matter the wishes of his father or mother.

Although the Dowager appreciated Arleigh's practical-mindedness when it came to the estate and the various houses the family owned, he always knew she had wanted a son she could hold up as a great beau for the young ladies of the ton to dangle after. It would be yet another feather of success in her cap. Aside from the unappealing nature of a marriage like his parents', Arleigh had rarely found an eligible young lady who could string ten intelligent words together, let alone keep his interest for a full conversation. He found balls and assemblies dreadfully dull unless his friends were present, and they were few and not always in Town. They, like him, enjoyed living on their estates. Very unfashionable.

Rachel had held his attention for a full two hours the other night. He had quite forgotten he was speaking to a woman. He had appreciated not only her knowledge but her insights and suddenly, her teasing had become bearable. In fact, it had become amusing. It turned out his wife was quite intelligent and funny. To be perfectly honest, it had shaken him a little.

"… so we are all ready for your departure, my lord."

Good Lord! Had his housekeeper been speaking at him that entire time?

He nodded. "Very good."

And it *was* very good that he knew he

could trust his servants. For it would not do to ask them both to repeat themselves. It would not do at all.

"Your horse, my lord."

Arleigh's tiger presented Sampson, his broad Irish draught.

"There you see!"

Rachel's sudden exclamation sent even the calm-tempered Sampson skittering sideways. It was just as well that the gelding moved his flank out of the way, for then Arleigh could gain a view of what had so excited his wife.

He struggled to maintain his equanimity when he saw the dishevelled state of both his wife's hair and her straw hat. Several items of faux fruit were scattered on the floor of the carriage and a few lengths of straw were pulled from the plaits around its wide brim, but there it sat, on the seat which would have been his.

Lady Arleigh was opposite, pulling pins from her hair and sighing.

"I am afraid my hair will never do. Nellie spent a full hour on it this morning tucking it beneath my hat. You see why I was loath to take it off now. She will have to do something with it when we change horses. Tomorrow I shall choose my chapeau with a little more care and a little less brim, for I am determined to meet your mother with my hair firmly under control!"

Arleigh took this speech in his stride, and assured his wife that, no doubt, his mother would know a good milliner in Bath who could repair the damaged hat.

"I am very appreciative. You know, with as much hair as I have under my command—or not as the case may be—it can be a loathsome task to find a hat that will fit over it all. At least the fashion is for large hair styles, for if it were not, I think I should have to shave my head."

"I sincerely hope that is never the case," said Arleigh.

Not riding with her was the right choice. Sampson's back might become uncomfortable after a fifty-mile ride, but it was certainly safer than a carriage journey with this woman. Three months. That was what they had agreed. Only three months.

"Shall we?" He took up the reins and hoisted himself into the saddle. The convoy began to leave London not five minutes later.

Chapter 7

"Doctor Smith commands me to drink it," said Lady Etheridge, her sharp eyes looking less than pleased. "Though I detest the stuff. Have you ever tasted Bath's waters? From the taste, one would never think it could be good for one's health."

"I haven't, Lady Etheridge, but many swear by it," Caro responded placidly. She had come to take her leave of Rebecca. Felton would be round with the carriage shortly. He had given her a strict quarter of an hour to say goodbye, declaring that she would be too exhausted if the visit were any longer, considering the drive they had ahead of them.

"Isn't it a happy coincidence that we are coming too," cried Rebecca, leaning conspiratorially towards Caro, her dark eyes sparkling with mischief. "And we are hot on the heels of my sister and Lord Arleigh. We can find out what it is they are hiding."

"Stop whispering like that! It's an impediment to my knowing *everything*." Lady Etheridge rapped her cane on the floor. "We shall be in Bath by early next week. When do you leave?"

"In less than a quarter of an hour," replied Caro, wondering how on earth she was going to break the news to her husband that all and sundry were descending on Bath.

"What? How abominably prompt."

"We decided yesterday, and Felton felt it would be advantageous to leave as soon as we could. We never had a honeymoon, you see," said Caro, hoping that the gently spoken words would find purchase in Rebecca's mind. "I left him taking charge of packing the house and overseeing preparations with the carriage. He is determined to leave today and we shall depart from your very door, Lady Etheridge."

"A man so intent on whisking his wife away, one would think loves you very much. Enough to take a sword for you," Lady Etheridge said, her merry eyes twinkling at Caro causing her to smile back.

"If this is a kind of honeymoon, does your brother not intend to come too?"

Rebecca avoided Caro's eye as she asked the question, drinking her tea and allowing her gaze to wander casually to her aunt.

"Mr Worth is back in Town? You failed to mention it, child," Lady Etheridge chided her niece.

"He is," Caro replied happily. "I believe Felton is happy for him to attend us after a few weeks."

"Well, I shall keep you company until then," said Rebecca, "for I am sure Mr Worth will be late. He is always away you know."

Lady Etheridge first eyed her niece and then sent a knowing and characteristically piercing glance towards Caro before speaking in her usual cutting way. "I do not think that Caro meant to say she wanted company before her brother arrives, Rebecca. I'm not sure a friend is needed on a honeymoon—or did I not translate that correctly, Mrs Felton?"

"Well... I..." Even Caro's quick wit did not have the speed to find a reply in time. She watched a wounded look overtake Rebecca's face.

"I remember how jealous my dear Roderick was of my time when we were first wed. I think you ought to leave them in peace, Rebecca. As for your sister, however, I shall make an exception when we get to Bath. I shall most certainly be visiting her and giving her quite the set-down after her lack of thought in *not* notifying me of her wedding. I am only glad that you had the wit to tell me, Rebecca, for if I had heard it from Lady Goring, I would have been forced to beat your sister with this cane of mine. Lord Arleigh, no less." Lady Etheridge's spoken thoughts detoured. "I am surprised at the man. He did not seem the marrying kind in his youth. Then again, men do have a tendency to surprise one. That Tobias Felton of yours is the perfect example. Who knew the scamp would someday become a respectable husband."

"Who knew," Caro echoed, an intimate smile playing on her lips.

The words were no insult when spoken by Lady Etheridge who knew both their stories so well. Caro still felt thankful towards the woman who had helped guide them together, though when she had uttered such sentiments to the widow shortly after her marriage, she had received a sharp command to desist such silly niceties.

"But if the rumours which that awful woman is spreading have any truth to them, then I am Queen Charlotte herself! I argued against her first match, you know. Cruel indeed to throw a young girl away on an old man, no matter his parentage. At least she has had the sense to choose for herself this time, regardless of your bullish father."

"Aunt!"

Caro was thankful that at that moment her ladyship's footman entered the room to announce her husband.

Felton's long legs and fine frame came gracefully into the room and he swept an outlandish bow to Lady Etheridge before he kissed the widow's hand. As ever, she appreciated the attention, swatting him away playfully and denouncing his libertine ways as unbecoming for a new husband.

"And how am I supposed to resist when faced with such intelligence and beauty?" he said with his mischievous grin. He greeted Lady Rebecca politely and then came to stand beside his wife, a protective hand immediately finding her shoulder.

"I am afraid I cannot stay. Bath awaits us and my wife has been tired of late, so I wish for us to make an early go of it."

Lady Etheridge eyed the hand upon Caro's shoulder and noted her sudden aversion to meeting anyone's gaze.

"A wise decision no doubt. It is a fool who attempts to go near Hampstead Heath in the twilight hours."

"Quite right, my lady, and I have no intention of introducing Caro to anyone of the High Toby variety. We will therefore bid you both adieu for the moment." He swept another bow and placed his hand under Caro's elbow to guide her upward. She tried to whisper something in his ear, but he was too intent on getting her away.

She had seen his look of concern the moment he had entered the room. Since he had learned of her condition, he was intent on swaddling her in as much comfort and unnecessary concern as possible. It had not mattered that she had argued thousands of women had undergone this natural part of life and she did not need to be bossed around by a boorish husband. He had only winked at her in response which really had not helped the matter.

"Yes, well, we shall endeavour to leave you to yourselves in Bath, for we shall be there next week."

"Yes we shall," said Rebecca. "And though I shall listen to my aunt's absurd suggestion that Caro may wish to spend more time with you than me, I shall certainly be expecting to see you both at the assemblies. Aunt says they are not the same since Beau Nash left us, but there will still be some entertainment from them, no doubt. Besides that, I am sure I can spend some time with my sister."

Felton's hand had tightened perceptibly upon Caro's arm.

"There is quite a host of us going to Bath then?" he said in the most relaxed tone he could manage.

"I have been ordered by my physician," said Lady Etheridge, "and Rebecca tells me she cannot wait to go and see Rachel again. I have no idea what so fascinates her, but she will not stop obsessing over her sister's new match. I should very much like to meet him and give her a set-down for not telling me of it, but apart from that, I believe they can be left quite to themselves."

Caro was pleased when Felton did not delve any deeper into the subject or offer any acidic remarks. He again bid good day to the women most amicably and left the house with his wife on his arm.

"So," he said, once he had settled Caro in the carriage with a blanket over her knees and a hot brick beneath her feet though it was summer. "We are to be invaded everywhere we go by whatever Rebecca's imagination has conjured up over her sister's match with Lord Arleigh."

Caro leant forward and took her husband's hand, speaking soothingly. "I am sorry, darling, I had no idea. But Lady Etheridge at least understands that we may not want to be disturbed. She already said to Rebecca before you arrived that we would like to be left alone. Actually," Caro said, releasing his hand and laying back on the carriage cushions as they rattled through London's morning streets. She bit her bottom lip meditatively which was never helpful for her husband who found this by-product of her thoughtfulness very attractive. "I think Rebecca was quite upset with me when I did not argue with her aunt's assumption that we wished to be left alone."

"Good! I like Lady Rebecca, but she can be rather invasive." Felton looked sour, staring out of the window as if someone had just stolen his favourite toy.

"Darling?" Caro questioned after half an hour of silence.

"Yes?"

"We are going away together," she said happily.

At these words a grin began to form on Felton's face. He caught eyes with his wife, his own twinkling, and then moved from the opposite seat to her side, putting his arm about her shoulders and pulling her close.

"So we are, wife." And he kissed her head.

Rachel's journey to Bath was proving quite different to that of the Feltons. By the end of the day, she had spent a total of eight hours in a carriage alone, being bumped about, and becoming quite unbearably bored.

When they finally arrived at the establishment in which Lord Arleigh had arranged for them to spend the night, she was quite honestly in a foul mood. She descended the carriage steps without a thought to her precious hat which still resided on the seat opposite hers. It had not proved a good conversational partner.

"Dinner will be brought into the parlour at six o'clock and then I think an early night is a good idea for both of us," said Arleigh, who had given his horse to a waiting groom.

"You may think what you want, but at this moment I am sure I do not care!"

Arleigh's brows rose at this but he remained silent as he stared at his wife. The fearsome expression on Rachel's face broke under his scrutiny.

"I am sorry," she said, rubbing her temples and drawing her fingers across her eyes. "I'm afraid the journey has worn on my nerves and I sound like the most spoiled chit you ever heard! I am not used to travelling. Sir Denby never once left his estate during our five years of marriage, and so neither did I. I have forgotten how weary it can make one feel."

"I understand." Lord Arleigh softened his tone a little. "I have kept you on the road too long. Come, you shall feel better after a cup of coffee and something to eat." He offered her his arm and without thinking, she took it. If she had not been so tired from the journey, she might have noted that this was the first time he had done so since their wedding day two weeks earlier.

They weaved their way through the public rooms of the hostelry and Rachel noticed that a great many people turned and stared as they did so. Some even tugged their forelocks. She frowned at the gesture, realising soon after that the crest on the carriage must have been seen by one of the lackeys in the stableyard and news had spread that a nobleman was in their midst.

"It may not be the most luxurious establishment, but I have found that it offers more peace than the others. I cannot abide acquaintances coming to my rooms and disturbing me during a tiring journey. I found this inn when I was riding down from Yorkshire and it serves some of the best pie I have ever tasted."

Rachel realised he was talking to make her feel better and she felt a sudden rush of gratitude.

"I am sure that Mr and Mrs Norris will have made it specially. They usually do when I let them know I am coming. It is why they stared downstairs. The locals are beginning to recognise me."

They entered a small parlour. It was furnished with a plain wooden table and chairs. There were a few small paintings on the wall and a pot of coffee already on the table, sending up a welcoming plume of steam from its spout.

"Sit down," Arleigh commanded and Rachel obeyed with only the merest look of defiance.

He took the coffee pot and poured two cups. Placing one before Rachel, he gave her another command, this time to drink, and again she obeyed. They were silent for a few moments, both gathering their thoughts.

"You're all wet," said Rachel suddenly.

After several gulps of the hot, bittersweet liquid, Rachel had begun to feel more herself. With the refreshment, she had finally taken in the state of her husband.

"It showered a little when we came out of London." He looked down at the mud spattered all over his boots and breeches. "It looks worse than it is. I must confess this is the state I usually return in when I have been inspecting the farms on my estate. I make a most unconventional sight, I dare say."

He no doubt said the last part in response to the glare Rachel was giving him. "Well, if it is to rain tomorrow, then please don't be so stupid as to keep riding. Just sit in the carriage with me. Honestly! It must have been when I drifted off. If I had known, I would have lowered the window and commanded you to join me. Goodness gracious, here I am complaining of being tired and you have been riding all this time and are still standing to wait on *me*."

"Commanded me?" Arleigh raised a brow and took a chair beside her, stretching his long legs out and resting one of his large arms on the table, droplets from his greatcoat rolling off onto the linen tablecloth.

"Don't you believe me? You should know by now what a Jezebel I can be. My father certainly does. That is why he was so odious the other day," Rachel said, avoiding Arleigh's eyes. They could be so very steady and relentless sometimes. She played with her cup, pulling the handle back and forth, twisting it on its saucer. "I am sorry you saw it. I get so angry at the time. Then after it is over, and he is gone, my temper cools and I can hardly blame him for being exasperated by me. I am not the daughter he wanted."

She had desired to say this since her parents' visit.

"He had no choice in it."

"No." Rachel's wide lips curled up in a rueful smile. "That's the problem. I rather think he likes to control things and it frustrates him beyond measure that I cannot be controlled by him.

"It is why I was married off to Sir Denby. I was told he was a decent match. Much better than the younger, less prosperous Mr Thayers who was nearer my age. And of course, in spite of the tears, an eighteen-year-old hardly knows that she can refuse to say the words at the altar. At least with me married off to some old gentleman, I was taken care of and kept from causing any scandals. Not that I had a taste for any. Romance is over-estimated in my opinion—forget the drama and be practical about the matter. Why can no one just think, 'Yes, I rather like this person, I shall do life with them?'" She was rambling, and she knew it, but she was too tired to care and Arleigh was too patient a listener. "But then, I guess it can't be like that with all these titles and lands and wealth, can it?"

She looked at him then, and found his gaze ever steady, his firm mouth pressed shut and his hands folded patiently in his lap. "I am talking nonsense. I feel worn out, I am afraid, and my head aches terribly."

"You will feel better for food."

She had expected him to stop there. To be

happy that she was not harping on anymore. To thank luck that he was no longer hearing her tragedy.

"You were only eighteen—how old was Sir Denby?"

"Fifty-seven when we married—sixty-two when he died."

Arleigh's brows rose and she saw the question in his eyes that everyone always had.

"We were man and wife for a time." She looked away, a blush stealing up her usually composed cheeks. "But I think he grew tired of making the effort and I can't say I was desirous of renewing his interest." She blinked, her eyes shutting for just a fraction too long, and then opened them again and met Arleigh stare for stare.

"Without a son to inherit and look after his dear mama, I was cast out." She spoke satirically of herself, not allowing him to ask the question she had seen in the eyes of all her acquaintances after her first month as a married woman. When would she be with child? Why wasn't it now? What could be... wrong?

"I suspect the cousin and his wife shall be far more the thing to run Godalming Hall. There," she said, a defensive flash of anger in her eyes. "My sorry story for you to pick over. Come, tell me, how much do you pity me?"

Her harsh words were expecting a retort, but still Arleigh sat there, calmly, steadily watching her.

"I find little pleasure," he said, finally speaking, "in hearing that a young girl was married off to an old man. Your father was wrong to do it."

His simplicity washed over Rachel in a refreshing wave. She felt the anger and resentment suddenly justified. No one had uttered aloud those inner thoughts of hers before.

"I should never subject my sisters to such treatment."

"Good."

They sat for a moment in silence until the inn's servants brought in their food. A crispy golden-topped pie was placed before Rachel. Her mouth watered instantly at the gravy-rich steam rising from the slits in the pastry. Cheerful green vegetables and a selection of carrots sat beside the pie and she did not need to be asked twice by her husband to begin devouring the exquisite meal.

"You were quite right!" she exclaimed at the end of the plateful, dropping her knife and fork and sitting back in her chair, hands on her full stomach. "I do not think I shall need to eat for a week!"

Chapter 8

The inn's servant girl brought in two glasses of fortified wine and cleared the plates. Once she was gone and they were alone again, Arleigh watched his wife take up one of the glasses and turn to face the fire. He could see the flames dancing in her eyes, the lids drooping, suddenly heavy with good food and weariness.

"Do you mind if I undress my hair? The pins are pulling."

Arleigh nodded silently. He watched as she placed her glass on the table and, turning back towards the fire, she started work on her hair.

He considered her afresh as he looked on. A childless woman, that was what she had admitted. Did that mean she could bear none? Was that the truth behind the dire straits that had led her to proposing their deal? And what did that mean for him? They had not spoken of children when they had discussed their deal. The separation was practical and no thought to heirs had been given. He was too concerned about his inheritance to think about his would-be heirs someday.

But was it such a bad thing? He should have been concerned by it, but his chief aim up until now had been to provide for his mother and sisters which he was able to do. There was always his brother Felix. If he should marry and have children the title and estate would eventually fall to him. Besides, Arleigh had never thought of having his own family. He'd seen enough of his mother's unhappiness to know that he could not inflict the same on some unsuspecting female. That is what made Rachel's deal such a good choice. And perhaps the fact that she could not have children served them both; there would be no danger of a child from unhappy parents as he had been.

He wondered if Rachel saw it that way, or whether her sudden harshness had been to hide deep pain. Whatever the case, she seemed calm now, pulling one pin out after another, the movements deft and silent and somehow intoxicating. He allowed the wine to flood his tired senses, dulling the aches from his long ride, and uncurling the muscles that had grown tight with the exertion.

She looked so appealing like that, before the fire, the warm light falling across her face, décolletage and strong pale arms. He watched each tumbling curl let loose, falling in wild tangles down her back and across her shoulders. He thought of Sir Denby, an old man, watching her so, night after night, when they had been married. The thought sent unpleasant feelings running through his arms, and his fingers curled tighter around his wine glass.

He caught the flicker of flames in the glass and the sight disrupted his thoughts. What was he doing? He shook himself mentally. What was he thinking? The drink was addling his senses. Before him sat a woman who was his wife in name, but that was all.

He looked at her again, but she had been unconscious of his gaze and his thoughts. She pushed the rim of her glass against her full lips and lay back in her chair, her stockinged feet, bare of shoes, raised towards the fire.

"D'you know," she said, bringing Arleigh up from the depths of his thoughts. "I can't remember the last time I felt so content."

She drank again, not justifying the sentence, and Arleigh couldn't help his brow from furrowing. What did she mean content? With their deal? Their journey? The prospect of her impending financial independence?

"Past your stuffy exterior, you are quite an easy fellow to get along with." She drained the last of her glass. "I mean it as a compliment, of course, before you become all offended. There are not many men who can tolerate me for long."

He could well believe that.

"But we can just sit here, like this, and it doesn't matter. I don't know that I've ever done that before. Usually it's all propriety and behaving and looking becoming. It's quite different with you, y'know." She looked over her shoulder at him, the tumble of her curls falling over the chair back as she slouched in an unladylike manner. "Perhaps marriages of convenience are no bad thing after all."

Why did she need to talk like this? Why must she constantly be sharing of herself in a manner which seemed to demand the same of him? But that wasn't what vexed him. What vexed him was that through her babbling, through her constant chatter, through her honesty, he was beginning to care, and damn it, he didn't want to care.

She was bewitching him in some way and this wine was pushing him over whatever edge he was standing on. His practicality, his common sense, all seemed muted in his mind. He was only happy she was over there and he was here, in this chair. Safe.

"I suppose I had better go to bed. We are up again early tomorrow—and it was your command." She had risen, that glorious mass of dark brown hair draped luxuriously over one shoulder and her imperious expression exchanged for an impish grin as she played on his previous words.

Arleigh rose to match her.

"There is only one room. Jeffries told me on arrival."

"Oh."

His wife did not look startled by the news. Rather, she simply appeared a little wrong-footed. He saw her brows knit a little, her mouth remaining partially open.

"Well, that is somewhat problematic."

"I can sleep in the chair before the fire if you take the room." Arleigh jerked his head towards the door, behind which a modest double bed lay. He had stayed in it many times before. Apparently one drawback of using a provincial inn, against its many positive aspects, was the lack of available rooms.

He was not looking forward to spending the night in the chair. He knew he would be trading one set of aching muscles for another, but he didn't allow his face to betray his thoughts.

"And ride tomorrow? Are you insane?" asked his wife. She drew her shoulders back and the imperious expression which so suited her large-featured face returned. She could never be described as pretty, but she was most certainly handsome.

"And you have a better proposal?" He was not really expecting an answer. He'd uttered the question without thinking. After it was said, it hung there like an awkward hanger-on.

Uncomfortable with the continuing silence, he left the room. He needed to clear his head and being trapped in a room with that woman was making it impossible. There was nothing Julius Arleigh disliked more than disorder and the disorder of his mind was completely unacceptable. He went to find Nellie, to send her up to get her mistress ready for bed, and tell Jeffries that he was not needed. That way, at least the servants would be kept oblivious to their master sleeping in a chair.

He returned some time later to an empty room but it did not stay empty for long. Lady Arleigh strode into the room, her hair in a manageable braid which fell to her waist, and the tatty banyan she had been wearing in the London house swathed around her, hinting at the hourglass shape beneath.

"Well, I have made the best of it, but I am afraid it will be a tight squeeze. Still, horizontal rest, if a little restricted, must surely trump any sleep to be had in a chair."

Arleigh had already taken in her figure, her dress, and her hair, before he quite realised what he was doing. When his eyes met hers, he couldn't hold her pragmatic gaze and took refuge in walking over by the fire.

"What do you mean?" he asked, unbuttoning his frock coat and hanging it over a chair. He sat down and began to work on extricating his feet from his leather boots, suddenly realising how essential Jeffries in fact was.

"I mean that I have created a sort of...

wall… which means that you can share the bed with me."

"Share the bed?" he said, his steady eyes finding hers again and seeing nothing of mischief there.

"Yes," she said, beginning to laugh. "And you needn't worry. I have no designs on your innocent person, but you do need sleep and I shall not be known as the woman who made her husband sleep in a chair."

She said everything so practically, so non-romantically, that it sounded sensible even to him. He had cooled off considerably since leaving her and, now that the madness that had flitted through his mind was gone, he really did wish to rest his weary muscles in a bed.

"If it will not inconvenience you."

"It will, considerably, for I am not the stillest of sleepers. I often end up upside down and quite turned about during the night. But I shall bear the suffering admirably. It is the least I can do for taking up your carriage seat with my hat."

Arleigh nodded and she disappeared through the door to the bedroom. When he did not follow her for half an hour, she came back out and what she saw set her off into peels of laughter. He glared back at her.

"I told Jefferies I did not need his help."

"Well, you lied, my lord."

She came over and knelt before him, taking the heel of one mud-covered boot with both hands.

"You needn't bother yourself," he protested, his body tensing at her close proximity.

"Don't be silly. I have tugged off my fair share of boots."

He relaxed only a little, allowing her to wiggle the boot and pull it at an angle from the heel that he could not manage himself.

"Well done!" he exclaimed as the offending item came free and she put it to dry before the fire.

She came back for the other but this one was harder. Arleigh found himself having to grip the arms of the chair just so that she wouldn't pull him off it. She was surprisingly strong.

"Goodness!" she said, and then mumbled something Arleigh was sure sounded like cursing. She tugged, pulled, twisted. All of a sudden it came free and she didn't have time to right herself. She was sent careening across the room falling against a pile of logs which toppled to the floor with her.

Arleigh leapt up from his chair, but she was giggling before he even got to her. The giggles transformed into deep rolls of laughter and caused tears to spring into her eyes. She was a sight to behold and it tickled him until he was laughing along with her.

"Let me take that," he said, finally stopping and relieving her of his muddy boot which she had been hugging to her chest.

It had left a large streak of dirt across the banyan, obscuring the oriental pattern. He offered her his hand and pulled her up. She was still laughing and hardly able to gain her balance, falling into him, making him drop the boot. He held her up against him, her body warm and surprisingly soft. Considering this woman was an imperious Amazonian she felt shockingly feminine against him. His shirt was half undone and her hair brushed his chest, her scent rising to him. And she was still laughing, totally oblivious of the effect she was having on him.

She pressed her hands against his chest and looked up into his eyes for a responding smile.

"You're filthy."

"It's your fault," she retorted, giggling.

When she caught the look in his eyes, however, she stopped. She made to speak but Arleigh saw words fail her. She stilled in his arms and he stared at her—at her eyes, her nose, her cheeks and then at her mouth. He wanted to kiss that mouth. He wanted to feel those lips against his.

"You'll need to take that off," he said abruptly.

"I beg your pardon?" Her eyes widened, her mouth parting.

"Your banyan." He let go of her and picked up the dropped boot, placing it with the other by the fire. "I shall not look if you wish to discard it. The fire will dry the mud by morning and you'll be able to brush it off."

Practicality. Sense. That was the best protection against whatever this was.

"Yes."

Her tone had changed and when he glanced at her, she was looking away, pulling at the cords which held her banyan together. He clenched his jaw, turned, and sought the bedroom for refuge. Choosing a side of the bed, he finally lay his weary frame down against the wall of blankets Rachel had made. His body may be tired, but his mind was no longer in the mood for rest.

He waited for her to come in, heard her blow out the candles and walk through the dark to her side of the bed, all without saying a word. He felt the impression she made on the bed as she sat down. He noted her movement until she lay still, just the other side of the pathetic barrier, the closest they had been at night.

Try as he might, he failed to relax beneath the covers. His fists were balled at his side, his breathing anything but steady and all ability to sleep deserted him. He turned, trying to find some kind of comfort, trying to ignore the woman he could hear breathing beside him. A woman in the same bed. A woman who was his wife.

Chapter 9

Arleigh greeted his mother and two sisters in the morning room of the family house in Bath. His mother had relegated herself and her two daughters to a set of apartments near the Assembly Rooms in the upper part of town. It was the correct thing to do with the arrival of a new Viscountess Arleigh, but he could already see she was not pleased about the matter.

"And where is this bride of yours?" She looked surprisingly young to be a widow and the mother of four children.

Arleigh's two sisters, the Honourable Diana and Phoebe Arleigh, took after their mother in height and hair colour. The sisters' hair was dark, almost black, but in the Dowager Viscountess' case it was streaked with grey. It made her look frighteningly superior. The look on her youngest daughter Phoebe's face hinted at the effects of her mother's imperious moods.

"She is not yet down. How are the rooms in

Green Street?"

The Dowager's eyes were a striking blue and she fixed them on her eldest son. "They are small."

"I am sorry that you felt you had to move, mother. You needn't have. I very much doubt my wife would have been averse to your remaining here."

"I had no intention of staying here." Her gaze became impossibly sharper. "I would hardly make myself a burden to your new household. Of course, if I had known that the marriage was to take place, I would have arranged for apartments before the rush and not left so many of our belongings here."

Arleigh skirted the chaise longue on which his mother was sitting, circling it to take a seat at its end. He stretched his large stockinged legs out before him, the skirts of his rather plain jacket flaring out to the side.

"Mother, you know that father's ridiculous behest made it impossible for me to deal well with the question of my marriage."

The Dowager said nothing.

"If I had not been quick about it, I would have failed to meet his request for my marriage within half a year, and we know what would have happened then."

"Is she pretty, Julius?"

"Don't be so impertinent, Phoebe. And hold your tongue when Julius is speaking with mother."

The fourteen-year-old Phoebe felt the best response to this curt rebuke from her older sister was a gaudy display of her tongue.

Arleigh felt a smile tugging at his mouth.

"And do you now speak like a native, Phoebe? You promised me when I last saw you that I would not be able to tell you were English born."

"Oui, monsieur, je suis devenu tout à fait compétent. Je parle comme le roi Louis lui-même."

"Oh, do you? Perhaps I had better introduce you at the French court next Season—then you may tell Louis yourself, oui?"

"Oh, do you mean it, Julius? In earnest, for I am sure I should be a delight to converse with."

"I am hardly sure of that." Diana's nose was ever so slightly hooked and she held it up in a habitually arrogant attitude when conversing with her younger counterpart.

Arleigh ignored the slight passing between his sisters and turned back to his mother.

"How have you been feeling, mother?"

The noble-looking woman did not catch his eye. She spent some time arranging the black skirts of her *robe à la française* and plucking at the delicate lace edging of her elbow-length sleeves. He watched the pinching about her mouth and the movement of her neck as she swallowed down the answer she might have given.

"Mama." He took the hand nearest to him, ignoring the squabbling between the sisters across the room. "Please speak to me. You have not spoken about father since his death."

"Felix fails to write me," she said, taking her hand back and keeping a pragmatic tone. "You will tell your brother that he may well enjoy his military duties but the duty to his mother comes first."

"I will tell him."

"You understand why your father asked you to marry, Julius?" she said, turning to him suddenly, her green eyes arresting his gaze. "You must secure an heir for the Arleigh name. We can trace our line back to the Conquest. Your father feared you would be content to remain a bachelor forever. You are not the man of Town and Society that he was."

"Well, I have obeyed his dying wishes," said Arleigh, releasing her hand and looking away. He felt guilty. Much like finding a hair in one's soup, guilt ruined everything. The satisfaction he had thought this visit would bring was dashed.

He knew that his father had wanted him to secure the family line, but his ridiculous bequest had jeopardised the whole estate. If Arleigh had not married Rachel when he did, he would have lost everything. He had been caught in a trap of his family's own making, and the only way out was to compromise. He had married quickly and conveniently and it had secured his inheritance.

He wished to arrange for their separation as soon as the lawyers and his family were satisfied. He had his half of the deal to uphold and he was a man of his word. The embarrassment would be born. It had to be, and hopefully could be done quietly.

"Yes, but who is this girl?"

Arleigh hardly thought the term girl could be applied to his wife. Rachel was anything but a young, green girl. She was more worldly than he had supposed. She was intelligent with good conversation and at the inn she had looked...

"She was the widow of Sir Denby, the eldest daughter of the Earl and Countess Fairing."

"But how could you marry in such ignominy? Without the proper attention that a viscount deserves." The Dowager pursed her lips. "I suspect it was all her doing—am I right? She was no doubt happy to secure such a brilliant match, especially if what I hear of her is true. She is called an eccentric."

"She is... an acquired taste," Arleigh conceded.

Just then, the door to the morning room was thrown open and the woman in question strode in. She wore the same silk banyan that seemed to be her home attire. Her hair, at least, was dressed, and Arleigh noted the fine line of her neck rising from the chemisette she wore with the man's garment.

She hadn't looked up from the letter she held in her hand as she came in and her Amazonian stride brought her to the centre of the family gathering before she was any the wiser as to company in the room.

"Arleigh, I…" she began, finally looking up from the document in her hand and jumping at the sight of the stern-looking woman beside her husband. "Goodness!" She turned around, catching sight of the sisters. Phoebe's mouth was agape and Diana immediately raised her nose at the sight of Rachel's dress. "What a gathering!"

"Lady Arleigh." He rose, taking her unencumbered hand and drawing her to a position that could be seen by all members of his family. "This is my family, all accounted for apart from my brother Felix who is serving as an officer in His Majesty's army. My mother, the Dowager Viscountess Arleigh. My sisters, the Honourable Diana and Phoebe Arleigh."

His mother did not speak, but continued to look scandalised at Rachel's dress. Phoebe was the first to break the silence.

"A pleasure, Lady Arleigh."

"Rachel, please."

Arleigh heard the strain in Rachel's voice and when he glanced at her, he saw she looked shocked. No more so than he. What was she about, dressing and entering in such a fashion with his family present?

"Lady Arleigh!" She recovered somewhat, curtseying to his mother and then to his sisters. "I must apologise. I was not told you had arrived." She quickly folded the letter that was in her hand and thrust it in the pocket of her banyan. "It is a pleasure to meet you all. You must all have been imagining who Lord Arleigh had married. I suppose I'm like a folkloric character to you all."

Arleigh could see she was trying her best to lighten what was a painfully awkward first impression.

"We had no idea what possessed Julius to marry in such a manner."

And to such a woman. That's what his mother meant. He knew her well enough to read between the lines. Apparently she wasn't going to help the situation.

"I believe it was your husband's will, was it not?" asked Rachel, drawing a shocked gasp from the Dowager Viscountess and two sets of scandalised eyes from Arleigh's sisters.

His mother's stare grew hard, but her lips pinched together in spite of the question. She would not answer. Having barely spoken about his father since his death, Rachel's blunt words could not be worse timed.

"Shall we have tea? I suspect Lord Arleigh has not ordered it yet?"

"No, he never remembers to," said Phoebe, her dark eyes sparkling with interest at the large woman dressed in oriental garb. "Are you liking the house?" Apparently Phoebe, oblivious to the tension in the air, would be filling the conversational void.

"I… yes, it's lovely."

"I know. My room had the best view of all Bath. Have you seen it?"

"Your room?" Rachel's brows puckered and she looked to Arleigh.

"My mother and sisters retired here after my father's passing," Arleigh explained.

Rachel appeared speechless at his words. It was the first time in their short marriage that he had ever seen her open her mouth without spouting an effusion of words.

"No, I have not. Would you care to show it to me?"

Phoebe seemed delighted at the suggestion and was already rising to accompany her new sister-in-law from the room when the Dowager Viscountess rose abruptly.

"We have clearly visited at an inopportune time," she said, glaring pointedly at his wife's dress. "Come, girls, we will leave your brother and his wife," she hissed, "and come again when they are better ready to receive us in *our* house."

Shortly after the cutting words, the Dowager Viscountess received a kiss from her son, gave a stiff and resentful curtsey to her new daughter-in-law, and left the room, her daughters in her wake.

"Well," said Rachel. "That was less than pleasant!"

As she turned, she caught sight of his face, and Arleigh was satisfied to see her surprised by his look of anger.

Rebecca was surveying the Pump Room with an unfriendly eye. If one more well-wisher came to speak with her under the guise of congratulations for her sister's recent nuptials with the real intention of sniffing out any scandal that may lay behind the impromptu wedding, she would scream.

Her aunt was enjoying catching up with old acquaintances who were spending time in Bath for their health. Rebecca watched the conversations which were taking place adjacent to her, for the first time without chiming in herself. She had no desire to. Since her interview with her sister, she had felt incredibly deflated. Rachel may have been married for the past five years but that did not alter sisterly bonds. If there was anyone whom Rebecca would have said knew her best, so entirely inside and out, it would have been her sister. And she used to feel the same about her.

"I have had a letter from your dear mama," said Lady Etheridge, turning to her niece, when the two older gentlemen she had been conversing with, dressed respectively in embroidered suits of puce and lavender, dissolved into the milling crowds around the taps.

"Have you?" asked Rebecca, her mother a distraction from her thoughts. "Have they deserted England for Greece yet?" They were due to spend their winter in the classical part of the Mediterranean.

"They certainly have, but your mother mentioned her trip to London. You know how she hates talking of the capital."

"Is she well?" They never came to London. The smoke didn't do her mother's lungs the least bit of good. That was why Rebecca always stayed with her aunt.

Rather than answering immediately, Lady Etheridge held out her hand to her niece.

"Come, come. I shall not stand about in this awkward fashion as if we have no one to talk to but ourselves. Besides, Doctor Smith told me slow walking was just the thing to help with sore limbs."

Rebecca placed her aunt's hand on her arm and they began another circuit of the Pump Room.

"No need to look horrified, my child, your mother is quite well. I have no doubt they have left port by now."

"But why did papa allow mama to risk her health? It was so foolish!"

"I believe to confront your sister over her hasty marriage—and it is clear from the letter that your mama was most upset by the interview. Though you know her, she will never say what she means, and that great lumbering oaf that is your father seems to have made a mess of the whole."

"I can't believe mama came to London."

"You may believe what you like, child, it will not alter the truth. Apparently your father was so displeased by the matter, and your mother so much shocked, that they felt it their duty to visit."

"They weren't happy?"

"You would think they had no reason to be anything else." Lady Etheridge's tongue was particularly sharp since her joints had been affecting her, and apparently now that her flattering, aged lotharios were out of earshot, she was free to hiss as much as she pleased. "But how can that bullish man you call a father ever be happy? I understand from the letter that he was much angered to find your sister had taken it upon herself to form her own brilliant match and failed to inform your parents.

"Your mother mentioned Lady Goring in her letter—nothing to do with anything—and so I am sure that it is a veiled comment over that trifling rumour concerning less than pure motives for their marriage. She writes to say that she saw Lady Goring briefly when they came to Town, for the woman was baying at their front door less than twelve hours after they arrived. I swear that woman has a better network of spies than the French court! I must source some of her informants for my own use."

Lady Etheridge's cane was tapping out a pretty little beat upon the polished wooden floors. The sound mingled with the conversations of all the other fashionable persons present, rising with them up to the stuccoed ceiling.

"Poor Rachel." Rebecca could well imagine her father's reaction to such a rumour and the hasty wedding. At the very least it *did* look like a wedding that had taken place to perhaps cover clandestine activities which would come to light in nine months' time. Was that why they had married? Why wouldn't Rachel simply have told her?

"I was inclined to think so — but then again, your sister is very capable of handling herself, something which endlessly vexes your father—and I only had to keep reading to find out that Rachel needs no sympathy. That man of hers, in your mother's words, 'is a very confident man who impressed Lord Fairing very much.' Of course, one only has to read between the lines of your mother's letter to translate."

Rebecca was already ahead of her aunt. Confident and impressive. That meant that her father had found him to be an intolerable up-start. But what did that mean? How could he have acted to provoke such a reaction? When Rebecca had seen him, he had seemed anything but animated. He had certainly been intimidating, but so was her father.

"I would have liked, very much, to have been at that interview. It would have provided a deal of amusement to distract me from these confounded knees and elbows of mine." Lady Etheridge struck her cane on the floor irritably causing several people nearby to glance over.

"Shall we sit a bit, aunt?"

Lady Etheridge reluctantly followed her niece's suggestion and they took two chairs at the edge of the room. It gave them an ideal vantage point from which to observe the swell of well-dressed people come and go from the establishment. There was the usual backbone of invalids who spent much of the year here, and then those who had come for the society and assemblies for which Bath was so well known.

"Oh, what is it that puckers your brows so, child?" snapped Lady Etheridge.

Rebecca's eyes shot round to her aunt.

"You have been like a lost lamb these past few days and now I give you an interesting story and you are like a corpse about it. And when Lord Fortnum and his old crony Sir Egresford were flirting quite outrageously with you, you did not even offer them a little smile."

"It was almost impossible to keep a straight face when Sir Egresford started to show us his new clocked stockings, aunt. If I had smiled, I would have laughed in his face."

"They were horribly obnoxious," she conceded. "However, that man's calves are as fine as a man's half his age. One cannot help but admire them and understand his penchant for silly stockings." Lady Etheridge paused for a few moments and then said quietly, so as not to be overheard, "You know you must stop fussing about this marriage of your sister's. One cannot always understand the choices of others, my child. The Lord knows my family did not understand mine, but Roderick was the best man I ever knew."

"It's just..." Her fine brow was puckering again. "Why could she not tell me? Not just that, but she is not herself, aunt. She did not speak one honest word when I saw her, only about the house and silly things I know she doesn't care one jot for."

"I believe we are called to love our family, Rebecca, not always to understand them."

Rebecca was just about to say that she could not be satisfied with such a situation when a stir at the entrance sent ripples of conversation through the crowd. Then, as the individuals parted, bowing and curtseying to the couple entering, Rebecca recognised Lord Arleigh. Next to him walked her sister wearing the most enormous straw hat.

Chapter 10

"**A**unt, may I present Lord Arleigh, my husband."

"A pleasure, Lady Etheridge," he said, in tones which hardly represented the words.

"And overdue," said Lady Etheridge, tapping her cane on the floor. "But you are quite the man, as tall as a tree I daresay, and such fine legs."

"Aunt," whispered Rebecca, knowing it was no use.

"So, tell me," said Lady Etheridge, drawing the couple away from the staring crowds and into a quiet corner of the Pump Room. "Was it really as scandalous a wedding as everyone is saying?"

No one spoke for a few moments. Rachel's eyes darted towards her husband. He would not be pleased. They had barely spoken since the interview with his mother and sisters. He had been keeping a meaningful distance, but whenever she caught his gaze, it was filled with displeasure. The problem was, the darned man didn't talk, he just stewed like some old, festering, boiled cabbage.

Lord Arleigh, without answering the question, declared that he wished to speak to Lord Fortnum on a stable matter, and asked if he could procure a glass of the waters for the ladies while he was away. He received their answers and left to fulfil them.

"A man of few words, it seems. Entirely the opposite of you then, my dear Rachel. Which reminds me, you have left me with a niece who is hardly a good companion. You should be ashamed of yourself," chided Lady Etheridge.

"Oh, yes? And how so, aunt? Is it because Rebecca could never match my conversation, wit for wit?" On the disappearance of her solemn husband there was suddenly much more room in Rachel's chest.

"Hardly," said Rebecca, almost snorting at the accusation. "This is the first I have seen you at the Pump Rooms. Are you both enjoying yourselves?"

"Yes, this is our first appearance," said Rachel, ignoring her sister's pointed stare, not to mention her question. "No doubt the reason we have caused a stir. Most disagreeable to have people aping after you as though you were some circus attraction. I do not think Arleigh likes it at all." Let Rebecca think that the reason for his foul mood. She could tell her sister still wasn't happy about the marriage and now, with the deal in such a precarious position, it was hardly the time to have her sniffing around.

"Well," Lady Etheridge replied. "If you had not rushed into getting married in such a fashion, I dare say Society may have found someone else to witter about, but I understand it was a rushed wedding, perhaps due to indiscretions…"

"A fine thing to say! Barely anyone has congratulated me—all I receive are accusations."

"What did you expect?" asked Rebecca, but her question was overridden by her aunt.

"Then let me offer my congratulations on a brilliant match. I hope that you will share the tale of the wedding shortly, for I am most vexed with you for almost allowing me to hear it from that vile woman, Lady Goring, first. You realise I may never be able to forgive you for such an infraction?"

"I must apologise from the bottom of my scandalous silk shoes, aunt."

"Well," said Lady Etheridge, making a show of looking mollified, "it has to be said, I admire your acumen for orchestrating the match. It almost makes up for the faux pas. It's just a shame your father cannot appreciate your skill."

"He is always displeased." She avoided her sister's gaze, the thought of her last interview with her father not pleasant, though it did bring up memories of Arleigh's intervention. A little smile curled at her lips, but it was gone again when she thought of how badly her first meeting with his mother had run.

"Have you heard," said Lady Etheridge, clearly pleased to have some news that her niece hadn't heard from other sources yet, "that your Mr Thayers is in Bath?"

"No," said Rachel, memories of a youthful love coming back through the mists of time. "I didn't know."

"He is visiting his sister and brother-in-law," Lady Etheridge explained. "Of course, you are quite tied-up again, so he has no new chance at your heart, but I remember how fond you were of him in your youth."

She *had* been fond of him. In fact, if she had not been forced to marry Sir Denby, there would have been a good chance that they would have wed. Yet here she was, married again, needing to work with her husband to gain his inheritance so that she might gain her independence. She pushed Thayers from her mind. In the future, a light flirtation was not off the cards, but for now, she could ill afford any distraction.

"What makes Rebecca such bad company, aunt?" she asked, turning the conversation.

"She is quite convinced that there is something suspicious about your hasty marriage. I suspect that could have been one of the reasons your father was less than pleased, though I have told them all it is stuff and nonsense."

Of all the people Rachel knew, her aunt

was probably the only one who could fully understand why rumours of a baby born on the wrong side of the sheets were unfounded. Though they had never spoken of it, her aunt had never been able to have children of her own, and Rachel's childless first marriage had been noted by the older relative. It was an unspoken understanding and one which meant she would be Rachel's best champion within the family against the salacious gossip.

"He can suspect as much as he pleases. There is nothing in the haste. And you must be kind to father, aunt. A man with no sons hardly has an easy life."

"Ladies," said Arleigh, just returned, offering glasses of Bath water to the three women.

"Tell me, is this your idea for a honeymoon or are you for the continent as well?" asked Lady Etheridge, lightening the conversation for the benefit of her new nephew-in-law.

Rachel appreciated the gesture, but the question was hardly one that could be easily answered. She glanced at Arleigh and then caught sight of her sister watching her. She took refuge in drinking, hoping that Arleigh would break his apparent vow of silence to answer.

"Not as yet, Lady Etheridge."

"Well, perhaps in the spring. There is nothing quite like springtime in Venice. One of the benefits of no children for myself and Roderick was the chance to travel as if tomorrow would never happen," said Lady Etheridge, a misty look softening her usually sharp blue eyes.

"It's hard to say what we shall be doing."

"Yes, quite," said Rachel, her words hot on the heels of her husband's.

"You mean you won't be going away for your honeymoon?" asked Rebecca, her dark eyes searching their faces.

"We haven't planned everything yet, Rebecca. We have barely been married a month. Besides, after such a hasty courtship and wedding, it is hardly surprising we have not worked these things out. One does not always plan months in advance."

The final sentence was uttered with a certain firmness that forbade any further questioning and Rachel hoped it would put her sister's probing to rest. How could she explain that the reason that nothing could be planned was because she would be living separately from the man in three months. At least, that was if their deal was carried through and she gained the financial independence she needed.

"Well, are you attending the Assembly Rooms on Friday night? The least you can do for not telling your aunt you have wedded a handsome viscount is to attend a dance and say the scandalous things you say best. Aunt would love that."

"It has not been decided yet," said Lord Arleigh, his tone and face as implacable as ever.

"Well," said Lady Etheridge, her tone a little clipped in response. "If you will abandon your aged relative at the assemblies and not tell me what I wish to know about your wedding, then I think your sister and I will take our leave."

Rachel kissed her aunt goodbye, causing a small smile to appear on the severe woman's face.

"I shall call upon you next week if that suits, aunt?"

"That will be fine."

"Dear sister." Rachel kissed her younger sibling's cheek. "Do not be forever glaring at me like that."

"Do not be forever lying to me," she whispered back.

Rachel pretended not to hear, only happy that her suspicious sister was gone. Now the real work must be done. She needed to speak to Arleigh. If their deal was to be upheld, something had to be done to shake words from the silent Viscount.

"We cannot carry on like this." Rachel turned on Arleigh the minute the morning room door closed.

He did not immediately answer. He was taking snuff and it was only when the box was snapped shut again and deposited in his deep jacket pocket that he looked at her. The anger that she saw there shocked her.

"Well, perhaps if you were not intent on alienating every member of my family, we might not be at this juncture."

"Alienating your family? Don't be so ridiculous."

"Was that not what you were trying to do when you met them dressed in a man's banyan and without even the manners to be formally announced?'

"You must be jesting. You think I intended my first impression to be made like that?"

"To be quite frank, madam, I find it impossible to discern any of your intentions." He had clasped his hands behind his back and was pacing with long strides about the room while she stood like some doll on a rotating pin following him.

"And that is why you are angry with me—though I am sure you have never said it? What is wrong with your tongue that you cannot speak your mind?"

"You do so for the both of us, madam. You are forever speaking. What made you think you could address my mother on such terms, and about such private matters as my father's death and will?"

"Well... I..." She didn't really have an answer for that. Remaining silent was the only course of action, but the look on Arleigh's face made her think she should make something up to fill the void. She had never seen him look so angry before. Finally, she fell back on the only adequate response. "Yes, that was wrong of me to handle it so. I... it's hard for me to understand it all."

"But you understand enough to know to greet your new family properly dressed?"

"Oh, for goodness' sake!" she cried, her hands flying up in the air and her eyes suddenly blazing at him. "I had no idea they had even arrived! You didn't deign to tell me they would be visiting that morning—only that they were visiting at some point over the next few days—and worse, you didn't even send a message to warn me."

He didn't immediately answer, although she was satisfied to see her outburst had halted his wrathful path.

"Goodness, do you think me so ill-bred that I do not understand the importance of dressing and acting in a proper way when meeting my in-laws? Your opinion of me must be low indeed."

He made to speak, but she cut him off.

"It is of no consequence," she said, waving him away. "No one's opinion of me is high—or so the gossip tells me. I only ask," she said, looking at him again, catching his steady gaze, "why you think I am a mind reader?"

"I… well… I must apologise."

She could see his teeth barely separate as he said the words.

"I was unaware that you were… unaware. But you must realise your dressing in a man's banyan is hardly appropriate."

"I believe, until I wish otherwise, I may dress as I like."

"Where did you even get it?"

She coloured then. "It was… er… Sir Denby's." Her cheeks were suddenly blazing hot.

He made no comment, but she saw his lips pinch and was suddenly shown the familial likeness to his mother.

"Do not look at me like such an ogre. I may dress as I like and I had no idea there were visitors."

"You have not presented my case well to my family. The will stipulated that I make a good match to a woman of equal parentage to my own. Good character and behaviour are implied."

"You doubt my character?"

Arleigh walked away from her again. "That is not what I meant."

"Oh, do not soften your words with me, for I am only your wife." She turned to look into the swept fireplace.

"We have a deal, Lady Wife," he said, his voice steady and worryingly quiet. He had come up behind her without her realising. She turned and looked into those steady grey eyes. "And you promised to keep up your end of it. Perhaps if you swallowed some of that pride you nurse, you would be able to play your part."

"Do not lecture me—I am not to be commanded. I may be your wife in name, but I am still my own being." She had stepped closer to him and could smell the soap he had lately bathed with. She ignored the pleasing scent, maintaining her scowl. "If you think for a moment I will be a weak-hearted lamb to be led whichever way I am commanded, think again. I will never be that."

She felt a sudden lump come into her throat. The emotion had risen unexpectedly within her. This argument touched a wound that was barely healed. She hated that it brought this out in her, that his words could upset her so. She pushed back the emotions which made her feel weak, the feelings she had no intention of showing anyone.

As if reading the thoughts in her eyes, Arleigh's own gaze softened just a fraction and he refrained from immediately answering her.

"I have no intention of forcing you to do anything," he said finally, turning away and resting both hands on the mantel. "You hurt her, my mother. You hurt her with what you said." He spoke quietly, "She has not been able to speak of my father since his death."

The feeling of anger began to thaw as she thought back to the Dowager Viscountess and considered whether the look on that hard face had been fractured by something vulnerable when she had mentioned her dead husband. Had she been cruel?

She sighed. "I am sorry for it. I never meant to be unfairly mean." She rubbed long fingers over her brow and at her temples. The tension of recent days had given her a headache that would not shift.

"We cannot go on like this — at odds," she said at length, in a voice far removed from that she had used earlier.

She came and sat on the chaise longue where his mother had been two days before. They needed to find a way past this. If the deal was to go forward and she was to be free, then they must work together to ensure his inheritance. If there was any hint of their marriage being false, it would be seen as illegitimate by the solicitors and he would lose everything. So would she.

"I think," she said, her hands now rubbing a pattern on the seat beside her rather than on her head, "we need to work together."

"Together?" he said, coming back from the window and sitting across from her, his hands loosely clasped between his knees.

"Your inheritance is essential to us both. If I am to gain my independence you must first gain yours. If we are to please your family — and the solicitors — then we must present a united front. But a united front requires teamwork just as a plough requires a well-matched pair. For instance, warning your wife of her upcoming appearance on stage before an audience of say, family members, would be helpful."

"I suppose it would. I had not thought."

She refrained from telling him that she had already realised he hadn't thought, and that perhaps his bachelorhood had lasting effects. They sat for a few moments in silent agreement and then, with the air somewhat cleared and their plan re-aligned, Rachel left him to his meditative state and went in search of burgundy.

Chapter 11

"All of London is to descend on us then," said Felton irritably as he saw James Worth enter the Pump Room. "We would have been better staying in Town if we had wanted a break, my dear."

"In fairness to James," said Caro calmly, "he has only just arrived back from his business and is no doubt starved of the company which has so rapidly left London. One cannot blame him for following sooner than we wanted."

"I certainly can, and I can blame you for encouraging him to come when you wrote to him."

"At least he insisted on finding his own rooms."

"Yes, indeed, for I would have turned him out of ours as soon as he arrived."

"You don't mean it."

"Don't I now?" Felton pinched her cheek affectionately. He had found a chair for her despite their relative scarcity in the Pump Room.

His wife knew well that beneath the easy-going façade of Tobias Felton was a will of iron. "If only your brother would realise the company he feels starved of is not ours," said Felton drily, moments before greeting James and taking his offered hand.

"How are you, brother?" asked Caro.

She was not allowed the pleasure of hearing his reply thanks to Felton's whispering, "Ah, his required company."

Her husband put a hand to her shoulder and she followed his gaze to the entrance of the room, seeing Rebecca arrive with her aunt.

"James, could you be a good man and fetch some of the waters for your sister?" said Felton suddenly, capturing James' attention before he could look to the entrance himself. "You should try some. Devilish, disgusting stuff though the physicians hereabouts swear by it."

"It's not that bad," said Caro, reluctantly relinquishing her cup to her husband who in turn handed it to her brother. She shot Felton a look of rebuke.

When her brother was out of earshot, Caro said, "You are being cruel, Tobias."

"No such thing. Everyone else is being cruel by invading our peace. If they will bring their theatrics to our door, I shall do my best to enjoy them."

Caro looked back to Rebecca. Lady Etheridge, already met by her elderly cortège, was wending her way towards some chairs they had earmarked for her. Rebecca split off from the party and started towards Caro. Felton had sent James away on purpose. He wanted them to have no warning of each other's presence.

"Good morning, Caro dear. Felton, I hope I am not intruding upon your time together— but, as you see, we are in a public place." Rebecca gestured with her fan across the wooden floors. They were milling about with all manner of polite Society currently residing in Bath.

"Not at all, Rebecca," Felton responded with more amiability than he had mustered up for his wife's friend in as many days. "And how are you going on? Are you still as sceptical as ever over your sister's brilliant match?"

Rebecca's dark eyes narrowed at the friendly interrogation. "Do not think me stupid, Felton. I know a mocking tone when I hear one. You are too pig-headed to understand."

"Am I? It must come naturally, for I am under no effort to be so."

Caro couldn't help the chuckle bubbling up her throat.

"How can you let him speak to me so, Caro?"

"You well know, I have no control over my husband's tongue, more sorrow for me. You are as unhappy as ever?"

"Unhappy?" James' voice made Rebecca visibly jump and she almost upset the full glasses in his hands.

Felton let out a laugh, but was quickly silenced by his wife's small fingers pinching his arm. They took the glasses James offered them in silence.

"Mr Worth! I had no idea of your being in Bath."

"I only arrived this morning."

"How was your journey, James?" asked Caro.

"Easy. One only has to travel across the Atlantic to think any journey within England's hallowed hedgerows a trifle. But what were you speaking of before I arrived? What is the matter, Lady Rebecca?"

"There is something the matter with my sister? Heaven forbid! I do not remember the last time she was ill. Tell me Becky, what ails you?"

It was Lady Arleigh. Caro had been so preoccupied with her brother and Rebecca that she had not seen the approach of the behatted Viscountess. Once again she was surprised by the Amazonian size of the eldest Fairing. Rachel was wearing a fine pale green robe *à la polonaise* with a contrasting yellow petticoat showing beneath the drawn-up skirts. In her hands was a fashionable embroidered muff which perfectly matched the petticoat, and atop her bountiful curls was the largest straw hat Caro had ever seen.

"Nothing!" snapped Rebecca.

"Lady Arleigh," said Caro, jumping in once

again, attempting to smooth over the situation. "Allow me to present my brother, Mr Worth."

"A pleasure—for if I were to say anything else, I am sure I would be lynched. Though with those eyes," she said, gesturing with a long-fingered hand towards Caro's brother's face, "it surely is a pleasure. So, are you my sister's beau? If you are not, I shall declare her the largest fool in Christendom."

"I… er…"

"Rachel! Do shut up!"

"Oh, sister, dear, if I were not saying something scandalous, I dare say I should be dead."

"It's quite all right," said Mr Worth. "I am growing accustomed to the Fairing family way."

"Oh dear. There is nothing to boast about in that, Mr Worth. We are all of us far too improper to be used to. And I must say it is not a tradition in all members of our family—mostly the women—speaking of which, is aunt E here?"

"She's being romanced by Sir Egresford and Lord Fortnum," her sister replied.

"They still charm her? One has to give credit where perseverance is found. Felton, I had not noticed you there — very quiet — quite unlike you."

"There are times when observance can provide as much amusement as witty repartee, Lady Arleigh." He bowed. "Congratulations on your marital match. Is your husband not in attendance today?"

"I believe he's riding—and do not think for a moment that the polite question has made me deaf to your first words. You are a scoundrel and a cad."

"I try," he said, bowing again.

"Caro, I do not know how you could have married him."

"Neither do I," she replied, "but there is no escaping him now."

Rachel's face broke into her generous smile. "May I steal my sister for a few moments?"

"Scoundrels, cads, improper women and now thieves," said Felton.

"There is no hope for me amongst such company," Caro lamented, a coy smile playing about her mouth. "You may have her."

It was only James who watched with a look of loss as Rebecca was taken off on the arm of her sister.

"My dear, I really wish you would stop looking daggers at me. It's most exhausting. Tell me what's bothering you?"

"What's bothering me?"

"Yes."

"You! You are bothering me!" Rebecca

turned angry eyes towards her taller sister.

Rachel had purposely made this trip to the Pump Rooms whilst Arleigh was otherwise engaged in order to confront her sister. She knew Rebecca would not be happy until she could have it out with her. Their brief interview in the London house had been cut short and even now, Rachel could see Rebecca was less than satisfied.

"Oh, not this again," said Rachel, as if surprised by the look of scepticism on Rebecca's face. "My dear, why can't you face the truth that I have made a sensible match for myself and that is the end of it."

"Because," began Rebecca, much too loudly. She drew the attention of several dowagers before regulating her volume and warding off their stares. "Because," she began again, "I should think that after your marriage to Sir Denby, you would not be in such haste to make another alliance which was not for... for love."

"Love?" Rachel laughed a little.

"Don't make fun of me. You remember as well as I the way we used to talk of making love matches. You remember mother telling us that we had handsome fortunes and could attract any man we wished."

"Father said no such thing."

That gave her sister pause and Rachel saw from her profile that she was thinking over the words, her fine brows puckering, her teeth biting down on her bottom lip.

"I know you never wished to be married to Sir Denby. I can still remember how you cried, but don't you see? That's why I find it so hard to believe that you can be happy with this new marriage to someone you do not love."

"Dear sister," Rachel said, squeezing Rebecca's arm affectionately as they walked around the Pump Room. "I do so appreciate your care and your concern, but I am happy, and I wish you would leave this matter well alone. It was a hasty marriage and I can see that you have concerns but..." She hesitated, wondering how much to divulge, knowing that telling Rebecca nothing would not satisfy her. "Arleigh and I, we made a deal." She paused her stride, looked her sister in the face, begging for her understanding. "I cannot tell you the whole, but trust me when I say that it is to our mutual benefit and you need not worry for my happiness."

Rebecca nodded a little and, to Rachel's relief, seemed the most satisfied she had been since bursting into Arleigh's London home.

"Now tell me," said Rachel, turning the conversation. "I realise I should be flogged for being so tactless before, but I really was poking around in the dark for fun. I did not realise there was something there. Are you in love with that Mr Worth?"

"Rachel!"

She saw a deep scarlet flood her sister's cheeks in confirmation and smiled.

"Oh, his eyes are lovely. He is a decent sort of chap?"

"Hardly the kind of man mama and papa would approve of. Don't you remember their father?"

"Died in infamy, if I'm not mistaken—but Caro has made a decent match and I hear that Lord Worth's son has a tidy fortune to his name, even if it is from trade. You know, for a romantic you do not seem very convinced by the notion."

"It's not that it's… I don't even know if he holds me in affection."

"How could he not?" asked Rachel, giving Rebecca another affectionate squeeze on the arm. The sisters exchanged knowing smiles and for the first time in many months, the bond of siblings sparked a little.

"You know what you must do," said Rachel with authority. "You must tell him." She was so busy burying her head as close to her sister's ear as possible that she hardly saw a gentleman approaching them through the chocolate curls.

When he spoke, the voice drew Rachel back through her memories.

"Good morning, Lady Rebecca, Lady… ah… Arleigh, I believe. It has been a long time. Mr Thayers, if I may help your recollection."

Rebecca had stopped short on their circuit of the room and Rachel, retracting her head from her sister, turned to face the beau of her youth.

"Mr Thayers," said Rebecca kindly, extending a hand and curtseying prettily. "Of course we remember. It is Lady Arleigh." Rebecca released her sister so that Rachel could offer her hand to Mr Thayers too.

As Rachel took in his face, as handsome as ever, she saw that age had only added lines which distinguished his attractive features. He was around the same height as her, his hair dark, his eyes a startling green, just like she remembered, and that smile which could set a frozen heart free.

"I am to offer you congratulations then, Lady Arleigh."

"I... thank you," Rachel managed to say, regaining her composure, shocked that such an old acquaintance could disconcert her so.

That deep-seated ache that had stayed with her for so many months after her first marriage reappeared without warning. She could feel the sorrows of her youth, the hopes that had dashed themselves on the rocks of her preordained future, the desires she had smothered in the name of fidelity.

She had seen him once after she had married Sir Denby, at a local Christmas assembly. The events which she had tried to forget unfolded before her. The way they had danced together, the whispers they had caused, the stolen kiss she had stopped, the offer he had made which would have ruined her, even if it would have given her a window of happiness in her life. She remembered the refusal she had given him, and the scolding she had received from her husband when they had returned home for being gone from the ballroom for so long.

"You look as well and as beautiful as always, Lady Arleigh. A rose by any other name…" He took her hand to his mouth and placed a second kiss on it, sending a fizzing feeling down the length of her arm as though someone had just spilled champagne on her.

"As eloquent as I remember, Mr Thayers," said Rebecca. "Tell us, has no bride succumbed to your charm?"

"I have yet to meet my match, Lady Rebecca," he said, turning his enigmatic eyes towards her sister.

Rachel was thankful for the distraction. Her sister had been too young to be told what had passed between the two of them. She knew there had been a tendre there, but Rachel had never told her the whole.

"And you have grown into the veritable beauty your sister is."

A smile curved Rebecca's red lips, but Rachel knew her sister well enough to see the knowing look in her eyes. She was no more taken in by flattery than Rachel.

He may be a flatterer, but there had been something between them in their youth, hadn't there? Was it still there? Three months. That was how long before her separation. Three weeks had already passed. She would gain her independence and then... What then? Would she give in to temptation if it was offered a second time?

"And how do you go on, Mr Thayers?" asked Rachel, tempted by the mystery of their time apart.

"Very well, I thank you. I am in Bath visiting my sister. She has lately brought another cherub into her family. Lord and Lady Crowley have a house north of The Circus. Do you stay in the Arleigh house?"

"Yes."

"And your husband—is he here?" He made to look around, but upon hearing that Lord Arleigh was riding, he sighed.

"And so you are left alone." He sighed again. "Well, I must return to my sister. She takes the waters after her confinement. But perhaps I shall see you again, Lady Arleigh."

"Perhaps."

He bowed and took his leave and after a brief moment of suspension, both sisters took up their promenade around the room once again.

"I may not be able to tell if another holds affection for *me,* but I can certainly tell that another holds affection for *you,*" said Rebecca, a saucy tone in her voice, shooting a smile at her sister.

They both erupted into giggles, provoking glares from all the surrounding water-takers. By the time Rachel had dropped her sister back into the company of her aunt and was taking her leave of the Pump Room, she was lost in her thoughts.

An unthinking glance to her side as she left locked her eyes with Mr Thayers, so that she took with her the feeling of his enigmatic green gaze. It had rested on her and she could not tell whether she was pleased or confused. In less than three months she would have her independence, but for the first time since planning it, she wondered exactly what that would mean.

Chapter 12

Rachel approached the garment on the bed cautiously. It was folded up in a neat square, and until she came upon it, she could not make out exactly what it was. She had not been expecting anything. She had barely had time to unpack, and her visit to the dressmakers on Milsom Street had only been a few days ago—hardly time enough for anything to be ready. Perhaps it was a wedding present sent from Rebecca or her aunt. But it was not wrapped.

She spread her long fingers over the material, tracing the embroidery, and gazing at it until she could make out the patterns on the brightly coloured silk. There were shapes of red flowers and white birds and, as she picked the garment up, it unfurled in all its richly coloured glory. It would have been fit for the Emperor of Japan himself.

"I decided that if you were going to persist in wearing a man's banyan, it should be mine."

She turned, startled to see Arleigh watching her from the doorway.

"Well... I... "

"What? Do you mean I have actually succeeded in making you speechless?" He entered the room and came to stand a little way off at the end of the bed.

Rachel was stroking the silk embroidery in wonder, only half listening, but she did smile at his question.

"I find it hard to understand how you cannot have married before, Arleigh. An adept present giver, one would think you know the rules of courtship well." She wasn't aware of the uncomfortable look which passed across her husband's face. She was too intent on the garment in her arms and the unsettling meeting with Mr Thayers that morning.

"It is more proper than wearing the other —you can have Nellie get rid of it."

She nodded, a generous smile pouring out from her mouth into her cheeks and eyes. She turned the look upon him, swinging the garment high and drawing it on over her dress.

"You are very tall," she remarked, pointing one of her feet and admiring the length of the robe which brushed just above the toes of her silk mules.

"So I've been told."

"But what about when we are separated?" she asked matter-of-factly, looking up at him and catching a certain hardness passing through his eyes.

"I barely wear the thing—you may take it."

She didn't respond. Take his banyan? It had been one thing to wear the banyan belonging to a dead husband, without sentiment, purely as a garment she enjoyed to wear at home because of its freedom. It felt entirely different taking this garment from a husband who was still living. From a man who would know she wore it. Who was giving it to her as a gift.

"Thank you," she said quietly.

She was suddenly very aware that she did not fully understand this man whose ever-present reservation made him, in equal parts, knowable and unknowable. Others were easily displeased, as he had been at first, but they stayed that way inclined. They rarely decided to speak to her as an equal, as he had begun to do. They didn't give her gifts. They never cared. Did he care?

"We are to attend the assembly on Friday, if you are happy to? My mother and sisters will be in attendance and I am hoping it will give us a chance to repair the damage that was done."

"Yes, of course."

He had said 'us', not her. He was keeping to their new deal, their unified front. Perhaps this banyan was a peace offering.

He inclined his head. "Thank you."

"I spoke to my sister this morning." She didn't mention meeting Mr Thayers. "I have allayed her fears, so hopefully she will be able to leave us alone, at least for a time." She took off the banyan and folded it carefully, laying it on the bed, and still he stood there.

"Good."

She caught his steady gaze and did her best to convey her gratitude for the banyan. He again nodded silently. Finally, after a few moments of no conversation, she spoke. "Is—" she paused, not wishing to sound ill-tempered. "Is there anything else?"

"I had been wondering," he said, taking a breath, "if you wished to come riding with me. I can secure a suitable mount for you, though I am unsure it will suit your exacting horseflesh requirements if it is a hired hack."

She smiled at that.

"However, if you wish to see your sister or friends, I have no objection. I shall ride out, whatever you decide." He shrugged his broad shoulders. "I usually go out in the mornings."

She suddenly felt guilty. The thought of another man's green eyes, of the thoughts she had been entertaining, of the pleasure she had taken in another man's compliments. They felt somehow wrong. This marriage relationship might be a falsehood, but her integrity was not, and she felt suddenly uneasy about just how solid it was.

"Well," she said, not looking him in the eye. "I had not even thought of it."

"My fault," he said before she could continue. "I had not offered it before, but I am used to riding most days when I am in Bath, and now I know how much you like to ride, I would be happy for you to join me, once a suitable mount is found."

She looked him in the eyes then. They were as steady as ever, but for some reason she was suddenly so much more aware of where they stood, in her bedroom, him at the end of her bed, his knees pressed against her coverlet.

Something had changed between them since their journey to Bath. There would always be tension between a man and woman, and she had felt moments of it with him, but she had not thought anything more of them. There could be nothing between them of that nature. It did not make sense. They had a deal and that could not be part of it.

"I would not wish to put you to any trouble on my account," she said in an unusually self-deprecating manner.

"It would not be. I think it will be far easier to select a mount for you than for my sisters. Phoebe will fall off anything with a mild cough, and Diana is awfully superficial in her selection. They must be fine greys for her to ride them."

"Families, Arleigh," she said with a sigh and a smile, "are a complicated thing."

"Indeed they are, and you may call me Julius," he said with his usual steady voice. "Calling me Arleigh hardly seems proper. Did you order new dresses?"

"Five, thank you. I shall never be accused of greeting your mother in anything less than fashion of the first stare again."

"Indeed, it would not do for the Viscountess Arleigh to be badly dressed." His eyes travelled to the banyan on the bed and a smile hovered about his mouth.

"Indeed," she echoed, his peace offering, their secret.

He explained that he was expected at his solicitors who had travelled up from London. He would be providing them with the marriage licence and certificate for their documentation in the move towards obtaining his inheritance. Then he left and she sat on the bed, the banyan draped across her knees, her fingers tracing the patterns, and thoughts of two men occupying her mind.

Arleigh was watching his wife on the dance floor with Mr Felton. She looked highly attractive in the new ball gown that had arrived this morning. It was made of a startling green which set off her rich brown hair to advantage. The design and detail was lost on him, but the fit was not. It drew in at her waist and flared out over her hips and up to her shoulders where a low, arcing neckline showed her pale, full décolletage.

He knew how long it had taken Nellie to tame her mistress' hair into a respectable style. It was braided several times over, wrapping back and forth across the crown of her head, and still she had curls falling down the nape of her neck and over her shoulder to lay teasingly across the swell of her bosom. He had watched her tug the locks free during their carriage ride to the Assembly Rooms.

She had teased him, asking if she was not the epitome of all that was proper and respectable. He had been unable to reply sufficiently, distracted by her attractiveness. She may look the epitome of those qualities, but his thoughts were certainly not. He had assumed that the night at the inn, when it had appeared that his control was weak, would be a unique event. He had blamed it on the weariness, the drink, the close proximity to a woman who was barely clothed. But his wife was very much clothed this evening and his control was very much withering away.

"I hope you were not offended by my husband's behaviour. He has a propensity for saying things that shock. It amuses him."

Mrs Felton was standing at his elbow. She had remained silent for some time, apparently as rapt by the dancers as he.

"I know little of your husband—but am I to think this is regular behaviour?"

"Yes." She fanned herself gently against the heat of the room and smiled up at the Viscount. "Please don't be offended."

"I don't claim to be," he said steadily. "Only, I find I am married to a woman who has the same inclinations."

The fair-haired Mrs Felton chuckled. "I cannot argue with you on that score, my lord. Her sister is a dear friend of mine and she appears to be a tamer version of her elder sibling. What are we to do, us poor spouses who must watch aghast as our better halves cause such havoc?"

"That is precisely what I have been wondering." Arleigh was not lying. He had been wondering what to do about this wife of his. They had made a deal, and he would uphold that deal as a gentleman should, but now it seemed there were... extenuating circumstances. His mind traced back over his conversation with Rachel in her bedchamber.

"I believe it's not only what I find most challenging, but also what I love most about my husband. His... less than usual manners and bearing have been... that is to say, he is a most honourable man, beneath the exterior."

"You love your husband deeply, Mrs Felton." Arleigh turned to her on his pronouncement and he saw a secret smile on her lips, her bright blue eyes drifting over to where her spouse danced, her fan wafting away not only the heat of the room but Arleigh's words as well.

"Entirely, my lord."

"But…" He turned back, not knowing how to finish the sentence, not even knowing what it was he meant to say.

"Yes?"

He could feel her gaze on him, but he said nothing. He saw from the corner of his eye her fan, steadily waving back and forth, a little of the air hitting his neck and cheek.

"I believe love is, well, it is the meeting of minds, my lord. You see, we might always find irritation in our spouse's manners or behaviours, but there is a fundamental understanding, a sharing of values, which underpins our characters."

Arleigh's eyes were once again drawn to his wife. He could see her laughing at something Felton had said, joy lighting her eyes, both the chin she so enjoyed turning up in stubbornness and the aristocratic nose she liked to look down, entirely relaxed.

"You are a fortunate woman, to have struck such a reasonable deal with a man whom you hold in affection."

"Deal? Yes, I suppose it is. A deal to live life together—though I believe you and I have both received the raw end of it." She laughed again.

Arleigh didn't respond. He did not wish to

interrupt her speech. The way she phrased herself, so like Rachel had in the inn that night, when she had spoken of doing life together. It was uncanny, and the way this woman, whom he barely knew, spoke with such genuineness, such honest truth, stilled him.

"Poor Mr Felton. We are as stubborn as each other. Marriage is a promise, a covenant, for a reason, my lord, is it not? For if we did not promise to be with each other forever, we would flee at the sight of the first hurdle, would we not?"

"Indeed."

His mother had not fled at the treatment of his father. She had been faithful even when his father had not. But they had hardly lived life together as Mrs Felton described. Everything had been separated and transactional in the late Lord's household.

"But I see you hold affection for Lady Arleigh, so you are as fortunate as I," said Caro happily, waving her fan at her husband who was approaching them with Rachel on his arm.

Arleigh's mouth fell open and he stepped forward to say something in response, but he was not given the chance. Caro had not noticed. She was already greeting her husband, the latter whispering something which made her giggle behind her fan.

"My wife is in need of refreshment, Arleigh, Lady A—will you excuse us?"

"Your husband is a reckless dancer, Mrs Felton—I sincerely hope we never dance again for the amount of times he stood on my toes during that minuet."

"Only because you insulted my action at the off, my lady. If you had not, I would not have felt compelled to live up to your pronouncement."

"Must you both go? We can send for some drinks." There was a tightness in Arleigh's voice that neither his wife nor the Feltons seemed to notice.

The other couple bid them adieu and Arleigh saw Caro throw a silent apology to Rachel as she was whisked across the room by her husband.

Arleigh bowed to his wife, to which she replied in mocking tones, "Oh come, I may look respectable, but we both know that there is no need to treat me as such, Julius." She smiled at him and he felt a sudden deep ache at the sight of her, her proximity, the waft of her scent.

She had used his Christian name. It was the first time since he had requested it, and it sounded somehow wholly right on her lips. Those full, red lips. There was a sudden intimacy between them which he had not expected.

"Is your mother here yet?" She looked around her and he noted her profile.

His gaze ran down her forehead, slipping down her nose, and then fell back over those full lips.

"She arrived while you danced." He coughed, trying to wake himself from this stupefying attraction. "I was awaiting your return to speak with her."

"Well, come on then," she said, taking his arm without asking. The touch only made the ache worse. He looked down at her and caught the heave of her décolletage in a way that would ruin any man. Damnation. This woman looked so attractive and it was inconvenient in the extreme.

He had been content in his bachelorhood. He had been content in his life. And then this woman had come barrelling into it and he was becoming a wreck of the man he knew.

His mother was sitting at the side of the Assembly Room. A coterie of female friends and his eldest sister Diana, who was out in Society, were scattered on the various seating. They all sat in beautiful attitudes so as to appear attractive to the assembly goers who passed by.

Arleigh strode through the centre of the circle and took his mother's hand, bowing deeply and kissing it with affection. "Mother, you remember my wife?"

The green-eyed woman did not incline her head in recognition of her daughter-in-law. Arleigh was pleased when Rachel ignored the slight and came forward with more grace than he had seen in her before.

"Lady Arleigh," she said, curtseying as deeply as he had bowed. "I am so pleased to see you again, and my beautiful sister-in-law."

The older woman raised a hand, as if to cast a spell. As one, the flock of beautiful birds rose from their chairs and flew away to other gatherings and dance partners.

Arleigh put his hand upon Rachel's to guide her to a nearby chair, but he felt her resist him.

"Lady Arleigh," she began. "I know that I should not be so plain-speaking, but in one matter I must be so before we continue. I believe I caused you great offence when we received you last week. Please accept my sincerest apologies. I was thoughtless in my attire, my reception and my words. I know that I have a dreadful tendency to speak the first thoughts that come into my mind, and I am horrified to think that it may have caused you or your daughters pain."

Arleigh listened to the speech with growing admiration. Not only that, but he could see the earnestness in Rachel's face. Her eyes were entirely locked onto his mother's, and the latter was shocked into fully listening to what his wife was saying. He believed her. He had spoken of how his mother had been hurt and she had not only listened but, from the sound of her voice, she was remorseful.

"I should like it if we could — if we might begin again — though I know that first impressions count for so much. I ask you, I beg you not to hold Julius to blame for my abhorrent actions. I did not do him justice in how I acted. Would you be so kind as to call on us again next week?"

"Well," said the Dowager at length.

Arleigh could see that she was gathering her thoughts and for a few moments he wasn't sure whether it was a good thing or not. Was she planning an attack or a retreat?

"That was unexpected, but eloquently put, *Lady Arleigh*."

He saw what it cost his mother to call her by her title. She had decided on acceptance. His wife's bold tactics had worked.

"Thank you, your ladyship." His wife curt-seyed again.

"Please be seated." The Dowager gestured with an ornate ivory fan to the seat beside her. "You are Lord Fairing's daughter?"

"Yes, though my parents are rarely in Society due to my mother's health."

And so it went on. The conversation was stilted at first, and entirely directed by his mother, but he was pleased to see that Rachel conversed in a most proper manner. "And your previous husband, Sir Denby?"

The question hung in the air for a few moments and Arleigh almost missed it. They had been speaking quite easily for some time now, so he had directed his attention away from the attractive figure of his wife. This brought him back.

"Mother, please."

"No." His wife put up a hand. "It's quite all right, Julius." She turned back to the Dowager Viscountess, matching her sharp green eyes, stare-for-stare. "I married Sir Denby when I was eighteen. He died ten months ago."

The Dowager Viscountess' dark brows arched pointedly. "Ten months. Your marriage to my son was still within your mourning period?"

"Yes."

Rachel said nothing more and the only thing to which Arleigh could attribute her calmness was her firm commitment to the deal. Her independence meant enough to her that she could bear this kind of interrogation. But then again, after the way her father had treated her, perhaps this was not new to her.

"Mother, I think my wife has been subjected to enough questioning for one evening, don't you?" He came forward and put a hand upon Rachel's shoulder.

"Diana—fetch something for your mama to drink," said the Dowager.

"But..." said her eldest daughter, a look of the utmost displeasure on her pale face.

"Now,   child." The Dowager's voice brooked no argument and the daughter was duly dispatched, clearly frustrated to miss whatever conversation was to pass between them in her absence.

"Your meeting with the solicitors did not settle the matter."

"How so?" Arleigh had provided them with everything they needed. He had taken the licence, the certificate. Short of the solicitors being witnesses themselves, he did not know how else he could prove it.

"The haste of your marriage has thrown speculation on its validity and they are demanding to see the curate who conducted the ceremony."

"Ridiculous! They had witnesses. I gave them the signed statements from the maid and my valet."

"Servants can be bought," said his mother in monotone accents.

"How can it be this difficult for a man to claim his birthright?" Arleigh was growing exasperated.

"Your father..."

"My father was the most cunning of them all—even from the grave he dictates my every move." His voice had not risen in volume, but the tone had changed to one of frustration and bitterness, his normally steady temperament failing him.

This had been going on for months. He had traipsed around London's ballrooms to find a bride, finding no one he felt he could subject to a loveless marriage. Now he had married a woman in a deal of convenience just so he could marry in time to stop his inheritance being entailed away. Still his father would not be happy, even in the grave.

"He only wanted…"

"He—" he began forcefully, but the sudden pressure of a hand on his forearm caused him to hesitate.

He looked down to see his wife's brown eyes staring up at him. "Perhaps we should…"

"This is none of your concern," he said, cutting her off. "You did not know the man. You can't have seen the way he controlled everything, and now, even in death, he must have his way."

"Julius." His wife rose suddenly from her chair, her hand tightening on his arm with a surprising amount of strength, and her face close to his. "This is not the place to lose the equanimity that so frames you. Come away tonight and you shall not regret your words tomorrow."

He found himself thrown on the back foot. Her eyes were challenging, and her height matched his. She would not relinquish her hold and he had a feeling that if he were to carry on, she would not be averse to making some kind of scene.

He kept his eyes locked on hers as he took in a breath, focusing on the strong brown of hers and the concern he saw there. He relaxed a little and as soon as she felt it, she released him.

"They will have their curate," he said. Then he turned, taking Rachel's hand and placing it on his arm, he escorted her from the Assembly Rooms.

They took the carriage home in silence. He could not think of what there was to say under such circumstances. He could not think at all. All he could offer her when they stood on the first floor of the Bath house, ready to retreat to their separate rooms, was a kiss on the hand.

He took it from her side without asking and drew it to his lips before she could protest. He held it there a moment, the warmth of her hand through her silk gloves touching the soft lips of his mouth.

"Thank you," he offered without looking her in the eye.

He released her and turned before she could respond. Entering his room he sent Jeffries away. Sitting before the fire, his hands clasped between his knees, he resigned himself to the fact he would not be sleeping tonight.

Chapter 13

Nellie woke Rachel early the following day. Apart from a few choice words thrown in her maid's direction, Rachel made no move to give up the warm bed in which she lay so comfortably.

"But, my lady, it is Lord Arleigh. He has requested I wake you for a ride," said Nellie fretfully, toying with her dress and looking at the heap of disarrayed hair and covers that was her mistress.

"Wait... What?" Rachel sat up suddenly, her heavy mass of curls obscuring the best part of her face.

"My lord Arleigh, he is awaiting you with a horse outside the house, my lady. I explained you weren't awake, but he wishes you to join him."

"Goodness!" Rachel turned over in the bed. She swung her long legs over the side, her bare feet reaching the thick Persian rug. Throwing out a few more choice curse words, she quickly began to get ready. The Gloucestershire-born maid was used to her mistress' language and showed no shock as she braided her hair into some kind of order, though it was particularly wild after being dressed elaborately for the Assembly.

The Assembly, that was what had happened last night. The events ran back through her mind as she dressed. Arleigh, or rather Julius, had kissed her hand, had he not? She was remembering now, how she had apologised to his mother to set all to rights, only for them to be told the solicitors were not pleased. What was it he had said about his father? Controlling. He had never spoken about him before, and she remembered taking his arm and holding it as hard as she could, fearful he might stride towards his mother and bellow. It was a side to him she had never seen before. He had always seemed so calm and measured, but now…

Whatever his mood was this morning, he was waiting outside with a horse for her, and she felt as if this surprising summons might have more behind it. Even if it did, she would risk it. She may be tired from their late night, but she had not ridden since being in Gloucestershire and the sudden proposal was tantalising.

She was ready in less than half an hour. Taking a look in the mirror, she observed the modish tricorn pinned into the braids of her hair, and the scarlet habit, far more daring than she had realised when she had ordered it to be made up in that colour.

"The master has a whip for you already, my lady."

She had managed only a slice of toast in all the hurry surrounding her getting ready and she was just popping the last piece in her mouth when she came out the door of the Bath house.

"I say, he's a corker!" she bellowed, making the fine, dark bay a groom was holding start a little and turn to face the loud woman.

"And a gelding too—I am honoured at your faith in my skill," she said, coming abreast of the beast and slapping his shoulder before scratching him under the chin. "A hired hack, are you?" she questioned the gelding. "Well, you are a fine one for all that."

After last night, she was unsure what mood her husband would be in, or the reason behind his summons. She used the horse as an excuse to gain a few moments in which to gather her wits before turning a brilliant smile upon Julius. He was already mounted on a heavy-set grey.

"Good morning." She then turned to one of his lordship's grooms and with some clear instructions was thrown into the saddle. "He's lovely."

Julius nodded, but remained silent. He wore a heavy greatcoat which was open and hanging slack over his thighs and, from this vantage point, they looked particularly muscular. His seat was firm and his broad shoulders thrown back as he held the leather reins loosely in one hand, his other spread across his thigh while he waited.

Rachel smoothed the skirts over her knee and threw the rest of them back over the gelding's flank to make them lay properly. Gathering her reins she looked to her husband.

"Ready?" he asked.

She nodded, taking the bone-handled whip he handed to her. They set off at a brisk trot along the streets of Bath. It took them a little under half an hour to reach open country, but the moment they did, Rachel was happy to have forgone an extra hour's sleep.

The Somerset countryside stretched before them in boundless wooded hills, glades and grazing fields. The sight of the open land sent excited springs into the steps of her mount and she enjoyed mastering his energetic temperament, keeping him steady, sitting back and upright in the saddle.

"There is a good stretch for a canter ahead."

He didn't ask her if she wished to take it. Nor did he ask her if she would be happy on her horse. He had glanced at her several times, she had noticed, but apart from that he had remained silent. He was leaving her to ride and she appreciated it. Riding had been a love of hers since she was a child and she had pursued the sport avidly throughout her teens and into her first marriage. It had been one of the few joys during her years with Sir Denby, and though she was used to riding alone, often preferring to be free of company, riding with Julius was proving enjoyable.

They followed a bend in the woodland which intersected the bottom of a valley until they reached the open stretch Julius had spoken of. He glanced once in her direction and she took this as her cue. They had been ambling along at an energetic walk, but as she shortened her reins, the gelding pre-empted her move and almost simultaneously, Julius' mount and hers sprang forward.

They bounded ahead, the wind whipping past their faces, the air fresh and clods of earth flicking up behind them. All was lost in a moment of undeniable power. Julius did not wait for her, his grey with its longer legs carrying him forward a head, then a body, and before long all she saw was the swish of the tail and her husband's forward figure, his coat flaring out around him.

At the end of the clearing he turned, reining in his mount until he had skirted the woods and turned back towards her. She gradually slowed to a walk and they came abreast, following a path threading its way around the foot of the hill to their left.

"I salute your choice in horseflesh," said

Rachel, forgetting the silence which had existed between them, and saluting him with the crop to her tricorn.

"I must apologise."

His abrupt words caused the smile on her face to fade.

"Whatever for?"

"I..." He was not looking at her and as she searched for his gaze, she realised he was actively avoiding hers. "It's... Urgh!" He whipped at a piece of foliage making his horse shy towards hers. Steadying the grey, a look of frustration marked his usually calm face. "Damn it all, I can't do this."

Rachel, for once, remained silent, not knowing what to say and fearing that saying anything would be a mistake.

"I am no good at speaking to females. Never have been. That's why my father was so insistent upon that clause in his will. Afraid I would let the family name go to another if I never married and produced an heir."

"You speak to me."

"You're..." He whipped out at the foliage again, but this time with less venom. "I should not have lost my temper as I did last night. I... I owe you a debt of gratitude for stopping me when you did."

"You already thanked me." She twisted her hands on the reins, remembering the kiss.

"I have a duty to provide for my family, and

yet here I am, unable to satisfy some law quack that I'm entitled to my birthright."

Rachel felt touched by his sudden honesty. She saw the muscles in his jaw were clenched and his hands tight upon the reins and whip.

He laughed then, his eyes looking sky-ward, "To think that you, my notoriously out-spoken wife, stopped me from speaking what I would later regret."

Rachel's lips curved into a rueful smile. "Life has a funny habit of turning most things on their heads."

Julius turned to her, a smile still on his face, his grey eyes alight with the same ruefulness she wore. "That it does."

They carried on quietly for a time. The birds were still singing their morning songs. The leaves of the trees were moved by a slight breeze, and up ahead they caught sight of a fleeing herd of deer.

"This reminds me of when you accosted me in the woods near Fenbridge House."

"It is rather similar," she replied. "That seems an age ago now."

"I couldn't quite believe that you had the audacity to follow me from Moreston's place, and propose marriage to me after one meeting and an overheard conversation."

"I can't quite believe it myself," she said, happy that he seemed distracted from his previous mood.

His hands had relaxed on the reins and he was looking about him a little.

"But after hearing your predicament from Moreston, it seemed the honourable thing to do."

His eyes darted to hers and she did not try to hide the provoking smile.

"You asked me why I never married," he said after a time, looking at the path between his horse's ears. "Truth be told, I have never had any desire to. My parent's marriage left much to be desired in my eyes. I had no wish to replicate it."

"And so you had to be coerced into the state," Rachel said humorously. "Do not worry. We shall not be under the same roof for long. You shall be free to enjoy a good semblance of your bachelorhood soon. Your improper choice of wife will be far removed from you."

She had meant it in frivolity, as a way of lightening his spirits. She had even said it with a smile. But he did not respond in kind. He maintained his silence and continued to look ahead.

They rode on, something lying between them, and Rachel was unsure what. Had he called her out on this ride only to talk? Did he feel the same stab of loneliness which afflicted her from time to time?

She could see that the weight of familial responsibility lay heavy on him. When they had first met, she had thought him too rigid, verging on dull, but now she was not sure she would draw the same conclusions.

"All that needs to be done," she said, hoping to once again draw him from his dark mood, "is for the curate to be brought from London. If they will not take the words of the servants, we must simply get the curate. We could send Jeffries to fetch him," she said pragmatically, working out the logistics as she went. "He would only be gone a few days and if we were to pay the curate for his time, he could not object to testifying to the solicitors. They will not argue against a man of God."

She leant across the divide between their horses and rested a hand upon one of his. He jumped visibly.

"We shall fight this and you will receive your birthright, Julius, I promise."

He nodded.

Before long, they had looped around the hill whose footprint they had been following and were on their way back to Bath. Julius spent the rest of the ride in brooding silence and Rachel did not interrupt it. The streets of Bath were far busier than at the early hour when they had left. Julius led the way to the mews at the back of the house. When they had dismounted and the horses taken away, he led the way to a tack room in the corner of the yard.

Rachel followed him to deposit her whip. She walked into the small room to be greeted by a wall of wonderful smells. The rich scent of leather, the must of horse sweat, and the sweet smell of hay all mingled in the dim interior. Saddles and bridles were hung on purpose-made hooks and stands and she skirted between them, following Julius to where he had deposited his crop and was removing his spurs.

"I'd forgotten how wonderful a tack room could smell," said Rachel, dropping her crop into the pot where Julius' now resided. "I can see why you insist on putting your own whip away."

She was turning to leave when his hand fell on her arm. He pulled her back to him, drawing her far closer than he ever had before. In fact, she couldn't remember if he had ever touched her like this.

"Thank you, Rachel," he whispered against her cheek, and then, without warning, he kissed her.

Just like that, he dropped his head, closing the little space left between them, and pressed his lips against hers. His other hand came up instinctively to cup her face and neck. His desire was evident, but then, as suddenly as it had started, it stopped. His lips left hers with a sharp intake of breath. Then he stepped back, looking more shocked than she did.

She had stepped back herself, her dark eyes watching his eyes widen. He passed a hand over his mouth, staring at her in disbelief.

"I'm sorry... I..."

For a man whom she was used to seeing in control, he looked shockingly off kilter.

She saw his grey eyes following the movement of her hands and realised she had done the same as him, touching fingers subconsciously to the reddened lips he had so recently kissed. Everything was numbed except the feelings he had awoken in her. A sudden heat coursed from her lips, down her neck, and lit a fire of desire in her chest so strong it startled her.

"That was not what I intended. I was grateful. I... I apologise," offered Julius, before brushing past her and out the door.

She was left there, leaning against the cold, stone wall, wondering what had just happened. When had their relationship changed so entirely? How had it happened? She had seen the glimpse of desire in his eyes before he had pulled away and for all she was worth, she didn't know what she thought of it.

They had a deal which she had thought pragmatic, but never... dangerous. Desire was something she had been ill-prepared for and yet her body had responded. What did this mean? Was she flattered? Was she fearful? Or was she... pleased?

Chapter 14

"**Y**ou seem a little off colour, oh niece of mine." Lady Etheridge sat in a corner of the Pump Room, her hands clasped on the top of her ebony cane, and her two flirts, Sir Egresford and Lord Fortnum, placed on either side of her.

"Do I?" Rachel had been ignoring most of what was being said by the septuagenarians whose saucy words and excessive adoration for her aunt sprang eternal.

"I shall give you cheer with my news," said Rebecca.

"Oh yes, splendid news, and she had it from the horse's proverbial mouth, eldest niece."

"And aunt is most pleased I came straight to her first. Though I must say, I only found out quite by accident."

Rebecca rattled on about calling on Caro and finding her throwing up in a chamber pot. Rachel's concentration was patchy at best. She could barely focus on what her sister was saying.

She had been like this all morning. Ever since yesterday when her husband had... had kissed her! She still couldn't quite believe it. And she had not even seen the man to confirm the truth of what had happened.

She had not seen him at dinner. He had dined out with his friend Moreston who had recently arrived in Bath, and when she had risen this morning, she found Arleigh had already gone out. Perhaps his conspicuous absence was proof enough. She had decided to visit the Pump Room by herself. She would not sit around the house all morning, stewing, wondering where he was, what he was doing, and what was to happen to them.

It was because of her preoccupation that she almost missed her sister's explanation of Caro's condition.

"Wait, you say she is with child?"

"Yes, Rachel—goodness, must I forever be ignored by those with whom I converse?"

"I shall never ignore you if you bring me such interesting pieces of news, my dear," Lady Etheridge said, before turning back to her aged beaus and laughing like a schoolgirl at their reminiscences of Seasons gone by.

Rachel quickly tuned them out. Caro Felton was pregnant? A familiar pain came back. The same pain Rachel always felt when she heard that someone was with child. When she had realised that carrying her own child was something she would never experience, every fresh missive of joyous news, from a childhood acquaintance or one of the few women over the years whom she would have called friend, was like a pin-prick to her heart.

"She is quite a way along too—I am sure that devilish husband of hers wished to keep the news all to himself, but she could not help spilling the beans—or the entire contents of her stomach for that matter—when I called on her. It explains why Felton has been so beastly towards me."

"Beastly?" Rachel clasped at anything that would take her mind off her own pain.

"Oh, the man claims I am a busybody—that I cannot be satisfied if I am not in the midst of some drama or other."

"Well..."

"Don't you dare!" Rebecca snapped her fan shut and brandished it at her sister.

"Becky, now do not hang, draw and quarter me just yet, but you are quite the truffle hunter when it comes to rich nuggets of drama. You have always enjoyed the stories that aunt E regales us with, ever since we were little. Perhaps you are a little too distracted with other people's circumstances."

"As opposed to what?"

"Well, Becky, I mean, I noticed the way you coloured when we saw Mr Worth—are you telling me that there is nothing there?"

Her sister did not reply, scowling into the middle distance and tapping her fan against the shoulder of her stunning caraco jacket.

"I don't mean to hurt your feelings, Becky, you know I don't. For though I am often brash, I care infinitely for you, do I not? You have alluded to much drama in the events that led to the Feltons' nuptials, and you have been trying to find out the truth of my marriage. Have you ever thought about your own feelings?"

"No... it's just..." She struggled with the words. "I could only be persuaded to marry a man whom I loved, deeply loved, and it is so hard to love a man who can barely string a sentence together."

Rachel chuckled a little at this. "I have learned, dear sister, that there is a lot to be said for a reserved man." Her smile faltered as she realised who she was praising.

"You know, aunt is right, you do look off colour."

"Oh, it's nothing, I just feel a little tired."

"Oh." Rebecca arched a provocative brow. "Do you?"

"Hush Becky, ah, Mr Worth!" Rachel turned to admit him into their circle. "How lovely it is to see you."

"And you also, Lady Arleigh, Lady Rebecca." James bowed to both a little stiffly and then stood awkwardly, all conversation gone.

Rachel looked between the two and saw

that Mr Worth's eyes were only for her sister who was purposely avoiding his gaze.

"Perhaps," she ventured, her voice far more gentle than normal, "you might take my sister on a turn about the room, Mr Worth, for I have a few things to discuss with my aunt and will have to leave shortly."

"Well," he said, a little surprised and then encouraged by the smile Rachel bestowed on him, "if that is agreeable to Lady Rebecca, I should be delighted."

"Rebecca?"

"That would be perfectly acceptable."

Rachel noted that Rebecca almost sniffed after her words. It seemed she really was upset with her beau, but perhaps this little interview was what they needed to see them on the right path again.

Rachel retreated to the side of the room. Standing behind her aunt's chair, she watched the couple join the crowd circuiting the large space. Her sister presented a fine figure, slightly smaller and more feminine than her own. She admired Mr Worth's stature, his square shoulders, and the ease with which he carried himself. Apparently it was only her sister that sent him into the guise of a young pup.

She could see he was doing most of the talking this time. Hopefully Becky would be pleased. Rachel wondered what they spoke of. She doubted it consisted of deals, of inheritances, or of parts to be played. She wondered where Julius had gone. Would he avoid her for the rest of their marriage? He had apologised for kissing her, but had it been needed? Though everything seemed to be cloaked in an indeterminable grey uncertainty, the one thing she was sure of was the fact that she had enjoyed that kiss.

It had been so long since she had spoken to someone with such familiarity as she had begun to do with Julius. They had spoken as equals, as friends, and it had only made her realise just how lonely she had been. Living with a man whose interests had been so averse to her own, whose age had been a constant barrier, and whose character was so opposite, it had felt at times like a perfectly gilded prison. There had been periods when her life had felt as constricting as an overtight set of whalebone stays. And yet, over the past few months, playing a role she had never expected to play, upholding a deal she had never expected to make, she had felt freer, more able to be herself than she had ever felt before.

More than that, she had *enjoyed* his company, something she would never have thought possible. He had a sense of humour beneath his fusty exterior. He even had a temper, which she had never felt needed an apology. She was only happy that he was human, that he erred. Goodness, was she really thinking of his pleasing attributes?

This must stop. They had a deal, and regardless of what she thought of the man she was married to, they would be separated soon enough. She would be gaining her independence.

Just as she had come to this conclusion, her sister came back to her, without Mr Worth, a look of bright-eyed anger on her attractive face.

"Well, sister," she said, almost panting after her energetic striding. "Mr Worth has just proposed to me and I have unequivocally refused him."

Rachel took a chair back to the Arleigh residence. She disliked being jostled around intensely, but she doubted Arleigh would have been happy if she had walked back, however much she would have enjoyed the time to think.

Rebecca's revelation had been positively shocking. Her younger sister had immediately demanded to go home with her aunt and Rachel had accompanied them. She admired Rebecca for managing to maintain some degree of composure in the Pump Room, but as soon as the servants were dismissed in her aunt's home, she had let out what could only be described as a shriek.

Her aunt could never bear any such noises. She had upbraided her niece soundly, demanding an explanation for their abrupt departure from the Pump Room. Rebecca had quickly relayed the proposal she had received from Mr Worth with wringing hands and tears of shock starting in her eyes. She had explained how ungentlemanly he had acted, what a fool he had made her look, for she had no idea of his desire to propose and, compelled by the need to escape the whole awful situation, she had refused him.

It took a glass of her aunt's best brandy to calm her sister and eventually, both she and her aged relative decided it would be best for Rebecca to lie down for a while. Rachel had left, not wishing to be gone too long, should Arleigh return and need her for the solicitors' business. To be completely honest, she had been relieved to leave. She wasn't sure her mind could cope with any further drama which might unfold, for it felt fit to burst.

It was thoughts of this, of her husband, of his inheritance, of that kiss, which tumbled in on her and made the small chair she travelled in feel suffocating. When they turned into the street of the Arleigh family's Bath house, the tiny windows of her small, upholstered prison gave her no preparation for the scene she was approaching.

The sight of her husband holding the bridle of the most splendid black gelding took her completely by surprise.

"Wh..." she began, as she looked up from batting down her skirts which had become crumpled in the chair.

"My lady," the chair bearer said, anxious to get to his next paying client, disrupting her thoughts.

Mrs Banshaw directed one of the footmen from the top of the steps to deal with the payment, leaving Rachel free to turn back to the horse.

He was twitching a little irritably, but those wide, intelligent eyes and alert, pincer ears only did him more justice. His coat was brushed and buffed to perfection. He shone like Alexander the Great's Bucephalus, and he must have rivalled the creature in stature. He was quite as big as Julius' grey, but his frame was finer. He had a deep barrel chest, long elegant legs and an attractive head.

"His name is Tarquin," said Julius, coming round to the side on which Rachel stood, admiring.

"He's magnificent," she replied, plucking at the fingers of her gloves to remove them so she could feel his coat. "Another addition for the stable?"

"Your addition," Julius said, his voice steady and his eyes focused on her reaction.

"My? Wait." Her hands stilled their stroking as she looked at her husband. "What do you mean, my addition?"

"I mean that he's your horse."

"Well." She had not expected this. He had disappeared all night and all morning and now this. "This is where you have been? Purchasing a horse for me?"

"Yes." Arleigh turned to stroke Tarquin. The gelding immediately began fussing at one of his pockets and Arleigh pulled a carrot from it and offered it to the horse. "Old Lord Fortnum had him. Claims he's got Marske blood in him. He drove a hard bargain, but I got him for a reasonable price. He's only eight. He'll be a good mount for you for a few years if you get on well. I'm sure I could persuade Fortnum to have him back if you don't suit."

"I… I can't believe that you bought me a horse."

"I said I would if you enjoyed riding out and…" he continued, refusing to meet her eye, "I thought you did."

"Yes, yes I did."

"Good." He stroked Tarquin's neck a few more times before calling a groom to take the horse round to the stables.

"Thank you." In spite of recent events, she couldn't stop herself placing a hand on his arm. "If I were a better woman, I would refuse this kindness as too much, but Tarquin is…" Rachel could not have picked a better horse had she tried. "He's wonderful. Does that make me greedy?"

"No."

She saw the smallest of smiles on his mouth and it pleased her. He had looked so stern when she first arrived. Perhaps he'd been… nervous? The feeling of his pleasure was warm and comforting.

"I shall choose to believe your lies."

The crease at the corner of his mouth deepened in response and he held out his arm. She took it and together, they walked into the house.

Chapter 15

"We are good friends, are we not Caro?"

Rebecca had demanded she attend tonight. She had insisted on Caro's presence at her aunt's small card party which was largely made up of her aged acquaintances.

"We are," Caro replied.

They had taken a seat in the small morning room which was otherwise unoccupied. The other guests were in the drawing room on the first floor. Pale green papers on the walls which would ordinarily have looked pretty and spring-like in the morning sun, looked dour and more akin to a night-time forest by candlelight.

"That is why I want you to know, why you must know," Rebecca said, biting her lip, her large brown eyes meeting tentatively with Caro's, "what has occurred between your brother and I."

Caro immediately raised her hand. She would not have this conversation. "James has told me of the facts, but the rest is between you and my brother."

She could still see James' downcast face when he had appeared at her door yesterday. It had taken a full hour for her to coax the truth from him and when she had heard it, she could scarcely believe it. For the first time since she had met Rebecca, she felt that her friend was not who she thought she was.

"But Caro, you must know why I made the decision I did. It is not that I wished to hurt James, it's just…"

"But you did," Caro said, trying her hardest to maintain her equilibrium. She had forgotten the feeling of her temper. It had cooled considerably since her troubles with the gaming hells of London had been dealt with. She had found no use for it, for she had been happy, and not even the occasionally irksome nature of her dear husband had raised it. "Rebecca, I can't be a party to this. He is my brother and he is…"

Should she say it? Should she put James so fully into a position of vulnerability? She looked about the room for inspiration, her eyes falling over the dark, archaic furniture and the shape of an aged harpsichord in the corner, cloaked in shadow. No one had been expected to use this room during Lady Etheridge's card party.

"You have wounded him, Rebecca. You have wounded him deeply and…" She felt the temperature of her blood rising. "I cannot understand it."

"But you see," said Rebecca, suddenly moving to kneel before her friend, taking Caro's hands and squeezing them in an act of supplication, "that is why I must explain myself. It is just…" She rose and walked away from Caro, her movements tense and awkward. "With my sister's marriage, it has been so distracting and…"

"Oh, Rebecca!" Caro rose suddenly, her blue eyes kindling. "When will you drop the subject? You have hounded your sister ever since you learned of her marriage, and you have spoken of nothing else to me. Can you not leave others' affairs to themselves?"

"Well, I…" She looked truly shocked. Words failed the open mouth that was ready to say them and her eyes shone with anxiety.

Caro spoke instead, "Your appetite for drama and scandal is amusing, dear," she said, her tone softening slightly. She rose to walk a little, her hand on her abdomen which strained against the stomacher she wore. "It always has been." She cast a kind smile towards her friend.

She did not wish to harm her, but there must be an end to this. Rebecca's ignoring of others' feelings in her desire to seek out truth that may be better left alone had put pressure on their relationship.

"It is half of the reason for our friendship — all that we have been through — but my dear, you who gave me advice and aid in my time of need, let me do you the same service. You are so focused on your sister, so focused on what others are doing rather than their feelings, I am afraid it has made you a little..." She steeled herself for the task at hand. For if their friendship were to survive, if they were to get through this, she must show what damage her friend was doing. "... callous, my dear."

"And is that what Felton thinks too? Do not think I have been blind to his obvious coldness towards me. If you had a sister, perhaps you would understand."

"I have a brother, Rebecca," Caro said, feeling her abdomen tighten with the tension in the room. She rubbed her hand back and forth across it. "We are great friends Rebecca, we always have been, but at this moment, you have behaved badly, for you know how my brother loves you and..." She trailed off, bending slightly at the sudden sharp pain which laced itself across her stomach. It came as quickly as it went and in spite of Rebecca's concerned looks, Caro wished to finish. "You love him, Rebecca, and don't try to deny it. It has been as clear as day since my betrothal."

"Are you well?"

"Yes." She waved her hand slightly. "I need a drink, I think," she said, touching a hand to her heated brow. She felt the perspiration there. The room was suddenly very close, but she had to finish what she'd started. "I do not tell you these things to hurt you. You know I love you, Rebecca.

You have been the best of friends to me. But I cannot watch you hurt those around you without you realising what you are doing, and I cannot come between my brother and my friend. Do you understand?"

She was satisfied to see Rebecca nod reluctantly and, feeling an urgent need for fresher air, she took her leave of the room.

The interview had been less than satisfactory. Rebecca felt as though she had been torn asunder. Now she was left to walk around as if everything were normal in spite of a bleeding wound. How could it be that her best friend would not listen to her explanation?

She was not a bad person. It was not her fault that James was so… well, he was so… James. Could she be blamed for wanting more than just a rushed proposal from a man she had barely seen for three months? In all honesty, she had been so shocked by the proposal that she had refused it out of hand without fully realising what she was doing.

The man had barely spoken three sentences to her since his return from business in the West Indies. Yes, it was true, she harboured a tendre for him, but she had never been given any indication that it was returned by his wooing her. And then to surprise a girl like that! It was too much, and yet, as soon as she had returned to her aunt's home, she had barely been able to stand. Had she really rejected the only man she had ever had some kind of feelings for?

And now this, her friend calling her out as callous. Was she callous? It was true she had not thought of others' feelings much recently, but there were reasons for that, her sister's mysterious marriage being one. She felt a growing indignation, a feeling which did not require much substantiation in fact, in which she could revel in order to dull the pain of what had just occurred.

They entered the room where the card players were gathered. Wending their way around tables surrounded by observers standing and chatting in groups, they parted ways. Rebecca watched Caro walk over to Felton and saw them whispering together. How could Caro understand? She had a husband who loved her, who had fought a duel for her, who had been stabbed for her. Felton was one of the most articulate men in polite Society, though his choice of subject matter was often questionable. It was quite different when one had a tendre for a man who was incapable of speaking his feelings. At times, Rebecca had even wondered if James was scared of her. How could she marry a man who was intimidated in her presence?

She moved absentmindedly through the crowds, ignoring the various calls on her attention which she would usually have responded to with a smile and a flourish of her fan. She found herself at the punch table, hand outstretched towards a freshly poured glass when another attempted to take it.

She glanced up to see who the perpetrator was and met with a set of bright emerald eyes. They twinkled at her as Mr Thayers smiled.

"Lady Rebecca, what a pleasant surprise."

"Hardly, Mr Thayers," she said with more sharpness than she meant. Her mood really was foul this evening. "This is my aunt's house."

"The charming Lady Etheridge. She extended an invitation to my sister and brother-in-law, and I could not resist attending myself." He passed her the glass she had reached for and took another, turning upon the room and searching the faces. "Is your charming sister in attendance?"

"She is," said Rebecca, following his gaze and seeing he had already found Rachel out. She was standing with Lord Fortnum and Sir Egresford. When Rebecca had left them, they were discussing horseflesh. From the animated look on her sister's face, Rebecca suspected that was still the subject of choice, though Arleigh was no longer at her sister's elbow.

"As delightful as ever. You will excuse me?"

He said it as a question, but it was the furthest thing from it, for he disappeared from her presence without awaiting a reply. She watched him make quick work of the crowd in between himself and her sister, and soon he was at her elbow, saying something charming no doubt, for a few moments later, Rachel erupted into peals of laughter. Mr Thayers leant in after the laughter had subsided and Rebecca noted with a furrowed brow that he touched Rachel's elbow in a far too intimate manner.

"Lady Rebecca," Arleigh said, ordering two glasses of burgundy from the servant before turning back to his sister-in-law.

"Brother," she replied sardonically.

Her tone caught Arleigh and he glanced down at Rebecca, observing the punch glass hung haphazardly from one finger, her general stance less than upright.

"I see my sister is still talking horseflesh."

"I doubt wild horses could tear her away from the subject." He paused, considering whether to continue the conversation. "You are enjoying your evening?" It was a risky question to ask. His wife had told him of Lady Rebecca's rejection of Mr Worth's suit, but when he had seen her earlier, she had seemed in perfect control of her faculties.

"Not in the slightest."

He wished he had not asked. She was clearly on the wrong side of sober and he was ill-equipped to deal with foxed men, let alone women. He took refuge in minimal words. "Oh?"

"There is no need to look so uncomfortable. Goodness, you are a very straight sort of man, Arleigh, it's what makes your marriage to my sister so..." She sloshed the punch glass from side-to-side trying to grasp at something.

"So?"

"Baffling."

Baffling? Was it that strange to think of him and Rachel meeting at another time, another place, when a deal was not needed, and finding...

"Yes. I mean, after her marriage to Sir Denby, I would have expected her to marry someone like Mr Thayers. Denby wasn't the liveliest of men, you see."

Rebecca wasn't even looking at him, but Arleigh's eyes were now fully locked onto her.

"And who is Mr Thayers?"

He'd heard that name before. Where had he heard it?

"Her childhood beau."

Yes, Rachel had mentioned him, that night at the inn.

"He's here, you know." Rebecca swung

round and thrust the punch glass towards him. "That's what baffles me about you two. What sort of cold fish can watch his wife being flirted with by the man who had her youthful heart?"

Arleigh, had he been asked, would not have been able to describe the sudden and violent series of feelings that coursed through his veins. The final feeling he was left with rocked his entire equanimity unpleasantly.

"What do you mean, my lady?"

"Well, he's here, don't you know—*that's him*." She thrust her glass in the direction of Lady Arleigh who was at that moment leaning back on the arm of a handsome, green-eyed gentleman, laughing. "He met us in the Pump Room the other day, just as besotted with her as ever. You know, if she were not…" Apparently that sentence was too much even for the drunken Lady Rebecca, for she stopped short and cast suddenly lucid eyes up at her brother-in-law, biting her lip in remorse.

"Oh, I…" She put her hands forward as if to stop him, but it was too late.

He made it across the room in five rapid paces and reached his laughing wife before she had finished her final peal.

"Oh, I say." The green-eyed gentleman, who could be none other than Mr Thayers, ceased his laughter and began a greeting, but Arleigh could not take his eyes off where that man's hand connected with his wife's back. "We haven't been intro... "

"I do not care who you are," said Arleigh, his voice cold as ice and his eyes bearing the full weight of his authority. "You will get your hands off my wife."

"Julius, I..." began Lady Arleigh, but he cut her off.

"Now."

He watched Mr Thayers look at Lady Arleigh and then back at himself. He then carefully removed his hand.

"A lovers' tiff, eh?" Lord Fortnum chimed in, chuckling as if it were all some lark. "A woman that knows her horseflesh as well as Lady Arleigh will be in high demand."

Arleigh did not wait to hear Sir Egresford concur with his crony. He took his wife's elbow and guided her forcefully from the gathering. He did not hear the whispered demands of explanation from his wife or see the looks of the card players. Even if he had, in that moment, he would not have cared.

Chapter 16

"What on earth has possessed you?" Rachel demanded.

Arleigh had just slammed the library door shut behind them in their Bath home. She had not been granted the opportunity to discard her hat, cloak and gloves on the servants when they had entered the house, for Arleigh had only just released her from the vice-like grip he had maintained since their exit from Lady Etheridge's.

"That man." The short explanation was offered in a tone of loathing. He looked like a crazed person, the way he was pacing, his hands raking furiously through his powdered hair, leaving it loose about his shoulders, and powder scattered over the cloth of his jacket. She had never seen him like this.

"What on earth do you mean?"

Though he did not look at her as he continued to move about the room like some caged animal, she could see the anger in his eyes.

"Mr Thayers," he said, as if that explained everything. "Your sister told me it was him," he added, answering her internal question. "Your childhood love."

Her mouth dropped open an inch and for a moment she was left without words.

"And what of it?" she said, command over her faculties finally coming back. "Mr Thayers was only conversing with me. I have done nothing to incur this wrath!" Her defiance was tempered by the smallest of doubts. She had not told Arleigh he was in Bath, that was true, but should she have? Was that twinge in her conscience telling her she had been remiss? They were not really husband and wife. This was a deal, wasn't it? "Why does it matter to you who I converse with?"

"Because you have the power to drive me mad, woman!" Arleigh almost shouted the words as he moved away from her towards the far window.

She had no answer for that.

The admission seemed to calm him, at least physically. His body still held the tension which seemed ready to burst from him, but he stopped pacing and instead turned towards her. His gaze was all but interrogating.

"What power?"

"You—what madness have you made come over me?" His urgent, plea-filled eyes cut her to the quick.

Her anger was washed away by a sudden wave of compassion.

"I can't sleep, I can't concentrate."

He came towards her then and, if she had been any less of the woman she was, she might have stepped back at the sight of the tall man barrelling towards her.

"I don't understand," she said. But she did. She did understand.

"No other man should touch you like that."

Other man. Was he the exception? Was he the only one that could? She could not ignore how attracted she was to him in that moment. He was a handsome man. She had known that all along, but she had always put him in a place that was out of bounds. Now she looked at him, as she had after he had kissed her in the tack room. With desire. She could see the longing in his eyes, she could see the attractive lilt of his lips, the masculinity of his frame.

This was dangerous. She might have ignored her attraction before, but he had shown her his already and now she was responding in spite of her restraint. She would not give in. She would not. She could not. No matter how attractive this man was. No matter what feelings she had developed for him. No matter how he had defended her to her parents, and cared for her, and listened to her. She would not. She tipped her chin challengingly at him.

But rather than answering her bold glare

in kind, she felt his hand upon her arm. It was there, just as Thayer's had been, but his touch, unlike others, sent sparks shooting under her skin. He kept his eyes locked onto hers, searching for her reaction, as he moved his fingers about her arm, tracing the line of her limb.

The sparks ignited a fire of desire in her chest and her breath was no longer steady. She exhaled, the air dancing over her lips, and her husband took that as his answer.

Julius wrapped his fingers around her arm, far more gently than he had done earlier, and drew her firmly towards him, his mouth falling on hers in a matter of seconds. It was like it had been in the tack room. His mouth was all that was passionate, and Rachel was just as surprised by the strength of his emotion as she had been the first time.

All steadiness, all firmness and all equanimity dissolved in a sea of desire and those feelings were transferred to her. She reached up instinctively, her hands touching his hair, running her fingers up between the locks.

He took her into his arms without a second bidding. He withdrew his kisses from her mouth only to descend upon her neck, down her shoulder, kissing the pale skin, sending more sparks shooting across her.

"You drive me mad, woman," he whispered against her, his breath tickling her collarbone.

She would have laughed if the sound hadn't been caught in her throat. This wasn't a moment for laughing. This was a moment for them.

He retracted from her and she could see the haze of desire in his eyes. He did not speak a word as he took her hand and led her from the room. The sight of two servants in the hall caused plumes of red to flood her cheeks but her husband was oblivious. He strode across the hall, his hand firmly around hers, ignorant of all distractions as he ascended the stairs.

They came to his door and Rachel heard the soft click as it opened, the door swinging wide revealing the private sanctum of this man who had all her attention. The papers and drapes were all rich greens and burgundies. This was a man's dwelling, and he drew her into it, shutting the door, bringing her before the bed. The fire was lit, blazing in the hearth, and candles scattered the wooden surfaces bathing the room in a warm glow.

Turning towards her, he only lingered for a moment. Whatever he briefly searched for in her eyes, he found, and he pulled her in against him, picking up exactly where they had left off in the library.

"Take out your hair pins," he whispered against her lips, and she did as she was bid, the great powdered mass of curls cascading over each other to swing low to her waist. He pushed his fingers through it, pulling her lips against his again, hungrily kissing her as if to make up for the months they had spent apart as man and wife.

Man and wife. That's what they were. This wasn't wise but... Rachel felt all resolve slipping from her fingers as they ran over his shoulders, and she didn't care. He wanted her. He desired her.

She pulled at his jacket until he obligingly discarded it, along with his cravat. Forgotten, like everything else, like the world, like all the pressures they had both faced. In this moment, solace was found here, comfort would be found. This was what they both wanted. Together, they had stumbled into a whirlpool of desire and together they would drown.

Rachel awoke to a feeling akin to waking after sleeping in the warm sunshine on a summer's day. The worries and stresses of recent days had faded away, and her whole frame was deliciously warm. It must have been morning, for she could make out light behind her closed eyes. She stretched against the crisp sheets, her limbs aching gently, and realised with a start that she was naked.

Cotton sheet ran against bare thigh and stomach. She froze, memories of a night of abandon flooding back. Her fingers brushed the skin of another's shoulder as they drew back to grip the covers and she stifled a giggle.

The other person shifted. "Am I to think you laugh at me, wife?" a deep voice rumbled from the depths of the covers.

"Not at you," Rachel replied, pulling the covers to her chin and laying back on the pillow. "I am simply used to a bed to myself. You... you take up rather a lot of it."

She heard what sounded like a grunt before realising Julius was actually laughing. She stared at the canopy above, too worried to look sideways at the man whom she was almost certain was as equally naked as herself.

They had spent the night together and she could barely believe it. But she could barely believe that the man she had been with last night was the same Julius Arleigh who had stared so stonily ahead at the altar on their wedding day. Last night he had been...

"What are you doing?"

Rachel halted. She had been making progress towards the dress she had so thoughtlessly discarded last night with the sheet clutched tightly around her.

"I'm getting up, Arleigh—Julius, that is."

She turned to look at him and coloured intensely as she caught his eyes, eyes that were so intently and deliberately staring at her. Apparently his reserved nature had been taken off along with his cravat.

"I... well." She spread a hand on the bed sheet that had nearly fallen to her waist.

Arleigh sat up suddenly, resting his elbows on his knees and staring at his clasped hands. She was given a clear view of a strong upper body.

"Rachel, last night I... it drove me mad to see that man with you."

"I understand—a man's passion is... strong."

She caught sight of a crease at the corner of his mouth and then a furtive glance in her direction.

"And what is yours?"

His eyes were softer than before. They looked at her, searching her face and lips for an answering smile.

"You started it," she retorted, pushing great curling locks from her face.

An awkward silence descended. In each person's mind, a hundred and one questions and thoughts tumbled over each other only to be overshadowed by the memory of the intimacy they had shared.

"Perhaps we should breakfast?" he offered, the hands which had been so relaxed now gripping together.

Rachel turned a suddenly relieved face

upon him. "That would be delightful."

"I shall go to my dressing room," said Julius, avoiding her eyes and suddenly regaining some of that aloof reserve. "And leave you to…"

"Cover my nakedness?" Rachel asked brashly, feeling it could be her only response in light of such awkwardness.

He nodded stiffly, all vestiges of last night falling away, and pulled one of the many bed sheets about his waist before slipping off the bed and out of the room.

Rachel was left on the large four-poster, sitting as it was on a raised dais, lost for a moment in this man's domain. What the devil of a mess! Here she was, in her husband's bed, and the said husband could not wish to be out of her presence quick enough. Perhaps that was to be expected. After all, what was last night? Had it just been a delightful mistake?

She could still smell his musk in the wake of his departure and with a sudden recklessness, flung herself back among the covers and inhaled. The scent filled her nostrils and if she were a schoolgirl, she might have been ashamed of the sudden desire it evoked in the depth of her stomach. As suddenly as she had fallen back into the memories of last night she started upright. What was wrong with her? She was acting the lovestruck debutante. Lovesick? Was that what this was? The feeling of desire, heavy upon her, creeping out from her stomach along her limbs in tingling sensations. She couldn't be.

"Rachel Anne Arleigh!" She chastised her wildly wandering mind, but even her own name brought back the man in question to her thoughts.

She had not viewed Arleigh, or rather Julius, in such a fashion before. He was handsome, that much was true, and she would own, but she had never found herself attracted to him. Perhaps it had been the nature of their relationship. He would never be hers, so why pine after an unattainable man? But now he had been attained, of his own volition, where did that leave her? Where did it leave him? It appeared as though he had left the bedchamber as soon as the realisation of what had happened last night had dawned on him.

Last night. It had never been like that with Sir Denby. There had never been much kissing, hardly thought to anything but the business at hand. She had been warned by friends that it would probably be so, that begetting an heir was a tiresome business. Well, last night had not felt like business at all.

She slipped from the bed and took up her dress and shift, to cover herself as best she could. Picking up her stays and accoutrements, she padded to the door, and with a last look back at the tumble of bedclothes, she opened the door and stepped out.

No. Last night had been about pleasure,

pure and simple. It had opened her eyes to what could be shared between a man and a woman, and apparently, judging by her side-tracked mind, it had quite ruined her for much else. But whatever desires Julius had awakened in her, and whatever experiences he had opened her eyes to last night, would have to be put to bed. He had left her quick enough, to return to his previous state, and so must she. But hard as she might try, she could not help her mind hovering delightedly over memories of herself and Julius.

Her scattered self entered her bedchamber so much distracted that she failed to see Nellie waiting for her beside the wash basin.

"Good morning, your ladyship..."

"Gracious child!" cried Rachel, jumping a full foot in the air. The jolt sent her stays clattering to the floor and the other articles of clothing soon after.

"I'm sorry, your ladyship, I did not mean to startle you."

"Oh, no matter, Nellie," said Rachel, wafting the hue of red away from her face with an agitated hand. "It's hardly your fault when I was sneaking into my own bedchamber. Can one sneak into one's own bedchamber?" Rachel was trying dreadfully hard to appear nonchalant in spite of her dishevelled state. She was failing.

"His lordship's valet sent me to ensure you are made ready for riding out with Lord Arleigh this morning, my lady."

Nellie's dimples appeared on her cheeks and she shot her mistress a knowing smirk.

"Really?" asked Rachel, a confused hand passing over her brow. What did this mean? Perhaps he considered this brief diversion into the realms of passion something in need of addressing and a private ride was better than the breakfast he had suggested.

"Your ladyship?" Nellie queried, still holding out the fetching green riding habit that had lately arrived from the dressmakers.

"Well, yes, I shall be ready shortly." Rachel held out the remnants of the wardrobe that no longer resided on her person, her maid taking them without so much as a word. "Thank you."

If it needed addressing as her husband obviously thought, she would be no coward. She would face him.

"If you can see to the taming of my hair as quickly as you can, we may not keep his lordship waiting too long."

And they didn't. In fact, Rachel was horrified that her toilette seemed to fly by when on every other occasion since she was sixteen it had felt like long-lived torture.

As Nellie placed a wonderful concoction of silks, fruit and stuffed bird on her mistress' head, Rachel's stomach began a small-scale riot in her abdomen. She was to face him. There was some comfort to be found in the fact that he would be dressed this time.

But how were they to speak? Were they to act like they always had? Ultimately, it all boiled down to one fundamental question in Rachel's mind—what of their deal?

Chapter 17

"**Y**ou know, I am not by any means saying that I understand females," said Felton. "Your sister continues to baffle me — more now than ever with her odd dietary requests — but is there not a reason that can be got at for Lady Rebecca refusing you?"

"Reason?" James asked glumly, his usual pragmatism lost in self-pity over his recent rejection.

The two gentlemen were trudging a path beside the Avon in the light of the afternoon sun. Swallows from nearby buildings swooped and wheeled above the flowing river as if teasing the body of water that it could not join them in the sky. The myriad of buildings, many newly erected in the typical Bath stone, were looking warm and inviting in the light, and other people were making the most of the good weather by walking too.

Caro would have been with them had Felton not insisted that she rest. She was as active as ever, but she was beginning to look wan with the added exertion of growing a baby within her. Felton had brooked no refusal, as was his custom now that his protective instincts were coming into their own, and Caro had stayed at home.

That was not the only reason Caro had agreed to try and sleep while they were gone. She was also pleased that Felton and her brother might have some time alone. She had not been able to coax much conversation from James since Rebecca had refused him and she thought that perhaps a fellow man might fare better.

"She didn't give me a reason."

"Are you sure? Ladies are inclined to be fairly talkative, even in the most extreme circumstances."

"The only thing she spoke of was the shock of it, and the fact that I had barely spoken to her."

"Really?" Felton's brows rose as he considered this new information. "I suppose she has a point."

"She has a..." James tried to muster an indignant tone but failed.

"Look, I'm not trying to kick a man while he's down, but there must be a reason for her refusal. We were all in agreement that she showed a marked partiality towards you."

"Not anymore."

"Not at the moment," Felton corrected without compassion. He wasn't trying to make his brother-in-law feel better with hollow words.

"Perhaps it is for the best," James sighed, the strike of his cane on the gravel path becoming a little stronger. "I have my business to think about, and with the way it has grown over the last year, I would do well to devote more of my time to it. There are opportunities in the north and in Cornwall I wish to explore."

"How many times have you spoken to Lady Rebecca since you met her?" asked Felton, totally ignoring James' turn in the conversation.

"I don't know."

"Approximately? A lot? A little?"

"I haven't been in the same country for the past few months," said James, on the defensive.

"Since you've been in Bath?"

"Maybe once."

"As I said, perhaps she has a point."

"Damn it all man! What good is it to dissect why she refused me. She just did, didn't she, and there's no changing it."

"Isn't there?"

"What on earth do you mean?"

"Well, if she does indeed have feelings for you, which more than one of us have noticed, then surely whatever it is that made her refuse you could be changed?"

"It's just…"

"Just what?"

"I'm not good at this talking. I'm not like her — confident and witty — or like you. I like to think things through, to consider. I can't just go about blurting out all these long conversations like others, so what am I supposed to say to her?"

"Are you saying that for the woman you love, you aren't willing to make a little conversation?"

"No, I just…" Again he trailed off, apparently giving up.

"Don't you see, it's not about the talking, James. A woman wants to know that you can take command. That you are confident. That you can take care of her when the need arises. How can she know you are capable of that if you cannot string a sentence together before her? Not to mention, a woman likes to be told that she's loved, especially before being asked to spend the rest of her life with someone."

"That does make sense."

"Yes, it does, doesn't it," said Felton, the shadow of a grin on his mouth.

"So what do you propose I do?"

Arleigh was standing in breeches and a plain, full-skirted, woollen coat, fit for riding. His hands were loosely clasping the reins of his wife's horse, and when she came near, she saw only a flicker of acknowledgment. He avoided her humorous eyes and smiling mouth. His own mouth was pressed shut. She saw a muscle in his jaw clench as she came beside him. He helped her aboard and took his horse from the groom, silently mounting and leading the way they had gone a few mornings before.

A mist hung heavily about the Bath streets, snaking between the townhouses and establishments, giving the city a forlorn atmosphere. The sound of the horses' hooves echoed eerily in the grey world, and for once Rachel was cast into silence. She watched the steady sway of her husband's horse and kept sight of his tall figure astride the tall animal.

They travelled thus for some time before the resort town's houses filtered away, leaving them in the pure countryside. The visibility was little better, but as they followed the meandering line of the valley floor, the sun rose and began to burn off the worst of the mist. Before long, warm rays of light stretched across the grass, causing a thousand drops of dew to shine in response. Tiny flowers, in yellow and white, were scattered amongst the long grasses, and birds sang to the dawn, raising the sun with their anthem. It was all beauty.

Rachel's mind had fallen back to last night, memories crowding in, mingling with each other, jostling for attention so that she thought of everything and nothing all at once.

She had begun to daydream, expecting the ride to be a silent one, when her husband's sudden speech brought her sharply back to reality.

"I never intended for last night to happen."

She kept her eyes fixed on the movement of her horse's dark ears, contemplating her answer. "No?"

"It was..."

She looked at him then, and was flattered to see a crease appear at the corner of his mouth.

"You need not explain yourself, Julius. I understand that..."

"Come with me," he said, cutting in and dismounting in the same moment.

He began to stride towards a section of the woodland where the trees grew close together and the morning sun was warded off by heavy branches.

Rachel was taken aback at the abrupt actions of the man who was apparently intent on surprising her. She huffed frustratedly as she watched him take long strides away. Looking down at the kid gloves in which her reins lay, she saw marks from the saddle-soaped leather across her palms. Her new horse was a little more impatient than the hack she had ridden last time. Right now she was tempted to let Tarquin have his way and take her from the confusion she felt, being in this place, with that man.

She glanced one last time at Julius who

had now all but disappeared between the trees and then looked to the path ahead. Before her lay the way she knew. She could navigate home. She didn't have to stay here. She didn't need to go where she did not know. To her right was uncharted, and the man she was venturing into it with was the most unknown of all. Did she want to know what he wanted to say? If he wanted to say anything at all? Did she want a verdict passed on last night? Right now, sat here, where she was, there was no danger, but in there, there was...

She dismounted as abruptly as her husband, causing her horse to skitter sideways and she took a few moments to calm him. Once he was placid, she took another few moments to persuade him that there was no bogeyman waiting for him in the trees, and then followed the deep footsteps her husband had left in the dew-laden grass.

Entering the woods, the warm rays of sun deflected from her green-clad shoulders and the sound of the birds echoed amongst the trees. Tarquin snorted ominously and pulled back on the reins before being coaxed once again further into the shadowed world.

Rachel could only just make out the tall quarters of her husband's horse, swaying between the undergrowth and trees. She followed in silent fashion, the only sound the brushing of leaves and branches. Where was he taking her? A fleeting thought of danger flitted across the forefront of her mind before she banished it. She must not be irrational, though she now walked alone through the woods with a man she barely knew. She had known him last night. His passion —there had been honesty in that—but still she could not match up the man she had been with last night to the one she had been married to for a month.

The trees were beginning to thin and strips of trunk were replaced by strips of light as the morning sun made headway in the war against the forest. In the next few moments, she was in the full glory of the sun. In the time she had been following her husband through the woods, the sun had burned off the last of the morning mist, and in this open glade at the very least, the dew had evaporated.

Rachel watched the swooping sparrows over the flowered meadow. For a few moments, her breath was caught at the beauty and secrecy of the scene. Only they were here to enjoy this. It was all theirs. At the thought, she turned to Julius and was surprised to see him watching her. He had barely looked at her since…

"I thought you would like it. I have wanted to bring you here, but I needed to be sure… it's a sanctuary."

It was his sanctuary. That was what he was saying, and he was choosing to share it with her. She found herself unable to hold his penetrating gaze.

"I don't understand," she said, her voice little more than a panicked whisper, one barely known to her.

She faltered as he walked towards her.

"Don't understand what?"

"What is it you want from... what about last night?" She hurriedly rephrased her sentence, not ready for the answer to her first question. Not yet.

"What about it?"

So that was it. She finally had her answer. His line was to ignore what had happened between them. The part of her that had yearned for more was to be denied.

But even as she came upon that conclusion in her mind, she flinched. His hand came up and cupped her cheek, slipped further back until his fingers were pulling at the back of her neck, drawing her towards him. She went willingly, the feeling in her chest demanding her to, until her lips were pressed against his. He was gentle, his lips asking, waiting for an answer before crying for more. His hand dropped to her lower back.

"You consume my thoughts," he murmured against her cheek when he paused. He pulled her against him and wrapped his arms about her. Her eyes opened to the clear blue of the sky and she realised he was embracing her. She had never been embraced by a man before, not even by her father when she was a child. The feeling was warm and safe. As though nothing could touch her within the walls of these strong arms. She felt a lump forming in her throat and cursed inwardly until the surprised tears backed off.

"Do you regret it?" he said, pulling back from her, though his hand still held onto her arm, unwilling to let her go completely.

"No, how could I?"

He smiled in response to her pragmatic tone.

"Neither do I." He kissed her again.

She wanted to ask what had become of their deal, but she didn't want to know the answer. She wanted to ask if they stood somewhere different now, if they were no longer merely traders on either side of an agreement. But she didn't want to know the answer. Not because she knew what she felt, or was sure of what she wanted. She knew neither, but she did know that last night had changed something and she wasn't sure she wanted it to be changed back. That embrace had given her something, and she wasn't sure she wanted to give it up.

They carried on their ride, still speaking little, but knowing more than they had this morning. When they arrived home, Arleigh drew her to one side in the hall of their Bath house.

"I have an idea," he said, speaking in hushed tones, causing the hairs on the back of Rachel's neck to rise.

"Oh yes?"

"Let us leave the rest of the world to itself for a while."

"How very tempting," said Rachel, her eyes warm with desire as she took her husband's arm.

Chapter 18

R ebecca was in no mood to be amused. In fact, if she had not been in public, which necessitated her keeping her countenance, she would probably be weeping at this present time. As it was, her beautiful face was twisted into something foreign as she sat in the Arleigh morning room awaiting her sister.

She wasn't quite sure why she had come. There was nothing Rachel could do to fix this mess. There was nothing that could be done to change what had taken place. She hadn't seen James in three days and she was sure she wouldn't be seeing him in the next three. Nor had she seen Caro, and though her friend had told her that they were indeed still friends, she had not felt it at their last meeting. Aunt Etheridge had insisted on keeping all her many engagements with her aged friends, but Rebecca was at the end of her capacity for small talk in the face of the life-changing decision she had just made. A decision she did not know whether she regretted or not.

But what had really been plaguing her mind on her journey over, were the final moments she had spent with her sister when last they had met. It was not every day that one's sister was carted off so publicly by her husband. Worse still, Rebecca had been the cause, and as with most recent events in her life, she could not stop the uncomfortable sense of guilt which threatened to overcome her.

So, perhaps her reason for coming was two-fold. She sought comfort for her own predicament, the way only a sister could provide it, and she was, quite frankly, worried over what she had caused to occur between her sister and Lord Arleigh.

"Good morning."

"Goodness gracious!" Rebecca jumped, swinging around to see a young woman, no more than a girl, peering curiously at her from a chaise longue near the window. "I had no idea I had company."

"What do you mean?" said the room's other occupant, a girlish giggle bubbling over. "Jeffries just told you I was here when you came in — that's why I smiled at you. I must say I thought it was strange you didn't smile back, but then some people don't, do they? My mother hardly ever smiles when she is smiled at — it makes her seem awfully ill-tempered, but I swear to you she can be quite cheery sometimes. Not like Julius. He always has a straight face, even when I stick my tongue out at him. He just tells me off. But now I have a new aunt, he doesn't seem quite so dull as he was. She's so funny. Have you met her? She looks like you."

Rebecca remained arrested, half-turned towards the young, dark-haired girl, and half towards the door as if she had just walked into the wrong house. She listened to the self-answering monologue and slowly came to realise who this young lady must belong to.

"Are you Lord Arleigh's sister?"

The girl nodded expectantly, her green eyes pleased at the realisation, clearly enjoying talking to a grown up.

Rebecca allowed one of her fine brows to raise questioningly. "Younger sister, I hazard?" For Rachel's sake, she hoped that this girl's observations on her brother's improved temperament still held true. The last time she had seen Arleigh, the look in his eyes had been frightening.

"Oh yes. I couldn't be older than Julius, he's ancient."

"Ancient, you say?" Rebecca relaxed a little and turned to face the girl with more friendliness.

"Yes. He was grown up when I was still a little girl. That's why he can be so boring. But as I say, aunt Rachel — for she bade me call her so — is jolly amusing. I came to see them both — is that why you are here?"

"It is indeed," said Rebecca, enjoying the blend of adult niceties and youthful questions. The girl was really rather sweet. "I came to see your aunt — she is my sister, you see, which makes us sisters-in-law." She only hoped that she would not see Arleigh and Rachel together as this girl desired. Rebecca had no wish to see her brother-in-law after the trouble she had caused the other night. He had seemed so angry and from the lack of affection displayed between the couple, it was frightening to think of the outcome of such emotion. "Might I ask your name?"

"Oh, of course, how rude of me — mama says I can be quite rude, but I don't always see it — I am Phoebe Arleigh, the youngest of my family."

"The youngest."

Phoebe nodded seriously, as if to impress upon her new acquaintance the disparity between that statement and her grown-up behaviour.

"And is your mother here?"

"No, nor my sister. They both wanted to stay in for a call from the Countess of Goring this morning."

"And you did not?"

"No — I think that woman is..." she struggled for a word that would sufficiently explain how she felt without sounding childish, but in the end her youth won. "Frightening."

Rebecca giggled at this, having taken a

seat on the chaise longue beside her companion. She discarded her muff and waved a hand over her face. "That woman is all paste and rouge, my dear, that is why she is so frightful. And no one has the nerve to tell her she looks ghastly for fear she will give them the cut."

"The cut — I have heard Diana talk about that, but whenever she realises I am listening to her talk to mama, she stops and gives me a scowl. Oh," said Phoebe, sighing and smiling dreamily. "I think I shall like your being my sister."

Rebecca smiled generously in response, the look lighting up the face which had, up until now, been downcast. A little distraction was proving quite the relief.

"Mama and Diana shall be so cross when they find out. My maid Lucy told me so, but I threatened to tell mama that Lucy sips at my chocolate in the morning, so she had to bring me."

"Well, you are quite the deviless."

Phoebe gasped, covering her mouth, her bright green eyes dancing above her hands.

"Oh, dash it — I oughtn't to say such naughty words, ought I?" said Rebecca, placing a gloved hand on the sofa between them in a gesture of friendship. "I shall not tell of your escape if you shall not tell of my cursing?"

Phoebe's hands dropped a little and then, quick as a flash, she placed a single finger to her lips in agreement and delivered her new relative a quick nod.

"Julius was supposed to come to mama's this morning. He was to fetch her to go to the men from London. They've come to see him about papa's will. So, you see, even if mama finds out I have snuck away, Julius will be the one in trouble."

The statement was spoken with great satisfaction, as if that settled the matter and protected them both from reprimand, but instead of settling matters for Rebecca, it brought her up sharply.

"Your papa's will, you say?" She paused, considering her approach.

She had already created a rapport with this girl. In fact, she was rather warming to her. The young lady reminded Rebecca of herself at that age and a certain secret trip to meet her father on a Boxing Day shoot one year. There was no doubt Rebecca would be able to get information from her if she wished.

And she did wish it. She had spent three days considering her own miserable situation with Mr Worth, analysing it until she was sick of the thought, trying her hardest to consider her rejection of James pragmatically, and realising that it made no difference whatsoever to her feelings, to her pained heart. On top of that, she had been worrying over the trouble she'd caused in her sister's new marriage. Her thoughts had been so consumed, she'd entirely forgotten the mystery of Rachel's sudden wedding.

"Do you mean solicitors?"

The girl nodded.

"And your brother and mama must see them about your papa's will?"

"Yes. I suppose aunt Rachel has told you about it?" asked Phoebe, looking sideways at Rebecca.

Rebecca opted for silence and a winning look, hoping that it would be convincing enough for Phoebe to confide in her.

"Diana says that papa made it so Julius had to marry within half a year of papa passing away. She says I would not understand, but that it has to do with papa's money and our houses. So the men from London must see Julius. I overheard mama saying they must have proof, though Julius and aunt Rachel are both wearing wedding rings, so I don't understand why the men from London don't believe them. That's why Julius was to come see mama this morning, you see. Did aunt Rachel not tell you? Diana doesn't always tell me everything — sisters can be quite annoying."

Arleigh *had* to marry in half a year? Inheritance—was that what this was all about? That would explain a hasty marriage, at least on his part. What it didn't explain was why Rachel had chosen to be the one he married. Her sister had promised never to marry without affection again. Was it really all a deception so that he could get his money and his estate? Did Rachel even know about the will?

At that moment, a servant came into the room to announce that Lord and Lady Arleigh had gone away and set no date to return. Rebecca looked at the servant and then at Phoebe. Gone without a word? Solicitors left waiting? Something clearly wasn't right.

"What, pray tell, do you mean, your sister is missing?" asked Felton, scepticism in his voice as he observed the agitated Lady Rebecca.

"I mean," said the Feltons' uninvited guest, clearly beginning to lose her temper, "exactly what I say. She is nowhere to be found since my aunt's card party."

"You mean the party at which you became more disguised than a Popish spy?"

He saw the words found their mark. Her lips pursed and there was a slight twitch at the corner of her jaw.

"Yes," she said, owning the insult.

Lady Rebecca Fairing had always been a strong woman, Felton knew. She proved it all the more now, but he would not relent. His pregnant wife was feeling exhausted and he knew about Caro's last conversation with Rebecca. Best friends they may be, but Caro needed protecting, and he bore that mantle. Besides, a plan was forming in his mind and he was conscious of the time. Rebecca needed to leave soon if he were to enact it.

"You saw the rage that Lord Arleigh was in. I am afraid..."

"That you caused the problem?"

"Felton," she said, rising suddenly with a rustle of silk skirts. "We have been friends for longer than your wife and I. Must you be so cutting?"

He paused, his green eyes absorbing the worn look on her face, sympathy lancing the hardened skin of his resolve.

"No—I must apologise for that," he said with a bow. "But you say they have left their residence. Is it not possible they have merely returned to London?"

"She would have told me."

"Would she?" asked Felton, a provoking twinkle in his eye. "She was remiss in telling you of her nuptials. Don't you think a trifle of a thing like returning to London might slip her mind also?"

"But didn't you see the scene Arleigh made?" she said, her voice permeated with despair.

"Yes, but you were the cause of that misunderstanding, from what you've told me, and

Arleigh is a steady man. There really is no reason to be alarmed, Lady Rebecca. Your sister is not exactly a retiring woman — there would have been a frank discussion, I have no doubt. We will find that they have merely returned to Town to escape prying eyes or some such." Felton opted for a softer tone. "What does your aunt say of the matter?"

Rebecca did not answer, and that was telling enough.

"Please let me see her."

"She is resting," Felton said firmly. He would not disturb Caro. James' rejected marriage proposal had affected Caro more than she cared to admit. She needed space. The baby needed a well-rested mother.

"Please," Rebecca whispered again, but his resolve had recovered, and he shook his head.

"Oh," Rebecca whimpered, wringing her gloved hands, and then, as if realising the involuntary display of her feelings, she stopped, pressed a handkerchief to her mouth and curtseying to Felton.

"Good day, Lady Rebecca."

She murmured something against the laced material, but Felton missed it. He had no doubt that if she were to pull it further from her mouth she would be unable to stifle the sobs that threatened.

At the moment of her departure from the morning room, the bell sounded.

"Damn," murmured Felton, following Lady Rebecca into the hallway and catching sight of the visitor at the same moment she did. "James." Felton came forward and took his hand, but the man's blue eyes were locked onto the woman who had turned down his proposal so unequivocally only days ago.

"Come through. Lady Rebecca is just leaving."

Perhaps this could work to Felton's advantage. He saw Rebecca avoid his brother-in-law's gaze and duck away from him towards the door. She acted as if she were no more than a servant.

Felton gently pulled James' arm as the front door closed, and guided him to the morning room, so lately the home of an awkward interview.

"Caro," said James suddenly, still not focusing his gaze on Felton. "How is she?"

"Well — she's resting," Felton replied and then fell silent, giving James time to launch into the subject which hung in the air between them.

"Good—tell me," said James, starting towards the door and then stopping, his hand rising to his brow and rubbing smooth the lines that had taken up residence there. "What..." He stepped back, as if to retract the beginning of the question, but it came unbidden anyway. "Why was Lady Rebecca here—what were her tears in aid of?"

Felton sighed, making as if he did not

wish to discuss it, and took a seat on one of the brocade sofas. He crossed his legs at the ankle and rested an elbow on the arm, cupping his chin in one hand and keeping his engaging green eyes upon James. He had tried to keep the two lovers from seeing each other, but realised how fortunate this was. The subject was broached without him having to bring it up himself. Excellent.

"It is of no import," he said, winding James up, knowing the desired result.

"Then you can tell me," James said, turning to his brother-in-law, placing his hands on his hips and surveying him archly. Felton knew that look. His wife had bestowed it on him many times, and he knew that it would brook no argument.

"Since the fracas at Lady Etheridge's card party, she has not seen her sister. Now she has found out that Lord and Lady Arleigh have left Bath. I suspect they have merely returned to London or perhaps to another estate of the Viscount's, but Lady Rebecca is worrying. She was not told, you see."

"Do you think it warranted?"

"Lady Etheridge sees nothing to be concerned over, and as that woman has the wit of a cunning fox, I trust her instincts."

James was frowning. That, thought Felton, was a good sign.

"But then..." Felton trailed off, planting the seed that was needed for James to take action. Rebecca had rejected James for not being able to speak to her, for not being some romantic figure, and though he would always remain the same dependable James, perhaps she could be forced to see why that was a good thing.

Chapter 19

L ady Etheridge insisted that her niece should take her for a walk while the weather held. Doctor Smith had told her ladyship to keep mobile, though she had thrown some choice words in his direction after the recommendation, and today was the first day she had felt well enough to venture out to one of her favourite spots.

It was not merely about her feeling well enough, however. The main reason for the outing was the fact that her niece was in less than roaring spirits. In her aunt's opinion, Rebecca needed to be out in the fresh air as much as her aged relative. As her niece was hardly going to venture out of her own accord, she would have to be coaxed, or in this case deceived, into leaving the sulking safety of indoors.

"If we follow the walk down the hill, we should find the bridge." Lady Etheridge did not look for a response. She knew that without a verbal thrashing, which at this moment she was not willing to give, she would not receive one. Rebecca was upset and she must have time and space before she could talk.

Lady Etheridge had explained she wished to walk in Prior Park. It held some of the finest views of Bath, and though her husband's old friend, Ralph Allen, had died some years earlier, the present owner had no objection to her walking in the park when she so desired. Of course, she was not fully aware of how much she intimidated others and that it was due more to this intimidation than any sentimentality on the current owner's part that she was allowed to walk freely through the estate. Lady Etheridge was not a woman to be denied.

As the Palladian bridge came in sight, stretching its five arches across the intersection of the lakes, Lady Etheridge smiled. She had come here with her husband many times in her younger days. They had boated on the lake and picnicked on the bank. There were so many happy memories here. The bridge, the view as they descended the valley, the lake; it was all so still, so beautiful. It was quiet now, as if the place reflected on those happy memories too. Apart from the sweet birdsong, the two women were alone here.

Lady Etheridge leant heavily on her niece's arm, the joints in her knees aching at the sudden exertion after so many days sitting and sipping the Bath waters. Curse her physician!

"Perhaps we should sit a while on the bridge?" suggested Rebecca, the first indication she was not entirely lost in her own thoughts.

"It will be well needed."

They came to the path leading up to and through the arches of the temple-like structure and found a cool stone seat within its confines. Lady Etheridge leant back and draped an arm across the expanse of the open arch in which they sat, looking out to the lake.

She spent a few moments in quiet reverie before speaking gently to her niece. "Come now, child, you have barely said a thing all morning and you know I keep you around for your conversation. You disappeared this morning to the Feltons' and came back gloomier than ever. There is nothing that can be done about your sister. She is married and they have their own affairs to deal with after my soirée. You are fretting about things that are not in your control."

"I just feel so..." She saw her niece's lip quiver and then pearl white teeth appear and clamp down on the involuntary movement. "I feel lost," she said succinctly.

"Oh, my child," Lady Etheridge said, taking both her niece's gloved hands in her own. "You are so very young, my dear," she said with a sigh, glancing at the still waters again, admiring a pair of swans that had just drifted into view. "You have yet to understand that many of us spend much of the time feeling lost. We grow up feeling so sure, thinking that everything works a particular way, that there are rules that all things must obey. What no one seems to realise is that a Sovereign God does not mean that he always works things in the way we expect. Sometimes that leaves us a little lost. You can either fight it and lose yourself even more, or you can accept it. You can accept the things that you cannot change, the situations you cannot fix."

A tired, rueful smile played briefly on Rebecca's lips.

"But you must also work on those you can. What of love for you, Rebecca? You are so intent on making sure your sister is happy, on finding out the truth of her feelings, but what of yours?"

Rebecca was crying now, clear round tears rolling down her cheeks.

"I don't know how to do that—how to..."

"Oh, my dear," said Lady Etheridge. She squeezed Rebecca's hands beneath her own and moved in closer to comfort her.

"I am not heartless!" Rebecca blurted out with sudden energy. "I know that is what others think of my refusal of Mr Worth, but I am not, I tell you."

"I never thought you were, child."

"It's just... I feel I hardly know him. There are moments," she said between small sobs, the tears still rolling, "when I feel I know him very well and there is something in his eyes I understand... but then he... he looks away from me and will not speak to me except to say, 'my lady this' and 'my lady that'... I cannot see that we would suit if we cannot speak to each other."

"A wise point, my dear." Lady Etheridge squeezed Rebecca's hand again and they were still for a time.

"Oh! Do not look, my child, but wipe your tears, for Mr Worth has just now appeared and is almost upon us, with a look upon his face of such urgency. Now." Lady Etheridge released her niece's hands.

"Mr Worth," said Lady Etheridge, rising and walking between her niece and the gentleman to give Rebecca time to regain her composure. "We did not expect to see you here, nor, I suppose, did the owner of this land. He and I have an agreement, but I doubt very much the same is true of you."

"Lady Etheridge, please." He was dressed in his usual plain way, a full-skirted woollen frock coat over buckskin breeches and a pair of hardy, but polished, leather boots. It was the look upon his face, however, that moved that most immovable of ladies.

She held his stare for a few moments and then, without turning, she cast words over her shoulder to her niece. "Rebecca, I have been remiss in not sending my regards up to the house. I shall be back shortly."

And without another word she turned on her heel and walked back the way they had come with a remarkable amount of poise for a woman with stiff joints.

"Lady Rebecca." James did not wait for her leave to carry on. "I noted your distress this morning at my brother-in-law's and I asked him as to the cause."

He had come to stand before her just as she had risen to face him with what little energy and resolve she had left. Though she stood before him, her gaze was averted to somewhere over his shoulder, as if some invisible individual resided there desiring to be watched. If she had ventured a glance, she would have noticed he did the same.

"I wished to come and lend whatever assistance you may require. Perhaps I can find out where Lord and Lady Arleigh have gone if that will alleviate your anxiety?"

"Well I…" She stopped, her mouth remaining open in surprise. How was it that he had come to her in such a manner with an offer of aid after all she had done to him? And with more confidence in these few minutes than he had shown in the last month.

"Do you truly believe your sister in danger?"

"I hardly know what to believe anymore. I am told not to worry by those around me," she said, forgetting the awkwardness and finding some relief in this shared confidence.

"You do not abide by the words of others when it comes to your mind, Reb... Lady Rebecca," James said, quickly correcting himself.

"When I..." said Rebecca. "When my heart senses that all is not as it should be, I trust it. I used to. Could I be so wrong?"

James did not immediately respond, and she felt the old stab of sadness. As much as she wished she could accept his silences, there were times when the urgency of the situation demanded more of a response, and yet he seemed so unaffected.

But then he did something that surprised her.

"The issue seems to be a lack of facts. The truth is, if you were furnished with the facts it would not necessarily allay your fears, but you would be satisfied that, whether it be good or bad, you would know the truth. I believe," he carried on in a pragmatic tone, "that you have been starved of the truth, and as a loving sister, have therefore been made unnecessarily anxious." He stood tall as he spoke, his hands clasped calmly behind his back, his pose all that was impeccable and manly.

How she felt for this man! She resisted the sudden urge to touch his arm, to ask him to take her into both of them, and satisfied herself with words instead.

"I could not have put it better myself. I have been made to feel the fool and an irritation for so long. What, I ask you," she said with sudden vehemence, "is wrong with caring for the welfare of a sibling?"

"Nothing. I know the feeling so entirely, and others are not always sensitive to the keenness of anxiety a sibling might feel for one's kin."

At his words, Rebecca was suddenly thrown back to a cold dawn when four men met upon a field, with swords in hand, and Caro's reputation at stake.

"I asked you what I could do to help—and now we have ascertained the cause of your discomfort we know the key—the truth."

His matter-of-fact tone had returned and the emotion that had so fully invaded his previous words was pushed back. A man who turned the tide with such control. How could she so wholly admire him and resent him for it all at once?

"Would it alleviate your anxieties if I were to make enquiries as to the whereabouts of Lady Arleigh?"

"Yes," said Rebecca without hesitation, moving forward and no longer resisting her urge. She pressed gloved fingers against the plain wool of his sleeve. "Yes it would." She thought of Caro then and her words. "But I would not wish to cause further upset. I have already done so much damage to you..."

"Have no fear," James said, removing his arm from her hand so that he could raise it to halt her speech. "I will find out the truth of the matter."

She felt the disconnection acutely. Had he done it to gesture or to sever contact? Had she not been the one to refuse him? The very fact he was speaking to her, offering her help, was a miracle after their last encounter. What had she thrown away?

As if reading her thoughts, but drawing the wrong conclusions, he spoke.

"I understand we cannot be what I had wished," he said, tension spread throughout his frame, "but I want you to know I care deeply for your welfare—no matter how things stand between us." He gave her no pause in which to offer a reply. "I shall report back my findings to you the moment I discover them."

He turned, his wooden heel grinding against grit that had gathered on the bridge, and walked away from her. The echo of his retreating presence sounded out among the arches.

Had he offered to help her from a place of pity or something deeper? Could he still feel for her after her rejection of him? It was the first real, frank conversation they had shared since Caro's misadventure over six months ago. Frankness was what made sense to Rebecca. She was a woman who spoke her mind, sometimes to her detriment. She had always prided herself on her honest and open nature, but now she wondered if her own character had cost her more dearly than she knew.

She was left bereft of any clarity of feeling. She was left alone, feeling as if she were the last person in the world.

Chapter 20

"Breathe."

Arleigh's words tickled at Rachel's ear, his lips close to her neck and his eyes following the line of her gaze down the shaft of the arrow.

His mouth curved as he glanced towards her and caught the concentration in her gaze. He could tell she was trying her best to ignore the feeling of his mouth so close to her, and the hands he held pressed about her waist under the pretence of keeping her body straight for the shot.

"Release," he whispered, the word left suspended as her fingers relaxed and the bolt was loosed. A moment of silence followed as they both watched the missile head for the coloured target some twenty yards away. At the moment of its hitting the second circle, his wife turned towards him with beaming eyes and a smile that could light up anyone's heart.

"Aha!" She jumped up and down, beating

the air with her bow and grabbing hold of him with her spare hand.

"Well done," he said, the sight of her joy making his chest ache. "You've a naturally good aim."

"And a good teacher — however distracting."

She had dropped the bow and was pressing both hands flat against his chest, her fingers finding their way between the buttons of his waistcoat as she leant against him.

"I accept no blame," he said, raising his hands mockingly and smiling at her as she continued to embrace him. "I cannot be held accountable for my attractiveness to an archeress."

"Oh can't you? I beg to differ." She began to giggle, but he cut her joyful outpouring short with a sudden kiss.

"Have we not had enough sun for today?" he murmured between repeated kisses.

"Julius, we have barely been out for the past few days."

Rachel and Arleigh had been sequestered away in Arleigh's hunting lodge, deep in the Mendip Hills, for three days. In that time, they had not left each other's company.

"Is that a bad thing?" he asked matter-of-factly, his frank eyes wondering at her reluctance. His gaze lingered on her smiling lips as they were always wont to do. He could not help it. Since first tasting those lips, he had found himself addicted and he had no wish to break his habit. "Don't you wish to return to the lodge?" he teased.

He relaxed, pulling her closer, and for a moment forgetting the desire to kiss. He had never felt like this with anyone, this calm, this at ease. It had never been easy like this, not even with family, but Rachel was...

She pulled out of his arms and bounded away towards Tarquin who was lashed to a low hanging branch. Apparently the gelding was getting used to her wild ways for he barely skittered at her sudden run, and waited patiently as she hoisted herself into the saddle in the most unladylike of movements.

"You want me, Lord Arleigh?" she cried, a devious smile on her lips and a challenging glint in her eyes. "Catch me."

He set off at a dead run, launching onto the grey and galloping after her towards the hunting lodge.

They arrived back at the lodge amid a clattering of hooves and laughter. The latter came from Lady Arleigh. The secluded nature of the retreat and the lack of house guests had nurtured Rachel's wild, unorthodox ways, and her great mass of rich chestnut hair was loose down her back with a single braid encircling her crown. A dashing crimson hat sat at a rakish angle, pinned to the single braid, with a trail of taffeta streaming behind. At least, it had been so positioned until that last bout of laughter set it loose and tumbling to the stableyard floor.

"Oh, blast it!" Rachel exclaimed, her gloved hand quick to confirm the bareness of her head.

It was an ill-timed accident, for the fluttering descent of millinery sent Tarquin skittering sideways.

The horse swung too quickly for Rachel to counter the movement and save her leg from being crushed against the stable door. Rachel was a fine horsewoman, but even the finest would have cried out in the same pain.

"Rachel!" Arleigh dismounted in one swooping motion, freeing his horse without a care.

A stable boy was already attempting to calm Lady Arleigh's horse with soothing tones and outstretched hands.

"Leave the horse and hide that," Arleigh barked, a finger pointing at the wild, red, flailing creation that spread its long, fearsome taffeta fingers over the straw-strewn floor.

Rachel clung with one hand to Tarquin's mane and clutched at her left leg with the other.

The tear of skirts disguised whatever damage had been done. She cursed in a very unladylike manner when Arleigh finally got near enough to touch it.

"Now, now, my wild wife—I am here to help. If you did not have such a penchant for oversized headwear we would hardly be in this predicament, would we?"

Rachel tried her best to scowl at him as his fingers prized her own away.

"I shall have to roll down your stocking."

"You have had good practice, so I expect you to do it most tenderly."

A smile hovered over his mouth before flitting away as concentration took over.

"You have broken the skin a little and an ugly bruise is already forming."

"Such ill manners, insulting the appearance of my leg," she said, funning through gritted teeth, trying to ward off the tears that threatened.

"You will not be able to dismount," he said, ignoring her provocation and maintaining the steadiness that so marked him. The characteristic calmness of his voice dulled her inclination to moan and instead, perhaps for the first time in her life, she listened to instruction without rejoinder.

He put one arm about her waist and waited with the other to catch her up. He told her how to move and what he would do to help her. Even had she wanted to, she could not have spoken any more provoking words, thanks to the pain from lifting her leg. She managed to get it over the horn and shifted sideways in the saddle, ready to disembark her exhausted beast.

Arleigh's arms were strong, and instead of placing her on the cobbled floor of the stableyard, he held her fast, eliciting an odd noise of surprise from Rachel. A sudden waft of male sweat and the scent of cloves crept into her nose and if she had not been in pain, she might have taken advantage of the close proximity of his lips.

"Now I am at your mercy, what will you do with me, my lord?"

His lips were slightly parted, and she wondered if he would give her the kiss she was yearning for. But he wasn't looking at her, and the look upon his face was anything but amorous. His gaze was fixed intently on someone across the courtyard and his eyes started at whoever they saw. He glanced down at her suddenly and there was a look on his face she had never seen before. He strove to hide it soon after, but it had been there. It was guilt. She followed his gaze and saw James Worth.

She summed up the situation and in spite of the pain, pushed against Arleigh's chest, forcing him to release her. Biting her lip against the discomfort, she regained her footing.

Arleigh tried to maintain his support but she shook free of him.

"Mr Worth!" she called, all bright energy. "We had not expected to see you here. We trust all is well in Bath with those we love?"

The gentleman in question took the greeting as his cue and dismounted, handing his horse to a waiting groom.

"Yes, they are well—I thank you, Lady Arleigh." He strode over to them, his face unreadable.

Rachel could not be sure whether this was down to his well-schooled countenance, or the pain clouding her usual acumen.

"But I fear you are not?" He stretched a gentlemanly hand towards her.

"Alas!" she said, smiling past the confusion she felt and clasping his arm with a gloved hand. "A bothersome hat has been my downfall." She could not tell whether Arleigh watched her, but her eyes avoided him regardless.

"What has brought you to these parts?" asked Arleigh in a clipped tone.

"I have business hereabouts and was fortunate enough to discover you owned a hunting lodge out this way. After you left Bath, I had thought I might chance upon you here."

"And chance upon us you have," said Rachel, smiling past the nagging feeling that told her James Worth's visit had nothing to do with divine providence. "I trust my sister was well when you left her?"

"Lady Rebecca was in good health," he replied, his steady blue gaze turning momentarily to Lord Arleigh.

Rachel chanced a glance. Arleigh was standing with his hands clasped behind his back, his body rigid, and his mouth nought but a thin line. She remembered that stance from before. She could sense the old coolness that had so marked their first acquaintance. What was wrong with him?

"I am glad to hear it," Rachel said, the amicable nature she was so known for winning over her bewildered emotions.

"Though she was anxious to send her greetings to you, since she had no opportunity to bid you farewell."

"Yes, quite. Poor Rebecca. Arleigh was insistent on coming away to his lodge. He wished to show me the countryside and we are such keen riders." She turned to Julius, looking for some sign of agreement with her pronouncement, or even a sign that he acknowledged her existence. But rather than respond, or even make eye contact, he maintained his statue-like pose, and she was horrified to see a look of haughty indifference upon his features.

Perhaps it was being caught out that had forced him off-balance. He was a private man, she knew. Perhaps this sudden change in mood could be attributed to an invasion of that privacy. The presence of the joyful Viscount, the one she had been getting to know over the past several days, had been snatched away. This ominous phantom was left in his place. Whatever the cause, she felt the victim of so sudden and complete a change.

As Arleigh seemed disinclined to do so, she took the role of host upon herself, attempting to give her husband time to adjust to the sudden intrusion.

"Mr Worth, won't you join us for tea? We were just about to go in." She refrained from asking for confirmation from her husband again. "If you would be so kind as to allow me to use this helpful limb?" She put pressure on Mr Worth's arm.

Leaning heavily upon their guest, Rachel began to move painfully towards the house, only to see her husband overtake them with a swiftness that bordered on rude and enter some twenty paces ahead.

Chapter 21

J ames Worth was bemused. Of all the situations he had imagined arriving in the middle of when tracking down Viscount Arleigh and his wife, this had not been one of them. A cry of pain from Lady Arleigh, his lordship shouting at his grooms, chaos with the horses, and then words of quiet affection passing between the two.

Yet that surprise had been short-lived in the face of Lord Arleigh's sudden change of mood. He had never seen a man's face alter so entirely in such a short space of time. In a flash, his expression had gone from humorous and relaxed to cold and guarded. The brief moment of affection that had existed between the two had given James hope that his news to Rebecca would be positive. But the atmosphere was entirely changed by his presence. As a private man himself, James might have forgiven Arleigh's embarrassment at being caught in such an intimate moment, but his coldness towards his wife surely wasn't attributable to just that.

By the time the small party had crossed the black and white hall of the lodge and entered a bright morning room, the tension was palpable. James and Lady Arleigh entered the room some five minutes behind the master of the house. Arleigh had taken up residence in the window embrasure of the old interior. The sun that streamed in outlined his tall form distinctly against the narrow, latticed panes.

"Would you be so kind as to pull that stool up to me?" asked Lady Arleigh after James had helped her to one of the ornate baroque sofas.

She had already pulled the bell and after a few moments of silence, a servant entered. Lady Arleigh asked for tea to be brought, together with some victuals for Mr Worth's refreshment. He appreciated the food. The ride had been long and in truth, he was quite fatigued. The fact that the majority of the journey had been spent with an aching heart and the face of a certain woman overshadowing his solitary thoughts had certainly added to his exhaustion. As he thought of that woman again now, he wondered just what he would be able to tell her when he returned to Bath.

"Your aunt sends her regards and, though I did not see your mother or sisters before my departure," James said, addressing himself to Lord Arleigh with the hopes of thawing the frozen man, "I believe Lady Rebecca was so fortunate as to meet your youngest sister, Phoebe, when they both visited your Bath home to call. Lady Rebecca told me of your sister's desire to see Lady Arleigh again."

"Did she now?" asked her ladyship, a smile starting on her generous mouth.

James, for the first time since his arrival, was provoked to respond in kind. He could not help it when the woman before him so resembled her kin. Her eyes lit in the same way as Rebecca's.

"She did. Apparently she was most insistent on seeing her new favourite sister."

Both conversational participants turned at the guttural cough emitted by the master of the house. He could see the tightness of Arleigh's fingers intertwined behind his back.

James turned back to Lady Arleigh for direction and caught the hurt on her face before she wiped it away. It was a valiant effort at disguise, but she had a face so like her sister's and neither of the Fairing women could keep their faces blank. The emotion seeped out in small movements or expressions as it did now. There was a slight pucker between Rachel's high brows which the false smile did not erase. There was a shield within her eyes that hid what true emotion lay there. There was a tension in her clasped hands that mirrored her husband's.

"And while we have been away, are there many new faces in Bath?"

"No, in fact it is the opposite. Many have

left for the Season in Town. There has been much talk of the balls and parties to be held in the capital, and, if I may be so bold, there has been much speculation on the activities of you both."

"Really? Oh, well, I suppose it is to be expected after our swift marriage. We have yet to hold our own ball. I should hate Society to think us remiss in not doing so. We should plan for it, should we not Arleigh?"

Arleigh, if it were possible, seemed to have become more rigid in his posture during the stilted conversation. But with that last question, he turned abruptly on his heel, and without ceremony or courtesy, he left the room, leaving the door flung wide open so that they could hear his heels clicking on the tiled hallway outside.

"Well, I..." For the first time since James had met Lady Arleigh she was utterly speechless. Still worse, he could have sworn that had she not been blinking so rapidly, tears would have poured from her eyes. She turned back to Mr Worth and mustered an excuse.

"It is no doubt the ride which has tired my husband out, and my foolishness in hurting myself. I do so vex him with my choice of millinery and there really is no excuse for the danger in which I put myself by not affixing the creation to my head properly. That was the cause of my injury, you see." She gestured to the foot she had up on the stool before her, cleverly taking the attention from the open door which she was unable to close.

James did it for her. It was the least he could do. There was a brief moment of silence. This was his chance.

"My lady, I must say, while we are alone, that your sister has been most worried by your absence. She has been concerned for your welfare."

"Oh, Becky, she will not leave well alone..." said Lady Arleigh, the tears which had threatened before starting back into her eyes.

"Forgive me, my lady, but you must not be angry with her. We were all worried after the card party at Lady Etheridge's. His lordship was... not himself and..."

"How stupid of me!" she cried suddenly, the tears finally falling and her hands quick to scrape them away from her rosy cheeks. "I had... Oh, poor Becky, it must have looked so... so terrible, but no, it was..." Her eyes wandered to the door behind which her husband, somewhere, brooded. "I... I cannot. I am quite all right, I must assure you. His lordship has been himself until..."

"You are quite well?"

"Yes, apart from..." She gestured to her foot again, her leather boot exposed from the edge of her riding habit on the silk stool. "It is becoming quite uncomfortable," she said angrily, huffing.

"My sister tells me that steaks are the best

treatment for bruises."

Lady Arleigh half laughed at that, but the movement must have caused more pain, for in the next moment, she was thrown back in her chair, her fingers burying themselves in her skirts.

"Perhaps my maid could be called?"

"Yes, indeed," James said, leaping up from the chair and pulling the bell. "Can I be of any further assistance?"

"Only this," said Lady Arleigh, breathing heavily. "If you would be willing to convey a message to my sister, telling her that I am quite well, her fears may be relieved."

"You have my word."

Her ladyship's maid came in then and as she set to work raising the skirts of her mistress to examine the injury, James retreated from the room. He conveyed his farewell to Lord Arleigh through a footman, guessing quite rightly that his lordship was in no mood to be disturbed, and left the house. He was most certainly more bewildered by the whole episode than when he had set out on his journey of discovery. He had a clear message for Rebecca, and it was not the one from her sister. Lady Rebecca had been right. Something strange was going on between Lord and Lady Arleigh.

Chapter 22

A month and a half had passed since James Worth's unfortunate appearance in the Mendip hills. Rachel's ankle had healed, but her morning rides with Lord Arleigh had not resumed. In that time, the couple had returned to London, along with the rest of Society, ready for the Season.

Their marriage had passed the solicitors' high legal demands and the Arleigh inheritance had finally been passed to the rightful heir. Rachel had upheld her half of the deal and now it was Arleigh's turn. But the subject had yet to be broached openly. It remained behind the veil of implied discussions while the main focus of the household was set upon preparations. It was time, the Dowager Viscountess had said, that they hold a ball at Arleigh House. Not only a ball, but one of the first and best of the Season so that all the ton might come and admire the new couple and any nasty rumours might be quelled. They owed that to the Arleigh name.

Rachel gazed from the window of her London bedroom onto the street below. It bustled with tradesmen who came at all hours to furnish the Arleigh home with enough food, drink and decorations to entertain all of Society. The house had never felt so loud and full of life, yet she had never felt such acute loneliness.

Since the fateful card party, she had not seen Rebecca and she was missing her. Rebecca and her aunt remained in Bath for the present and Mr Worth had been called away to Cornwall on business. No doubt they would all come to London for the Arleighs' ball. It made Rachel both look forward to and dread the event.

In the meantime she lived in a realm of solitude. Arleigh would not speak to her. He was constantly absent from the house on business or with friends at his club. He had barely even looked at her, not since he had spoken those fateful words.

"We have not thought. We made a deal."

A deal. Was that what it had come down to? The nights they had shared, the kisses that had lingered. All that she had given to him of herself after so many years keeping everyone at bay, and he had thrown it all away.

It felt as though all she had thought she'd known and believed in had been destroyed. Arleigh's actions on Mr Worth's appearance at the hunting lodge had been like a stone thrown inside the glasshouse of her carefully constructed hope. Arleigh had struck at the summit and from that initial impact, fractures had begun to appear. They were exacerbated by Arleigh's refusal to speak to her, his constant absence from the house, and his refusal to call her to his bed again.

Those cracks had run into one another, spiralling ever downward, threading their way through the clear construction until they weakened its very foundations. Then, with a great inward groan, the whole structure had split and fallen apart, tumbling down until there was nothing left, and her belief, her faith in what they had shared, was gone.

He had taken all that he wanted from her. He had stripped from her companionship and comfort and now he no longer needed her. Just as her father had passed her off to an old man, and Sir Denby had used her until he saw no fruit, Arleigh had cast her aside. She could barely breathe for pain at the thought of it.

Sat as she was in the window seat, her tears causing the glass to steam before her face, she felt despair creeping into every fibre of her being. Even the silk banyan wrapped around her was like some mocking caress from her absent husband. She wished she had never thrown away that old, tattered banyan that had been a sign of her independence.

A deal. They had made a deal. They may not have spoken of it, but Arleigh had as good as said it would be followed through. She had as good as admitted her inability to carry a child. He would have been a fool not to understand. That was why he had bedded her willingly and cast her off just as easily.

Was that all she had been to him? She could have sworn that in those tender moments, when she had seen who she thought was the real man, he had held her in affection. But she had been wrong. No man had and no man would. Her one function, the sole reason for her being married, the main purpose of her womanhood, was to produce children, and she could not.

Had it all really been an elaborate ruse? Had he play-acted with her, giving her his banyan, acting the jealous man, understanding and playing to her humour and conversation? Had it all been a lie? The cold man she had been confronted with over the last six weeks was proof enough. But however much she tried to drag down her heightened feelings and bury them deep beneath resolution and determination, she found that his coldness was still the lancing ice blade it had been at the beginning. It cut her, and now she felt weaker than she ever had before. If this was love, it could go to the devil.

"My lady, can I not tempt you with sweetmeats?" asked Nellie.

She must have come into the chamber in the last few minutes, but Rachel had not noticed. Her sobs, though stifled, deadened everything else to her.

"No, Nellie." Rachel dabbed the lace handkerchief at her eyes but kept her gaze on the view outside the window.

"But you have not eaten for several days, my lady. You must eat something."

"I said no, Nellie, please! Let me be until I must dress for dinner."

"Yes, my lady."

Rachel felt a stab of regret.

"You may do whatever you like to my hair later," she said, as a peace offering, turning her red, puffy eyes towards her maid.

"Yes, my lady." Nellie smiled gently, bobbing a curtsey, and left the room once again.

The deal had turned out more dangerous than Rachel could ever have imagined. Alone again, she turned back to the window, and the despair she could no longer fight overwhelmed her.

Chapter 23

"Oh, Tobias, it is too much!" exclaimed Caro, her eyes bright with surprise. She reached long, graceful fingers out and touched the beautiful green silk of the newly made gown.

Felton said nothing, smiling mischievously at his wife.

"Honestly, Tobias, do not look at me so. You should not have ordered this."

"You said yourself that none of your ball gowns fit you anymore, and how else shall we attend the Arleighs' ball? You have flatly refused my numerous requests to attend soirées in the same fashion as Eve in the Garden of Eden, so what am I to do?"

She swotted the embroidered fabric of his frock coat, making him swish the beautiful new dress away from her to avoid any further strikes.

"I was able to loosen them so far, but this baby seems intent on enlarging me!"

"If you are so averse to it, my darling wife, I

shall take it back to the dressmakers and demand they undo their artful work and give me back my money."

Caro's fine brow puckered as she unleashed a scowl upon her husband and then a sudden smile flashed across her mouth and the look in her eyes turned to one of challenge.

"Very well, perhaps I should take you up on your requested dress and attend the ball as naked as a babe. I wonder exactly what all the men would think of my naked body and my belly swelling with child?" An elegant brow rose in provocation.

The look on Felton's mischievous face faded and he took on one of compliance. "You will do no such thing. Where did you ever get the notion that I would like other men to see what is only mine? My vixen wife, you must wear this extravagantly expensive dress." He swung it high so that it fell with a great swooping of silk, ruffles and bows over the brocade sofa of their London home.

"Thank you, husband," said Caro, coming before him and rising on her tiptoes to plant a kiss upon his clean-shaven cheek.

Felton wrapped his arms around his wife and the bump that was pushing their embraces further apart by the day.

"This may be the last glorious ball you enjoy before your confinement."

"You promised," she said to his smiling

face, "that you would take me to your family's country home to be confined. I cannot stand the idea of being cooped up for so long in London."

"You shall not. The first breath my baby's lungs take will be one of fine country air, I promise, my dear Caro." He kissed her. "No doubt Frederick will think it his right to be the child's godparent, but I shall be thrown to the dogs before he is allowed to bore my child to death with his dull lectures on the moral responsibility of a Felton to the community and country at large."

"Frederick makes some good points," replied Caro gently, taking a piece of her husband's fair hair and twisting it about her finger.

"He very well may, but the man is an absolute fool, and even your forgiving heart cannot argue with that."

Caro pursed her lips against the smile that was threatening.

"You know he would like to be asked."

"You're right. We should ask my brother. And... what of godmother?"

Caro pushed away from his embrace and went back to the dress on the sofa, running her fingers over the tiny ruffles that edged the open-fronted gown.

"I know you are not happy with me for bringing it up," said Felton gently, "but do you think you will ever forgive Rebecca?"

"I never said I wasn't happy."

"Oh no? And when did your not saying

something ever mean that I could not tell what you felt?" He winked at her.

"Urgh! You don't know how I feel. And I am driven quite mad by your assumptions."

"Am I wrong? Ah, those flashing eyes, you are angry with me. Very well, I will not *assume* you are unhappy with me, but I shall tell you that I do not regret the question. The woman might drive me mad at times, but you and she are good friends." He tried to pull Caro back into his arms but she refused to come.

She wanted to turn back to him. She wanted to pretend she was fine. That she was not upset. That everything was just as it ought to be and that she had no reason not to be happy. She should be happy.

"I am angry, but not at you. It's just... I expected better of her."

"We don't all make the right decisions in life, Caro," said Felton, a certain tenderness in his voice. "Sometimes, one feels pushed into a situation, for whatever reason, and we make decisions we think are for the best. Later, we might realise the mistakes we've made."

She knew what he was implying, the history he was pointing to.

"I thought Rebecca was vexing you," said Caro archly.

"She was. Many friends vex me. That does not mean that they cannot be forgiven, as they forgive my antics." He came to one of the chairs beside the fireplace and sat down. "I have heard from James."

"James? He did not write to me."

"He went to see Rebecca when we were still in Bath. I encouraged him to."

Felton's words lingered in Caro's mind as she took on their full meaning.

"You did what?"

"Rebecca came to the house upset, one day when you were especially sick in the morning. I turned her away so that you might not be further distressed after your argument at the card party, but I could not help feeling that she was seeking not you or me, but James, and they crossed paths while they were there."

Caro remained silent, the full import of what Felton was telling her impacting every sense and thought she had.

"Sometimes love needs a little… push. I know that from personal experience." Felton carried on too quickly for her to interject as he must have known she wished to. "In James' letter, he writes of going to see Rebecca to ensure that she was all right after her upset at our home. She told him of her fears, and he said the most logical thing was to ascertain the truth of the matter to alleviate her worries."

That sounded like James and ordinarily the pragmatism that so characterised her brother would make Caro smile. But the fact that he had gone back to the woman who had so carelessly denied his love, to chase after her fancies, enraged her. He was only going to get hurt again.

"He is of the opinion that Rebecca was right to be concerned over her sister."

The words sent a sudden stab of guilt through Caro. She had dismissed those same concerns.

"He said that he came upon Lord and Lady Arleigh at their country retreat, and when he did, he thought that something was distinctly off."

"When did he write to you?" asked Caro finally, not addressing his revelation.

"A week since."

"What? Why did you not tell me before now?" She could not help the indignation in her voice. Even if she could have, she would not have wanted to in this moment.

"You needed rest, and you had already told me you wished to leave Rebecca to herself since your harsh words with her at the card party."

"James agrees with her?"

"Yes."

Caro watched her husband pull a snuff-box from the deep pockets of his coat and proceed to take some. All the time, her thoughts sped over her conversations with Rebecca—those that concerned her sister and the final conversation that had resulted in a break in their friendship. But now James agreed with her? What did that mean?

"You need not feel guilty."

"I don't feel guilty!" Caro's voice rose with her temper. "I feel angry. Being with child does not mean I am incapable of dealing with other situations. Goodness gracious—when were you going to tell me of all this? I have not even spoken to Rebecca in over a month. She has written to me numerous times, but I had…"

"You wanted space. What good would it have done to bring this up before?"

"That's not your decision to make. First you encourage my brother back to the woman who has broken his heart, without my know-ledge, then I find you are conspiring together with Rebecca to find out whatever it is her sister is involved in. And now I find you are delaying telling me that James is now in agreement with Rebecca." Caro felt a lump enter her throat and forced it back. This pregnancy was causing her emotions to get the better of her and darn it, she had no wish to cry.

"Don't you understand?" she asked, lower-ing her voice as she tried to control the tears which threatened. "It's as bad as lying to me, To-bias. No," she corrected herself, "it's the same."

"Caro…" He had risen, but she pulled back from the outstretched arms that begged to touch her.

"No! We were honest. I was honest with you, and this is how I am repaid? You know everything about me, and you chose to keep things from me." She raised her hands, the sudden feeling of vulnerability forcing the desire to protect herself. "I can't be in your presence at the moment."

She turned towards the door and was thankful that Felton let her go. She passed by the newly made dress and retired to her room and solitude.

"You must invite Lord Castleford for he was one of your father's closest friends," said the Dowager Viscountess Arleigh, her eyes fixed firmly upon the figure of her son before the fireplace.

"Yes, papa did like him so," chimed in Diana, her nose held a little too high and her eyes darting towards her mother seeking approval.

"Papa used to say how in his cups Castleford always was at the hunt ball," said Phoebe, her sweet voice at odds with her words, "but when I asked papa what he meant, he told me not to be so nosy. I am not nosy, I only thought it preposterous to say a grown man might fit in a cup. I knew there was another meaning, but he would not tell me."

"Be quiet, Phoebe." The Dowager turned back to Lady Arleigh who was seated at a pretty walnut writing desk. "Did you get that, Lady Arleigh?"

"Yes, thank you," Rachel replied, her quill flicking here and there as she added the names of Lord and Lady Castleford to the list of attendees for their grand ball.

As it was to be the first held by the new Lord and Lady Arleigh, the Dowager had been over almost daily to help her daughter-in-law with the preparations. All must go well for their acceptance into polite Society after their some-what unorthodox wedding.

"In that case, I think we are very nearly done. The guest list is complete. We planned the menu yesterday." She looked about her at the scattering of lists and notes, nodding to herself. "Yes, excellent. You have done exceedingly well, Lady Arleigh." She looked at Rachel who was slow to set down the quill and look up.

When she did, the Dowager saw the same lacklustre expression she had seen since they had arrived back in London. Jane Arleigh had noted it before, and considered it the first cloud in the couple's young marriage. The eclipse how-ever had yet to pass.

She had been shocked by their sudden marriage, and she had to admit that she had not been convinced in the slightest with her son's choice of bride. But it seemed that this woman before her, with her wild curly hair, tall statu-esque figure and odd taste in fashion, had been determined to prove her wrong. First with her passionate words of apology upon their second meeting, and then by her calm, diligent work towards this ball.

That being said, there was something of her original enthusiasm that had not come back with her from Bath, and the Dowager could no longer ignore it. Even a blind man could see that there was a rift between the couple. They were as polite as could be with their guests, but not once had they looked at each other, and they had an odd way of speaking of the other when they were both present instead of addressing each other directly. The Dowager had been married long enough to recognise the difference between a simple lovers' tiff and something much deeper.

"Mama, please can I come to the ball?" pleaded Phoebe for the umpteenth time.

The Dowager turned to her youngest daughter and cupped her soft, round cheek tenderly. "No, my dear, you are too young."

"Oh, but I wish to. I would be good. I could be as boring as Julius. Look." Phoebe proceeded to mimic the pose of her elder brother, hands clasped behind her back, and mirroring his sour face.

"Phoebe, stop it," her mother chided.

Julius did not respond, merely scowling towards his younger sibling, and then casting a fleeting glance towards his wife.

"Come, my dears, let us leave this young couple to have a few moments of peace with each other amongst all these preparations." The Dowager rose, pulling on her kid gloves and throwing commanding glances towards her daughters who responded with varying degrees of obedience.

"Rachel, please will you let me come to the ball. I shall be so good."

"Oh, my sweet tyrant," said Lady Arleigh, a sudden soft animation in her voice. "I do not think you can come to the ball. You are so young and there will be far too many boring old people there. You wouldn't like it at all."

"What if I stay upstairs and watch? Lady Sophia Cleverson said her mama let her do that." Phoebe cast a condemning glance towards her mother. "And I could sleep here, in my old room, I would be no trouble, I promise you."

"Well, I…"

"Of course she cannot! Mother, bridle my sister's impertinent tongue."

"Julius!" The shocked Dowager put a hand around her daughter's shoulders just as Phoebe began to cry. "There is no need for such hard words."

"Is there not?" he asked, a sharpness in his voice which dissolved with his next words. "Forgive me—mother—Phoebe." He put out a hand, but the girl cowered away.

"Of course you may all stay the night of the ball," said Rachel quickly. "It was remiss of us not to ask before. Will you? We can have all your old rooms made up."

"That would be delightful," said Diana, uncustomary excitement invading her voice.

"How kind of you—we would be delighted to accept," said the Dowager, unable to take her eyes off her son. She saw a haunted expression on his face and as Diana and Phoebe said their pretty goodbyes to Rachel, the Dowager turned towards her son and spoke with compassion. "You are not yourself, my son. A young bride, a ball in the next few days, and you are not happy."

"Mother." He raised a hand to brush off her sentiments, but she brought him up short.

"Do not ignore me. I have not seen you speak to your sister like that since you were but a child yourself. Not that I am rebuking you, for there is clearly something causing this, and whatever it is, I suggest you sort it out. Your bride looks no happier than you, and however unconventional she may be and the issues I have with that kind of behaviour, it is of far more concern to me to see her so downcast."

"Rachel is quite well."

"Ignoring her feelings as well as your own? You two have not looked at each other once when in my company these last two weeks. Remember, my son, as much as this ball is to give your marriage the legitimacy it lacks, it is for you to celebrate your bride and your joining. Do not forget it.

"Your father had his foibles, as you well

know. Perhaps you saw and heard things that happened between us that you did not… like."

Julius remained silent, but his mother could see the past running across his eyes. The unhappiness of her marriage known and reflected in his youthful memories.

"But I do know, though we had a marriage you perhaps did not envy, that speaking to each other is all important. Perhaps if… you should talk to your wife."

Her son did not reply. After a moment he inclined his head in acceptance of her words. With Diana already leaving the room, and Phoebe thanking Rachel again and again, the Dowager made to leave.

"Come, Phoebe, your sister-in-law heard your thanks the first time out of the twenty. Hush now and let's take our leave. Goodbye, dear." She placed a kiss upon Rachel's cheek in a rare show of affection and left the room.

Chapter 24

A rleigh took in the figure of his wife silhouetted by the morning sun. She was still before the window, tall and silent, and for the first time in days, he let himself really look at her. He hadn't noticed the new braiding of her hair, taking away some of the wildness of it, and forcing it into a well-schooled style, looking demure under its powder. She was dressed appropriately, her body clad in a green silk robe à l'anglaise. He had not seen her wear the banyan in weeks. His banyan.

She walked back from the window, where she had been paused in some unknown reverie, to the table on which the papers for the ball lay. He could see the tiredness in her usually animated face. Then there were her eyes, intent on steering away from him, and somehow vacant in their gaze. It was as though all emotion had been gathered up and put away. As though she chose to think of nothing deeper than the task at hand. Everything about her seemed repressed. He was the cause of that.

The same intense guilt that he had felt when he had seen the shock on her face in the Mendip hills came back. Everything had seemed so easy until the moment of James Worth's arrival, when real life had come crashing in upon their stolen paradise. They had been away from the world, away from Society and their pasts. They had been able to enjoy themselves, enjoy each other, but the invasion of the outside world had brought with it all the niggling worries Arleigh had forced away before.

It had been easy to ignore his family's past when Society had not been present. The fear that he would tread in the footsteps of his parents' marriage. Yet, as soon as James Worth had appeared at the Hunting Lodge it had all come flooding back and shaken him with its ferocity. The vision of his father had risen up to taunt him, and as he had retracted from Rachel, he had seen pain in her eyes and he knew from experience it would only get worse. He was doing the very thing he had sworn never to do. He had realised in that moment that he was too much his father's son and she would be better off alone than subjected to a marriage like that of his parents.

After that, he had done something abominable. The only thing he could think of to push Rachel far beyond where he could hurt her. He had told her that her barrenness had not been part of their deal, and that, though they had not spoken of heirs, he had not planned for it. It had been a lie, of course, he had already considered heirs and decided Felix's future marriage would continue the Arleigh name. But his aim had been to inflict damage and inflict damage he had. It had been a simple thing, after that, to resurrect the agreement of their separation without protest. If he could keep her away from him then he would not risk becoming his father and forcing her into a long, unhappy marriage with him. This short-term pain would be just that, short in duration, and she would be happier without him.

He had begun on this foolhardy deal from a place of desperation, seeing it as the only route to not hurting some innocent girl by inflicting on her a marriage of no affection. He had not seen Rachel as some innocent girl, but a hard-headed woman. He had been wrong. She was innocent, an innocent woman, and he'd hurt her.

Even as he watched her, his feelings stirred. He had missed her closeness and companionship. Loneliness had encroached on their marriage. But how else was he supposed to resist hurting her again, falling into passion again, and building upon those feelings he had so foolishly cultivated? He would not be his father, but even now he knew himself capable of inflicting the same level of pain upon his own wife.

He willed himself not to go to her. Not to pull her close. Not to kiss those lips and to comfort her. He wondered if she would let him if he tried.

Just as the thought came into his mind, she finished gathering up the papers and headed for the morning room door.

"Wait."

He saw the flash of surprise run through her frame and the sudden rigidity that took over at the sound of his voice.

"I am tired, my lord," she said, neither expanding upon the statement nor turning, only waiting for him to release her as she assumed he would.

"I have not seen you much of late," he started, his calm and steady tone overriding the mix of emotions he felt. "I wished to ask how you are?"

She did not answer immediately, and he thought she was considering her answer. Perhaps she would speak in a small, hurt voice.

"You wonder at my health and well-being?"

The tone was anything but gentle and he realised how wrong his thinking had been. She laughed, harshly, not the usual loud rolling peals that denoted joy.

"He asks me how I am? How condescending of his lordship to deign to ask the woman he has quit bedding how she is?"

The words were sharp and sour. They flowed from her like spoiled wine spewing from the cracks of a broken barrel.

"Do you truly believe that I shall be some meek and mild woman who will take mistreatment without question?"

No, he did not. Only a fool would think that Rachel Arleigh was anything akin to meek and mild.

"I've explained my actions," he said, for the first time a pleading tone in his voice. He willed her to understand his position. How could he make her understand…? "You know why it must be like this."

"What I know," she said, whirling towards him, brandishing the papers and squaring her shoulders, "is that you have done what all others have never failed to do. You have taken what you wanted from me and then…"

He saw sudden tears glistening in her eyes, but the unconscious action of her body seemed to rile her even further. She swore loudly, turning about and throwing the papers on the chaise longue so she could rub at her face before any tears fell.

He started forward, raising his hand to instinctually offer his handkerchief.

She did not acknowledge it. "It was only a deal, was it not, my lord?" she said, suddenly carefree and full of forced gaiety.

"Rachel, don't be like that… Have we not been honest with one another before?"

"Before," she echoed, her gaze drifting for

a moment. "What was that? All of it was false-hood."

"No," he cut in, halting abruptly as he real-ised that what he had to say would only make things worse. The truth of his feelings, of what had happened between them, it would only make things worse. There were things he had never said to her and telling her now was needless.

"I wait only for you to give me a date on which you will arrange for my settlement and establishment. It is up to you to give me the in-dependence you promised, and you have made it clear you intend to stand by your word as a gentleman. There is no need for false concern."

"I only wish to know you are well. My valet has it from your maid that you have not been. Are you sleeping? You look…" He had moved to-wards her again, countering her evasive moves, until they were by the window, facing each other, the noise of London barely held at bay beside them.

All his strength, all his resistance, he would give himself this, he would give her this. He raised his hand and stroked the only loose curl back from her face as she turned away, her eyes closing and her lashes fanning out over pale cheeks.

"Don't," she whispered as his fingertips touched the skin of her cheek and threatened to caress it.

He stilled them, but they remained there,

and he was connected to her for the first time in weeks. It felt like touching hot embers, the feeling shooting through his fingertips, the warmth drawing him in. But she had said no. She had requested that he not touch her. No, she had *pleaded* with him not to touch her.

He retracted his hand. "I know we have not spoken since… It is for the best."

"Is it?"

"It's impossible," said Arleigh. Everything was. The situation, the feelings he felt, the things he wished to do, the fears that bound him. It was all… impossible.

"As you say, my lord. You wished to provide for your family and all I wish for was freedom. Neither of us could have predicted how dangerous this deal would be."

She walked away from him and he did not stop her this time. He watched her regather the papers and leave the room. As she did, a mist came over his eyes and he found himself unable to move. When eventually he did, he retired to his rooms to change for a ride, the only thing he knew would clear his head. Passing by his wife's room he heard the muffled sound of someone weeping. He paused at the door, unsure whether to go in, but the sound stopped soon after and with a heavy heart he walked away.

Felton's knuckles knocked softly against the door of Caro's room. The sound was small and lacking confidence and he waited anxiously for a sound from within.

"Come." He heard his wife's voice sounding firm but far away.

Entering the room slowly, he saw his wife with her back to him, bent over various chemises and gowns strewn across the padded bench at the end of her unused bed.

"Libby, I don't think I can wear half of these things now—my belly is absolutely monstrous. I'm not sure what we will do about my dress for the Arleighs' ball." Felton saw her pick up a puce silk dress from the bed and hold it up against her. "Though this gown is open-fronted, and I remember having it taken in once, so there is probably plenty of material if it were to be let out again. Oh, that will do very..." She turned and caught sight of Felton leaning uneasily against the door, his hands still on the handle in case he needed to make a hasty escape.

His wife's blue eyes studied him carefully, the dress still held tightly against her burgeoning stomach. She dismissed Libby and, on the maid leaving, lapsed back into silence, her red lips pressed shut causing little dimples to appear either side of her mouth. The pregnancy really was making her bloom. Her hair had never looked so glossy and in the afternoon sunlight, it shone like gold.

She had never looked more beautiful and he had never felt more sorry he had hurt her.

"You will not wear the green dress I ordered?" he asked, feeling a coward for choosing to speak of dresses rather than their argument.

"Perhaps," said Caro, her usually full lips pursing. Felton knew he must dive straight in.

"I came to apologise."

She maintained her silence, but there was a slight incline of her head and she slowly placed the dress back upon the bed. She moved to where a simple wooden chair stood, one of the remnants of their pre-married lives, and seated herself beside the fire.

Felton came forward instinctively to hold the back of the chair while she descended. She gestured towards the bench, on which a small space was naked of clothes, and he took a seat.

"Caro, I never meant to hurt you. I just... no, that is not the way to start. I do not wish to justify the actions which hurt you, but I do wish you to understand why I took them. Will you hear me out?"

"Yes," she said immediately, and then her hand came thoughtfully to her chin and she changed her mind. "No." She leant back in the chair with a sigh. "I do not wish to know why. I only wish that you would have told me."

"If I had, you would have disagreed."

"Yes, but you could have made the decision just the same. At least then I would feel that you trusted me—I would not feel betrayed."

"I know." His eyes traced the patterns on the carpet and the buckles on his shoes. "But I wished to give your brother the best chance of happiness. In the circumstances, I feel that chance is with Rebecca. Whatever her faults, she is your friend."

"Oh, I know that! Of course I do."

Neither of them said anything for a few minutes. All that could be heard were the far-off sounds of John and Libby seeing to the running of the house and the distant conversation of people passing outside.

"Tell me of James' suspicions."

"Well," said Felton, leaning back, resting his elbows casually on the bed. "He does not have any fixed idea on what the truth is, but he says they were acting awfully strangely when he came upon them at Arleigh's hunting lodge. Apparently, they were all affection until they noticed his presence, and then Arleigh became as cold as a fish."

"Couldn't that just be his character?" asked Caro, an eyebrow arching as she looked at him.

"Your brother seemed to think it was something more than that. Said Lady Arleigh was as perplexed at the Viscount's behaviour as he was and sent James off as soon as she could. I've heard from some of my acquaintances that since Arleigh's been back in London, he's been abroad most nights at his club and friends' places, but never once seen with his wife."

"Has Rebecca seen her since to ask about it?"

"She has not come down from Bath as yet. I believe she will arrive for the ball, but at present, her aunt wishes to remain in Somerset for her health, or so James says."

"Well, that fits nicely," said Caro, rising and going to her dressing table to retrieve an already sealed letter. "I have written to her to invite her to stay with us so that we might make amends. Perhaps if she comes early for her sister's ball, she might finally find out the truth from Rachel."

"A capital idea!" Felton leapt up from the bench to accept the letter from his wife's hand, but before he was allowed to kiss her, she stayed him with a hand.

"Do you forgive me?" he asked.

"It is not just about forgiveness, Tobias, it is about rebuilding trust. You cannot deceive me like that. I know deception played a part in our courtship, but that was different. We are married now and have a child on the way. We must be honest with each other and ever on the same team or we will not be able to carry the weight of life equally and keep pace with one another."

"You are right." He knelt before her, wishing her to know how much he agreed, and took up the hem of her gown, kissing it. "Forgive me, wife."

"I had forgiven you already," she said, taking his hand from her gown and beckoning him to stand. "You may kiss me now."

He watched with relief as a little smile appeared on her lips and he kissed her lightly on the mouth.

"I shall see that this goes with the next post," he said, brandishing the letter. He squeezed her hand gently and, with a renewed spring in his step, went to see that it was done.

Chapter 25

Rachel felt another wretched heave coiling around her stomach and tossed the remainder of her breakfast into the chamber pot.

"You had better empty it, Nellie, before last night's dinner makes an appearance too," she said, wiping her mouth with her handkerchief and handing the basin to her maid.

"Yes, my lady." Nellie bobbed away, disappearing into the closet.

Almost in the same instant, there was an abrupt rap at the adjoining door.

Rachel did not answer it. Firstly, because she had absolutely no desire to test her nausea by getting up from her bed where she sat wrapped in a banyan feeling wretched. Secondly, she had no wish to see who was on the other side of that door.

"Oh, my lady, do not worry. I will get it for you," said Nellie, who had evidently heard the knock and dispensed of the basin's contents doubly quick. Before Rachel could stop her with an urgent whisper, the maid was across the room and opening the door.

"Your lordship, my apologies, but my mistress is not feeling well." She bobbed a curtsey. "Perhaps you can come later?"

"Not well?"

There was Arleigh's steady voice, and even after everything that had happened, Rachel was loath to accept the calming effect it had upon her exacerbated nerves.

"Does she need a doctor?"

She did not need a doctor. Most certainly not.

"No, my lord."

"What's wrong with her."

"She has a..." Nellie was bobbing violently now as she struggled for a lie.

"A migraine. I need no doctor," Rachel called. "I shall be fine once the vomiting ceases. Nellie, be so good as to bring the chamber pot back for I am due another round."

Nellie, more than thankful for being saved from lying to her master, scurried back to her mistress, leaving the door to swing wide. Rachel took the chamber pot between her legs where it had been before and proceeded to bring forth yesterday's dinner.

When the bout was over, she slowly sat upright, her stomach muscles sore and tender, and dabbed at her mouth once again. As she did so, she was horrified to see her husband standing at the foot of her bed.

She drew her shoulders back so that she might face him with seeming strength despite feeling absolutely rotten.

"You are unwell," stated Arleigh quite unnecessarily.

Realising that he was not going to leave, Nellie hastily withdrew.

"The migraine. They have had the same effect on me ever since I was a child. Immense pain and then the contents of my stomach has a penchant for daylight."

She rubbed at the skin beneath her eyes, painfully aware that she must look dreadfully pale and drawn. As she did so, she felt the wild curling mass of her freed hair either side of her face. She saw him observing it too.

"I shall be well presently. I need to rest a while—was there something you wanted?"

"Will you be well enough for the ball—if not, there is no need to..."

"I shall be fine," Rachel replied, not able to keep the prickle from her voice. She had no desire to be seen like this. She had already shown this man more vulnerability than she had shown any other. Seeing her physically sick made the exposure worse.

"You do not look well," he carried on, his head drifting to one side as he examined her, a furrow appearing in his brow. If she had been a fool, she would have thought him genuinely concerned.

But she did not need his concern. What she needed was for him to leave the room. There were other reasons that he could not see her so.

"Honestly, Julius," she said, using his Christian name in the hopes it would drive him from her. She had learned that closeness to her was repugnant to him. "I shall be quite well. You may leave me."

She had used his Christian name. She had not done that since the hunting lodge. His fingers had been brushing the covers on the end of her bed, but now he moved to the side of it and sat down upon its edge. This was the closest they had been in over a month.

"You do not look well. I could…"

"You can do nothing. The ball is set, and I shall attend as well as half of fashionable Society."

He said nothing, only looking at her tired eyes, her drawn face, her grey skin. She had grown worse since they had returned to London. He had expected her to be upset by his treatment of her. He had known his actions would hurt her and the hurt was visible. But the extent of the damage he had done pained him. He felt it deep within his chest, like a constriction, preventing him from breathing.

"Will you not allow me to call the doctor? They would be here and gone before the ball. At least then you should know the cause of the ailment."

He watched her gaze drop to the covers, her eyes somewhere far away from here and him. He had sent her away in exile to that other place.

"I have told you," she said, slowly, quietly and definitely. "I have a migraine."

She warned him off, much as a dog might warn off an intruder. Her fangs were bared, but even so, he could not bring himself to leave. Not just yet.

"It shall be gone presently, and I shall be myself again."

But she wouldn't. He knew that. He had seen who she was. He had been privy to her thoughts, her dreams, her body. He had held her as a wife. But he would not do so again. The thought was frustrating, and if he were being honest in the depths of his soul, it scared him. No one else was like her. He could not be himself in the same way with another.

But that was their deal, was it not? Friendship had never been part of the deal. He remembered even now the sharp words they had exchanged on the sham of their wedding day.

Their companionship had never been agreed upon, never needed, but it had grown, nonetheless. And their first night together. That had not been part of their deal. He remembered how he had woken in the night and for a brief moment, before sleep had retaken his senses, he had seen her there, next to him, her eyes shut and her face all that was peaceful. That was the first time he had seen true peace transposed on those features. And he had stolen that away.

When was the last night he had slept as well as he had then? It had not just been Rachel who had found peace in their moments together. All those years of striving to be the man his father envisioned, demanded. Those last months before his death were not spent in celebration of his life or their familial love, but rather in castigating his eldest son for lack of a lineage. There had been no fairness in that. No justice. The remaining moments with his father had been filled with derision and unfulfilled hopes. The legacy the late Lord Arleigh had left was one of angst, hurt and upset for his whole family.

That's how it had been before her. His calm façade had hidden a sea of family troubles and personal disappointments, and then Lady Rachel Denby had appeared. She had barrelled into his life as she did into everything. Her very appearance of chaos had repulsed him at first, but there was something about her, something that... worked. She knew how to speak to him, unlike any other female he knew. She had broken through his mother's grief and communicated with a woman whose hard exterior had been formed by years of her husband's demanding ways. And she had become like a sister to his own kin.

Was he really going to rip her away from all that?

Here she sat, all strength in weakness. Determined that he would not be let near again. He did not blame her. He felt the frustration he had been quelling over the past weeks in trips to his club and drinking with his close acquaintances.

The fear he would tread in the footsteps of his parents' marriage was costing him dearly and part of that price was already being extracted from Rachel. He would extract no more. He had seen what marriage was, the pain it could exact upon the participants. He had cut out the variables he had thought might lead him towards making the same mistakes. He had not chosen a naive miss, he had not courted and romanced with false promises that married life would always be thus, he had removed feelings entirely in the hopes that their exclusion would protect them for both parties. But here they were, the pain Rachel felt evident on her face, in her words. And what of his feelings? Was it pain he felt? Was that the deep crushing feeling in his chest?

He could not answer and his feelings did not matter. He had been a fool to think that he could protect Rachel from hurt when he was his father's son. Going through with their separation would remove him from her life and any chance he might inflict more pain. He would not have to look into her face anymore and see the shattered emotions that lay there, or acknowledge the muddy waters that now lay between them like cloudy confusing pools impossible to navigate.

Was he really going to do it?

His hand had crept forward unconsciously, and without thinking he took Rachel's fingers in his own. They were cold. Instinctively, he clasped them tighter. They stayed like that for a moment. Peace hovered over the couple and, for the briefest of times, it was possible to forget all that had happened. To forget his father, and expectations, and the pain of the past. To go back to that joy-filled paradise, and pretend that nothing would change.

"Julius!" she said suddenly, pushing his hand away. He expected a sharp-worded rebuke to follow, but instead, he watched her head disappear as she threw up again in the chamber pot between her legs.

He shifted to her side, a hand rising up to her back in comfort and another taking the curtain of wild curls and pulling them out of her way as she continued to heave. He could feel the tension that wracked her body and discerned a stifled moan as she finished the bout and slowly uncurled to sitting up once again.

He continued the rubbing motion of his hand upon her banyan-covered back, unconsciously mirroring the same comfort he had received from his childhood nurse.

"Please, Arleigh."

And he was back to Arleigh. Julius had merely been an unconscious slip of the tongue. She wanted to push him away as he had done to her.

"I must get dressed, that I may oversee preparations for the ball."

"I do not mind if you wish to wear your banyan for the day, if that is how you should feel most comfortable."

"My comfort," she said, her eyes not rising to meet his, her voice steadier than he had heard it, "is not your concern. I have told you I am well, and if you have decided to uphold our deal, then there really is nothing more we have to speak of. Showing any kind of forced affection and care does neither of us any favours, my lord. I shall be your loyal wife at tonight's ball, and then our communications may end, for you have made your decision clear."

"I do not want this."

"If it was…" She broke off whatever it was she had been meaning to say. He could tell from her tone it would have been provoking, but she gave in. That's what she sounded like now, someone surrendered, and he hated it. "Do not say what you cannot mean."

He felt the words keenly, though they were uttered without malice.

"If you did not wish it to be this way, it would not be. But we made a deal, and you intend to uphold it. I know your feelings on the matter and as I said to you before, now I just wish to be free. Then you also may be free to live your life without me."

She looked pained and he did not want to see her so. He rose from the bed, ceasing all contact, and finally left the room. She was right. After this ball, there would be no need to wait any longer for their separation, and yet he hadn't arranged for her own establishment. He needed to. Time was running out. But her words still rang clear in his ears, *live your life without me*.

Is that really what he wanted to do?

Chapter 26

"Well, I will certainly make the most of this ball, for I shall not be out in Society again for a great while."

"What? Caro enjoying Society? I never thought it possible," said Rebecca, fanning herself against the heat of the swell in the Arleighs' ballroom. Of course, the fact that the fan hid the smile she flashed at Caro's expense was merely convenient.

"Yes," said Caro, swatting her friend with her fan just as Rebecca always did to her. "I am."

"You know, motherhood is really changing you," said Rebecca, the teasing tone still in her voice.

Caro grinned back at her and then her eyes lit up as they caught sight of something across the room. "Rebecca, be quick, for I see a spare set of chairs by the wall and we will be lucky if we come by some again."

"Yes, indeed." Rebecca linked arms with

her friend and for the hundredth time today, prayed thanks that their friendship had been restored.

They had made it halfway across the packed room when Rebecca caught sight of her sister. It was the briefest of glimpses of the hostess, but immediately Rebecca knew something was wrong.

"Caro..."

"I have already seen her—she is walking from the room. Come this way."

Rebecca's arm was taken and she followed in the wake of a large, pregnant Caro. Unlike the usual experience of traversing a ballroom where people deep in conversation would not move easily, Rebecca found that travelling with a pregnant lady caused the sea of people to part like some biblical miracle.

They made their way through several of the gaily decorated and considerably full rooms of the Arleighs' London home, up a set of richly carpeted stairs, and into a room set aside for the ladies.

"Rachel?" she called as Caro moved aside.

Her sister paused at the call, her hand about to open a side door.

"Oh, Becky, darling," she said, coming forward.

Rebecca noted the dark hollows beneath her sister's eyes and a drawn look on her face.

"How are you?" asked Rebecca, her eyes

searching. She saw Rachel look about her at the various other ladies present who were attending to their toilette and chattering in groups.

"Come with me — Caro too," she said, turning back to the door she had been about to open and venturing through it to a small ante-room aglow with candles and home to a well-banked fire burning merrily in the grate. It was clearly not meant for regular ball attendees as attested to by the lack of decoration and intimate feel.

The tapestries which adorned the small room's walls, floor to ceiling, gave it a distinctly cosy feel and had there not been so much tension in the occupants, it might have seemed quite a homely meeting.

"Rachel, how are you?" Rebecca repeated her question, her eyes searching her sibling's face, but upon her sister turning back towards her, she stopped. Rachel looked suddenly much paler, the expression on her face considerably altered, and her breath rapid and shallow.

"Just give me a moment... Becky... to catch my breath." She sat down beside the fire, a hand to her stomach and another to her forehead. The other ladies joined her and Rebecca reached out a hand to touch her sister's arm.

"Whatever's the matter?" She put a hand to Rachel's forehead, feeling the clammy skin and seeing a glazed look in her eyes. "Here, you must lie back. Shall I call for Lord Arleigh?"

"No! Heavens, no!" Rachel panted out the words, only causing Rebecca to worry more.

She considered whether her sister might be delirious. Perhaps it was the heat of the ball, the pressure of hosting. There must be nearly three hundred people downstairs.

Caro rose. "I shall fetch some brandy."

"There's some there — on the sideboard," Rebecca said. She pointed to where a crystal decanter glinted in the firelight, its amber liquid rich and inviting.

"I shall be all right in a moment." Rachel's authoritative tone and confident words faded into tension and something else. Rebecca remembered her sister only sounding like this once before, when she was told she must marry Sir Denby. It was the sound of fear.

In spite of her natural inclinations, Rebecca did not speak for some time. She offered the glass of brandy supplied by Caro to her sister, who sipped at it slowly and continued to stare into the firelight. After about five minutes had passed, Rachel's breathing had slowed, but the pained expression on her face did not disappear.

"Sister, what is it? You can tell me."

"I can't." Rachel's gaze was lost in the flickering flames of the fire. "It is too awful."

"Nothing is too awful, dear sister. I love you, you silly fool, and you shall tell me what is wrong, whatever the matter is, for it makes me feel wretched to see you so. What's worrying you?"

From the corner of her eye, Rebecca saw Caro rise slowly, and go to the far side of the small room.

"I hate to see you so unhappy and you have told me not to worry, but since aunt's card party I have been sick with the feeling of it."

Rachel's face puckered at the words, as though she were sucking on a lemon, her lip twisted and then suddenly she was crying.

"Oh," she moaned softly, taking a hand-kerchief from the bosom of her ballgown and dabbing furiously at her face. "This is absolutely wretched! Just fancy me sitting here and bawling my eyes out like a silly schoolroom miss, unable to hold her emotions in check. It's ridiculous! If this is how you have been feeling all these months Caro, then I simply cannot advocate getting with child to anyone!"

The other two women stopped short, their heads snapping up at the brashly spoken words. They immediately converged on Rachel who lay prostrate on the sofa.

"What do you mean—is it true? Are you with child?" asked Rebecca.

"Oh, congratulations, Rachel—Arleigh must be thrilled."

Rachel rose abruptly and walked away to stand before the fire with her back turned towards them.

"Oh, I do not think he would be if he

knew," she said quietly to the flames.

"You have not told him?" Rebecca noted the queer tone in her sister's voice. "Why have you not? Surely he will be happy at the news."

"Oh no, I don't suppose he would be. Our marriage is one of convenience and that is the end of it. We shall not be one joyous happy family —that was never the deal. An agreed separation with individual households, that was what we planned." She swung round, her eyes as large as saucers and her hands wringing the hand-kerchief that was clasped between them. "You must never tell him—either of you. You must not breathe a word."

"I knew it," uttered Rebecca in nothing more than a whisper.

"But he cannot separate from you if you are with child—whatever is he thinking?" Caro's practical words cut through the deductions of Rebecca's thoughts.

"It was the deal," said Rachel, suddenly crumpling into a chair beside the fire and look-ing far smaller than she had ever done before. "It all sounds so sordid now, now I speak it aloud to others, but it made sense before. Our marriage of convenience would get him his inheritance and me the independence of wealth and my own es-tablishment. This," she said, gesturing a hand to her abdomen but not able to bear looking at it, "was a foolish mistake when I thought a man could choose love over his own selfish desires."

"And you do not plan to tell him?" asked Rebecca, the desire to chastise her sister on her deceit evaporating in the face of such brokenness.

"Why should he know?" countered Rachel. "He made it clear when he thought me a barren woman that he would take his pleasure in my body and leave me by the wayside. He has no right to know that…" She faltered.

Rebecca saw the look of doubt in her eyes. Rachel spoke from anger, not wisdom, but who could criticise her for it?

"I…" Rachel looked into the flames as she spoke, the stalled words unstopped from a secret place within her. "I cannot force him to be a loving husband and father when that was not what he wanted. Not when he doesn't love me. I know I sound insane, but if you were within my mind, my heart, if you felt what I felt, you would understand that I cannot be with another who does not love me. I cannot bear it. Better that I get away with the independence he promised. The child and I can live somewhere secluded in the country away from prying eyes. I could even take another name."

"Rachel." Rebecca took one of her hands in her own but said no more for the time being. What could be said? What good would it do to say anything more?

"Do you love him?" asked Caro.

Silent tears rolled down Rachel's cheeks

and glistened in the firelight.

"I hate myself for it," she said finally. "For falling for it."

"Are you sure of his intentions?"

Rebecca looked at Caro in surprise, not seeing past her sister's hurt to the logic of the question.

"I do not say it to cause pain," Caro said, seemingly reading Rebecca's thoughts, "but what you are saying is a huge decision to make unless you are sure."

When no response was given, Caro spoke again. "I have seen the way he looks at you, Rachel. And though he is a stern and quiet man, I have watched him with you. He is not a man indifferent to his wife."

"Caro!" Rebecca rebuked.

"I shall call for food," Caro said after a moment's pause. "In your condition, you had best eat."

"I'm not hungry. And what you say cannot be true, Caro, however well-meaning you believe it to be. He has told me himself he means to follow through with our separation. No man who had feelings for me would make that decision and not with such certainty. I won't entrap him with a child. I cannot bear another loveless marriage. You would not understand."

"That's true—but I urge you to be sure. For now, you need to eat."

"I've told you. I do not wish it."

Caro came round the chair and bent down as far as her swollen stomach would allow to look directly in Rachel's eyes.

"From one woman who has been through traumatic circumstances to another, you will feel better for food, even if you don't feel hungry." She spoke sternly, as if she were a schoolmistress, and it seemed to have a rallying effect upon her charge. "Besides, you must eat for the child. After that, we may think of the future, but not before." She went straight to the bell and pulled it once sharply.

The servant was not long in appearing and Caro ordered turtle soup up to the little tapestry room. They encouraged Rachel to eat a little, then helped her to her feet and checked her face and hair. They then stoically returned to the ballroom and the rest of the evening went off as if nothing had happened.

People laughed and danced and ate and danced again. Music rang through the rooms of the Arleighs' London home and all Society went away considering the unorthodox wedding of the Viscount and his wife quite an acceptable thing. That was how it had all been planned after all.

That was what his mother had wanted and that was the plan that Rachel had agreed to.

Arleigh watched the servants removing the spoiled food, used porcelain, and spent wine glasses from the entertaining rooms. His mother and sister had already gone up, and he was standing at the foot of the stairs. The housekeeper and his butler were speaking to him about arrangements for the food, what could be kept and what would be given to the poor. They talked of the servants setting the house to rights early tomorrow morning, ready for the day ahead. They kept blathering on. It was their job after all, it was what he employed them for, but at this moment he cared nought for what they said.

"No, allow the servants some rest before they set to their chores tomorrow. Lady Arleigh and I are not expecting visitors, so there should be no need for the house to be restored immediately." Arleigh failed to keep the weariness from his voice. He passed a hand over his eyes and felt the puffiness of the skin there. The brilliant blue embroidered silk suit he had worn this evening was crumpled and tired, much like its wearer. "The food should of course be saved as best it can. The servants may have it tomorrow and we, I'm sure, can enjoy some of the ball's repast again. The remainder, as you say, can go to the poor. But for now, let us finish the immediate chores and put the house to bed."

The servants agreed with their lordship's

suggestions wholeheartedly, shadows of exhaustion over their own countenances as well as their master's.

Arleigh wondered where Rachel was. He had not seen her since that final dance she had taken with Mr Worth in lieu of Mr Felton who had promised it, but been required to take his tired wife home.

As he passed through the rooms in search of her, the servants could be seen pottering back and forth, hastened in their tasks by the thought of their beds and the promise of a morning off. The great chandeliers had been lowered and, one by one, the candles were snuffed out, their light disappearing much like the ball-goers, and in its place only shadows of what had been before.

He thought of the laughter and intimacy he and Rachel had shared and was suddenly afflicted by deep longing. The feeling ran through his limbs and hands, a desire to embrace her again. It ran through his stomach. And it ran in deep cracks across his chest.

He had been congratulated tonight, even sincerely by those who saw the value in Rachel and in his marriage, and superciliously by others who could not see past the secrecy and scandal of the wedding or the outspoken nature of his wife. They had all come to gawk and make merry and he had entertained them as he ought. He had done his duty, and now all he wished was to take refuge in the arms of the wife he had hurt, who no longer wished for his affection, and who would no longer be connected to his presence within a matter of weeks.

And that feeling came back, strong and unsettling, or rather it was a voice that questioned his motives, his decision, his soon-to-be actions. He thought of his mother's words earlier this evening.

"It has gone off well, Julius. Your father would have been proud."

Would he? All those staring eyes and inquisitive faces. Rachel had born it all with grace and an uncharacteristically silent tongue. He had watched her from afar and seen the paleness of her complexion and the lines about her mouth and brow, though she would clear them as soon as they had appeared and replace them with a pleasing smile and a look of deference to her guests.

On failing to find her in any of the public rooms, he ascended the stairs, lights snuffed out behind him by the servants, and a candle in his hand. The room that had been set aside for the ladies' powder room was vacant, so he carried on until he was outside Rachel's bedroom. The door was slightly ajar, the light of a few candles throwing itself out the door, and he stood in such a way that he had a fair view of the room.

He did not catch sight of her at first, expecting to see her either before the fire or in the huge bed. His eyes flew straight past her and then came back, as a cloud drew back from the face of the moon and the light from that celestial orb outlined the figure of his wife. He could see from her outline that she had discarded the tight stays needed for the ball gown she had been wearing and must have been clad instead in the banyan he had given to her. She was his banyan bride, but not for much longer.

He stood there, watching her; the outline of her figure and the steadiness of her head as she stared out of the window at what he knew not. He wanted to know. He wanted to read those thoughts of hers that had been so freely shared at the beginning and which she now kept hidden. Her heart and mind were locked away in a fortress and there was no way of scaling the walls. There was no way of knowing what lay within the citadel. He had built that citadel, brick by brick.

Arleigh's gaze drifted from where she stood to the fire, so he missed her turn and her sudden words caused him to jerk.

"Was there something you needed, my lord?"

His eyes looked back to her and she stood there, her arm wrapped around her, a handkerchief clasped beneath her chin. When she moved a little, not towards him, but further away, he noticed that she must not be wearing anything beneath the banyan as moonlight caught a pale strip of exposed skin.

Her arm moved to cover herself. He realised the candle he held illuminated his face clearly to her. She had seen the direction of his gaze.

"I only came to check that you are well. The ball did not tire you too much I hope?"

What a ridiculous thing, to ask such a question at past four in the morning, with the horizon beckoning the sun to rise.

Apparently she thought so, for she did not answer, but turned back to the window and somehow it seemed an invitation for Arleigh to enter the room. He paused only a moment longer on the threshold before entering and coming to stand beside his wife at the window. A few lone link boys trotted past the house below, their lights recently snuffed at their customers' doors and a farthing no doubt nestled in their pockets. Apart from that, the outside world was deserted at this hour. The buildings were largely unlit with only the moon to cast its unbending light across jutting architraves and porticos leaving the rest of the landscape to the night.

Everything was still. The servants must largely be abed, apart from Arleigh's valet who no doubt awaited him in his dressing room. He should have sent him to bed. Arleigh could undress himself tonight and besides, he was unsure when he would come to bed. Leaving to give the orders now would break whatever moment this was.

"You did well this evening," he said, the words sounding lame, as if he were praising a faithful hound. He metaphorically kicked himself.

Again she did not answer. Her silence uncharacteristic. So was the fact that she had not sent him from her presence.

"So they believe it," she whispered. "That our marriage is real."

He jerked his head in assent. The candle glowed between them.

"The deed is done. Can you believe it?" She spoke without anger or malice. "We shall soon be separated and no longer see each other. It is quite incredible."

He felt as if a lead weight had taken up residence on his chest.

"Your mother and sisters are abed?" she asked.

"They are."

"Then I shall go too."

And that was his cue. He left her by the window, but when he turned to close the door, she had not moved. She still stood looking through the panes, her thoughts secret from him.

Arleigh returned to his rooms and after undressing, ordered brandy and sat before his fire drinking. He could not sleep, and he wondered if the woman next door still stood by the window, staring out into the night, just as he did into the fire.

In one way the future was clear. The separation would be arranged, their paths would part, and he would return to his old life. But that future was wholly unappealing and in this moment, the words of Caro Felton came to him from that night at the ball, '... I see you hold affection for Lady Arleigh... you are... fortunate... a deal to do life together... marriage is a... covenant... if we did not promise... we would high-tail at the sight of the first hurdle... love is... the meeting of minds... '

Chapter 27

C aro was surprised to learn they had a visitor early the next morning. At least, it was before eleven, and therefore long before the time that either she or her husband had intended to get up after the ball. It had surprised her and Felton all the more to learn that it was Lord Arleigh who had arrived at their house and now awaited them in the morning room.

"What do you suppose he wants?" Felton pondered aloud as he shrugged himself into a woollen jacket.

"I should imagine," Caro started, realising that she had not had a moment in which to tell her husband of the conversation with Rachel and Rebecca the previous night, "that it is to do with the future of his marriage."

"His marriage!" Felton exclaimed, turning with surprise to his wife.

Caro sat clothed in an open gown at her dressing table with Libby dressing her hair as quickly as she could.

"What on earth about his marriage? We certainly have nothing to do with it and it has only just been exhibited to Society."

"Yes, well…" Caro caught Libby's eye in her looking glass and the old maid bobbed a curtsey.

"Right you are, madam, right you are. I shall disappear." And Libby did so, leaving Caro to turn to her husband and recount the conversations she had been privy to the night before.

"Well, I'll be damned! James said there was something going on, but I had no idea about this. And she is sure she is with child?"

"Over a month. It is early yet, but she is sure."

"And Arleigh has no idea," Felton repeated, his eyes looking into the middle distance. "But why is he here? We barely know the fellow."

"I have no idea, but it can't be a coincidence after what I learned last night," Caro said, rising from the chair and feeling as much in the dark as her husband.

"No, I guess it can't be," said Felton, offering an arm to his wife and escorting her downstairs to their unexpected guest.

Upon entering the morning room, they found Lord Arleigh looking out the window, his hands clasped behind his back, apparently having quite forgotten that he was in someone else's house and expecting their presence at any moment.

When Felton greeted him, before guiding his wife to a comfortable seat beside the fire, the Viscount looked quite as startled as if they had just appeared unexpectedly at his own door.

Caro watched him recover his countenance and incline his head to them both. He enquired after their rest and whether they had enjoyed the ball, but soon after, lapsed into silence.

Caro looked at Felton, whose own eyes belied a feeling of helplessness at the odd circumstances. He shrugged his shoulders and raised his eyebrows.

"And is Lady Arleigh well and recovered from the ball?" asked Caro, failing to make eye contact with the Viscount, who seemed to be busy studying the legs of her chair.

"I left before she woke this morning."

"Ah, I see."

She cringed inwardly, trying vainly to find something to say, but wanting all the time to ask him outright if he loved Rachel. She decided that it would not help the situation.

"Is there something we can do for you?" Caro asked gently, not wishing to appear rude.

"No."

"I think what my wife means," Felton began. Caro shot him a warning look which he ignored. "Is that coming to us so early after your own ball seems a little unusual. Especially as— if you do not mind me pointing out—we are not overly acquainted with your lordship. We can only assume that you wish to discuss something with us."

"Tobias!" Caro spoke under her breath but Arleigh talked over the reprimand.

"I must apologise for arriving at your home in such an unorthodox style. I just..." He trailed off and looked wholly unlike the usually aloof and commanding Viscount that they had met before.

"It is just that Mrs Felton said something to me a short time ago and it has played upon my mind of late. I came with the express purpose of speaking about it, but now I am here, I—I hardly know how to start or what it was I was going to say." He bowed awkwardly. "I will leave."

"Leave? Don't be ridiculous, Arleigh. I was hardly casting you out. Forgive my brash words —it is only that I assumed you wished to say something particular. Take a seat, man!"

"I shall ring for coffee," Caro chimed in. The Viscount had obviously come for a reason, and with all that they both knew about Arleigh and Rachel's current predicament, it would be plain foolishness to let him go without trying to help. It was obvious he was conflicted, and Caro and Felton had both agreed that Rachel's plan of raising the child in secrecy and alone was quite preposterous.

"What is it my wife has said to upset you so?" asked Felton, a mischievous smile upon his lips. "I am forever telling her not to say outlandish things."

Even Arleigh's straight mouth curved a little at this.

"Coffee would be most welcome."

"Excellent. Now do sit down. I am sure your feet hurt as damnably as mine after all that dancing last night." Felton gestured to a chair.

"Most kind." The Viscount took a seat and a short silence fell over the gathering again. After the coffee was ordered, he spoke.

"Perhaps I may ask you a question, Felton?" Upon a nod, the Viscount continued. "Do you consider the emotion of love to be able to overcome all obstacles in a marriage?"

Caro wondered if he knew of the child. Was he considering reneging on Rachel's deal in light of the news?

"I think the idea of love as simply a feeling is to completely misunderstand it. A man might feel a sense of honour in his word, but it is the action of him keeping it which is where the real power lies, is it not? Feelings are just feelings, but love demands action. I suppose you know a little of how Caro's and my courtship began?"

Caro wondered how much Felton might divulge. They had not told another person of what had happened between Felton and the Marquis of Ravensbough that fateful morning. It had been essential to keep her honour intact.

"I heard of a duel."

"Yes, Society rang with it for a while. I am

sure you can imagine that Caro had little affection for the idea of my duelling when I told her of it." Caro tensed a little at the thin ice on which Felton was treading, hoping that he would not fall through and show Arleigh that they knew everything. "That is why I told her after I called the man out. She had made me promise not to do anything foolish, but I had to do it in order to protect the woman I loved. I would have proven myself dishonourable in not protecting her. I would have disproved my love. What is a man's love for a woman if it is not willing to take action?" Her husband turned to her and let slip a wink. She felt the same old thrill run through her.

Arleigh had crossed his arms over his chest during this time and was rubbing his chin.

"Perhaps I am not a good person to ask," Felton said. "At least according to others."

"Don't be silly," Caro snapped. "You are a man of your word even under threat of death. That shows more honour than others exhibit in their whole lives." She thought of that silver scar on his abdomen where he had taken a sword for her. A wave of fresh love for the man she had married washed over her. He would make a good father to their child.

"That is why I wished to ask you both, though I know you say we are not well acquainted. When you spoke to me at that ball, Mrs Felton, you said that love was a meeting of minds. You spoke of hurdles..." He trailed off, clearly unsure how to word what he was trying to say.

"We have not been married long, but we have already overcome several hurdles—have we not, wife?"

Caro smiled back at him, knowing he hinted at their recent arguments.

"We must learn to be a team, like a fine pair pulling a curricle. That is how we see it. Sometimes we disagree, but we always pull in the same direction in the end, we must choose to love one another through it all. We both want our marriage to succeed."

Arleigh sighed.

"Then the question becomes," said Caro very gently. "Do you love your wife?"

He did not answer.

"If you do, then your duty is to her in both sentiment and action. For marriage is a covenant."

"But we do not know what it is you speak of," Felton said, glancing at Caro and continuing when he saw her nod. It was not their place to make decisions for this couple, no matter if they thought they knew what was best. These were not their lives to live or play with. "So it will come down to you. I would just urge you to remember that we only get one chance on this earth."

Caro and Felton both fell silent, allowing their words to settle in the Viscount's mind. He rose after a few minutes, saying he must return home. He thanked them, though they had no idea what they had helped him to decide, and Felton saw him out.

When her husband came back, Caro had her arms wrapped around her swelling abdomen, deep in thought.

"How did I do?"

She smiled at him. "Very well. It is so hard, is it not, when you see two people in love, not to encourage them to find each other." She held out a hand to him, squeezing his when he gave it. "Do you think that is why Lady Etheridge told you to marry me so bluntly? She saw we loved each other and said what she already saw. I can... I can see why you made the decision to do what you did with Rebecca and James. I would still want to know, but I see now how you must have thought, and why you made that decision."

He bent and kissed her.

"So many people in love, and we can only hope that they will find each other," she said.

"Thank goodness we have already done that. The whole thing is quite exhausting."

"I couldn't agree more. Perhaps we should go back to bed for a while."

"Perhaps we should."

"The ball was a great success," said the Dowager Viscountess, "You were quite the hostess."

"Thank you," Rachel replied.

Phoebe and Diana had yet to rise and so, after breakfasting, the Dowager had asked Rachel to walk with her in Hyde Park. They were strolling slowly, arm-in-arm, and for the first time since they had met, Rachel felt the Dowager was quite relaxed in her company.

"You know, you must have the family jewels. I have them in safekeeping. The tiara is with the bank, but the necklaces and bracelets that have been with the Arleighs for over a hundred years are all in my care. I shall have them sent round."

"Oh no, you need not do that yet."

"Nonsense—I should have given them to you before, so that you could have worn them last night. All this business with the solicitors had quite put the thought out of my mind, but now that it's settled and your marriage has had its societal debut, it should be done."

The sun was warm upon them. Rachel had thrown up again this morning, but recovered enough to be in company. Now however, although the nausea had abated, she felt a little faint in the heat. She pushed away the feeling and tried to concentrate on what the Dowager said.

"Perhaps we can wait a little." The meeting Arleigh was having with his solicitors this morning would not be 'settling' the matter as the Dowager so confidently asserted. He had left early, and there was nowhere else he could have gone. He must be arranging her settlement. "There is no rush."

"I would like to send them. The late Lord Arleigh gave them to me on my wedding day and I had always imagined giving them to my son's bride on her wedding day." She patted Rachel's hand. "Not that I am chastising you. I really am quite happy for you both. Now that we have this little time together, I can be honest, for I think we know that we had a tense beginning, but I am so happy for Julius. Even your refusal of the jewels tells me you are well suited. He needed a strong wife."

The Dowager smiled at Rachel, but the kind words and loving look only made her feel more faint. She had made up her mind last night, after being so close to telling Julius, that she would continue to keep the baby a secret. And then he had been gone this morning. She could only think that he had left to arrange her freedom. It was hard to hold him at arm's length, but at least he knew the deal. What about his family? His family were going to be so hurt by the separation.

"My husband was a strong man. He and I never seemed to share the equal footing that you and Julius do, even after such a short time. I... I admire that."

Rachel's step faltered.

"Are you all right, my dear?" The Dowager held Rachel's hand firmly on her arm, keeping her balanced. "Come, let's sit." She led Rachel to a bench and once she was seated, she looked her over critically. A sudden, small smile appeared upon her severe face.

"It was the same when I was with child."

Rachel felt the colour draining from her face. "What?"

"I thought it last night. I suspect my son has no idea. Men never do."

"No, no I am not," said Rachel vehemently.

"Very well, I apologise. It is probably not my place. I shall not say a word." The soft look was still on the Dowager's face and she appeared surprisingly indulgent, offering to keep the secret.

It only made Rachel feel worse.

"It is easier when you have had children of your own, to guess the condition in others— that is, if you *are* with child. We shall wait here a moment while you catch your breath and then we shall return home. You were not what I expected in a wife for my son," she carried on, sitting down next to Rachel and plucking at her skirts. "But despite your unorthodox ways and what I had heard of you, you are a most loyal wife to my son. You understand the duties that are demanded of a viscountess, and you performed them so well last night. All of our family acquaintances were quite taken with you. Arleigh said that it would be trying for you—he has the same dislike for society that you do—but you would not have known it last night."

Rachel suddenly understood that this was necessary for the Dowager. She needed to be allowed time to give her approval of her daughter-in-law, almost a rite of motherly passage, but it was so hard when Rachel knew the truth. If things had been different, she would have seen this as the beginning of their future relationship. They could have been a mother and daughter-in-law who saw eye-to-eye not dagger-to-dagger. They could have lived alongside one another. They could have been a family. It was her grandchild who grew within Rachel even now.

"He was intent on steering the most trying of the guests away from you all night. Though Lady Goring got through, I know. You dealt with her very well until Arleigh was able to bring her daughter alongside to escort her away."

She hadn't known that. That Arleigh had watched her all through the ball. That he had tried to spare her from the worst of it. That he had remembered how she hated Society gatherings, that she had been ridiculed at them, and people had judged her unorthodox ways. That was why he had kept certain people away from her. To help ease the burden, so she would not lose her temper or feel judged. He had cared for her.

She thought of how she had turned him away last night. All of her had wanted to go to him apart from that anchor of protection that held her in her secret, safe harbour. Had he come to her room really to see after her welfare? It had seemed he had wanted to say something more, but she had not encouraged him. After he had gone from her room, she had barely slept and every now and then, she had heard the clink of glass and wondered if he was awake for the same reasons as her.

But this morning had brought with it harsh reality. The separation was being brought about even now and he would no doubt do it as quickly and quietly as possible. She had wanted to stop him last night, to tell him the truth, but she could not live with another man who did not love her. She just couldn't.

"Well, I suppose I had better get back before my daughters arise and cause havoc in your house. Phoebe could not be kept away from the sweetmeats last night and I've no doubt she is pestering the housekeeper or might have even snuck into the kitchen by now. She is by far my most unruly child. It is always that way with the youngest." She glanced at Rachel's stomach, smiled quickly again, and then rose, offering her arm to her daughter-in-law.

"Come. Perhaps your husband has come

home by now."

Rachel took it thankfully, but did not respond to her comments. How could she, when her mind was in such utter turmoil? The Dowager thought her son at some club or other. Rachel knew better and she could not be there when he came back.

Chapter 28

A rleigh had needed time to think after speaking to the Feltons. Now, he was resolved on what needed to be done and the sooner the better. This whole palaver had gone on long enough. He was a pragmatic man and when he saw the logical end to something, the actions that needed to be taken were better done as soon as possible. More hurt needed to be avoided. Seeing the Feltons' love for each other had told him that. It was cruel to let something go on when a simple end could be obtained.

He returned home early evening, ready to act upon his resolve, but was shocked to learn that not only had his mother and sisters left, but so had his wife.

He was handed a letter by one of the servants immediately on entering the hall.

"Her ladyship left this for you, my lord, and…" The servant hesitated.

"What is it?" Arleigh asked impatiently. He had things to say that could wait no longer.

This deal needed to be ended now.

"Her ladyship took the carriage and a… a portmanteau. I believe she has gone away, my lord."

Arleigh did not respond to this, waving the servant away with a quick jerk of the hand and breaking the wafer on his wife's letter right there in the hall. It read,

Dear Arleigh,　　　　*27th February 1776*

By the time you read this missive I shall already be gone. I am headed to the hunting lodge. Forgive my presumption, but at this point, I am sure you are not shocked by it. I have taken my sister with me—you will forgive me that luxury. I have no wish to be in London when you arrive back with news of our arranged separation.

I have been a coward, I know, for I thought myself strong enough to face all this — the deal I promised to uphold, but after speaking to your mother this morning, I simply cannot. I cannot bear witness to the pain we are about to inflict on those around us, and ourselves. We were foolish to think such a deal could be struck and followed through without affecting others, without affecting us.

Send me news of when the deed is done and we no longer need see each other. Don't you think this is for the best?

I understand the duty you have to your family, but I have a duty to my heart also. It will not withstand more and so I must leave you.

Forgive me.

R

Arleigh dropped the hand which held the letter. This would not do. That damnable headstrong woman. What would Society think at the abrupt departure from London of the Viscountess Arleigh, directly after their ball and without her husband? After a few seconds, the fingers which held the paper were so loose with absentmindedness that the letter fluttered to the floor.

The Viscount's perfectly controlled countenance suddenly cracked. His fists clenched and he drew his shoulders back, letting forth a fearsome bellow.

"Fitz!" he shouted immediately after.

The scandalised servant appeared before his master.

Ignoring the servant's fearful countenance, he demanded the time that Lady Arleigh had quit the house.

"Just after midday, my lord."

Arleigh cursed himself for taking so long. He had wanted to be alone to think after speaking to the Feltons. If only he had come back sooner this mess could have been avoided. Rachel had managed to appear the picture of normality for the entirety of the ball, but apparently it had cost her too dearly.

It was gone five o'clock. She was well beyond London already.

"Is there a full moon tonight?"

"No, my lord. When she asked Dobbs, he suggested leaving right away if she wished to go. There can be no travelling tonight."

"Damn it all! I must remain in London until tomorrow. My solicitor will be arriving in the morning—tell my valet to pack a bag. I shall dine directly."

"Yes, my lord." The butler bobbed and scurried away like a mouse from a cat.

Arleigh went straight upstairs to wash and change for dinner. He ordered the meal to his library. He had paperwork to look over before he left tomorrow and he did not know how long he would be in Somerset.

He seated himself at the desk, flicking the skirts of his jacket out of the way with a precise movement. The line of his mouth was as firm as ever as he pulled a sheet of paper from a neatly packed bundle and laid it atop the fine leather surface of the desk. He opened a case lying before the inkstand and took out a knife and quill. He worked in quick, accurate movements, crafting a new tip and dipping it in the black ink. He set to work.

∞ ∞ ∞

"My Lady Arleigh."

The landlord of the inn they had arrived at barely ten minutes before had come to meet them at the entrance to the taproom. His face was rosy from the heat of the bustling inn and his eyes surprised but merry at seeing the Viscountess Arleigh so soon again at his establishment.

Rachel managed a wan smile. "Mr Norris, sister, the proprietor of this fine establishment."

"My lady." He bowed, smiling at his illustrious guests.

"Might we have a room for the night?" Rachel tried her best to sound heartened, but the journey had been long and arduous. She had asked Arleigh's driver to keep the horses going as long as he could. They had been travelling most of the day and well into the evening, as far as the daylight would allow.

"Yes, of course, my lady. And is his lordship travelling with you also?"

Rachel felt a muscle above her lip tighten at the mention of her husband. It must have made her look as though she were sneering at the poor, little landlord. She tried her hardest to relax and ignore the pain conjured within her heart, but she could not bring herself to answer. The journey had wearied her beyond bearing and her usual wherewithal was lost.

"Lord Arleigh is still in London. We have come to the country for a short break away," Rebecca said, filling the breach and carrying on in a tone that was both friendly and firm. "Would you mind if we were shown straight up to our rooms, and if you would be so good, have the cook send up some stew and bread for us both. We are quite famished and as you can imagine, wholly exhausted from the journey."

"Well... well, of course," said Mr Norris, smiling at the noblewoman he had never met before and only glancing once more at the worryingly pale Viscountess Arleigh. When he turned back to Lady Rebecca, he saw a certain look in her dark eyes that sent him running to the other room to order the food.

"Mr Dobbs, if you will unload our portmanteau in readiness before the carriage is taken away?"

Rachel could hear her sister, but she seemed further away than reality. Everything did. Everything was mute and she was numb. She had no wish to speak, a desire quite unnatural to her. She had nothing to say, she could make no sense of the thoughts in her head. There was much to think upon and nothing to say. And that which there was to think upon was painful, and after a time, she had just thought of nothing.

Numbness had stolen over her, starting in little waves, and now she was quite submerged.

"My dear, come, we are to follow Mr Norris."

Rachel felt her sister place her hand under her elbow and guide her forward. The chatter of the taproom, busy as travellers came in for supper, was like incomprehensible bubbles under the water to her.

They came to the same private parlour attached to the bed chamber she and Arleigh had been given the last time they were here. It could not have been anywhere else, for it was the only private parlour in the establishment. That's why she had asked Dobbs to stop somewhere else on the road, but he only trusted Mr Norris' stable lad to give the horses the proper seeing to they deserved. So they had come here.

It was the same as before. A little fire burning merrily in the grate. The table scrubbed clean and spread with fresh linen for their arrival. The room she had stayed in with Arleigh. It was like walking into the past. She blinked, screwing up her eyes, forcing those memories away, for she remembered laughing then and sharing of herself. She remembered trusting him then.

Rebecca guided her to a chair, and she was happy to be off her feet. She had been sat all day in the carriage, but to be still, without a lurching motion making her nausea all the worse, was such relief. They were left alone for a short time before the food came. Rebecca was saying something about the portmanteau and whether Nellie should unpack it now or later. Rachel wasn't listening.

When the door opened with Mr Norris and a servant girl bearing food, Rachel's head jerked upright, and she was suddenly aware that she had fallen sound asleep at the table.

She caught her sister's eye, but Rebecca said nothing until Mr Norris and the servant girl had retreated.

"We went rather too far today. The sight of you is fearful, I'm afraid. You are like the walking dead, my dear, and to think…" She glanced towards Rachel's stomach, obscured by the table. "We should perhaps have stopped earlier, but Dobbs was so insistent about the horses. You would think there were horse thieves working every other inn from London to Bath the way he speaks! Something about *priggers of prancers*. Poor Nellie looked frightened half to death by the way he was going on, whispering ominously. I had to stare him down quite ferociously to silence him, you know."

She was speaking a little too loudly and a little too brightly. She was trying to steer Rachel's mind away from her sombre thoughts. But those sombre thoughts would not leave Rachel tonight. They could not. She had chosen a path, five months ago, that would change her life forever. On that path had been a crossroads and she had decided on this way. There was no turning back now. Her life would change again and there would be no changing back. No harking back to those five months.

Rebecca rose from the table as soon as she had finished her repast and set to organising their things with Nellie in the bedchamber. It left Rachel alone to her thoughts and she realised, as she stared into the bright white embers of the fire, that her hand rested gently upon her stomach. There was a little comfort in the action. She almost resolved to move it when, for the first time since she had decided to leave Arleigh, she realised that she was not totally alone. Within her was a life, however small, however insignificant at present. Perhaps there was a tiny speck of light in the sky above the broken glass house of her heart. One day, it might shine upon her.

She glanced at the stew and bread which sat on the pewter plate before her. With less reluctance than in the last few days, she picked up the spoon and took a mouthful.

Rachel was unaware of her sister's eyes upon her from the bedchamber. She missed the brief smile of relief on her sibling's face. Apparently her sister was so frightened of disturbing this turn of events that she chose to quietly close the bedchamber door and leave Rachel to consume her first full meal in weeks.

∞∞∞

"You realise aunt Etheridge will be livid when she finds out you have gone with me."

"Nonsense!" Rebecca snapped. "Aunt E will fully understand my need to be with you at this time from my missive—oh don't look at me like that—I hardly told her you were with child. Although, knowing our aunt, she has probably guessed as much by now."

Rachel nodded, her expressive brow raised in assent at the conjecture.

"Perhaps, but she should be kept from any evidence of it if I am to keep the child a secret." Her gloved hands rested lightly on the small protrusion of her stomach and her eyes now followed the wall of the deer park that led up to the hunting lodge.

"Have you thought of where you shall set up once you have your independence? I have been thinking," her sister carried on before Rachel could reply. "If you were to settle within an easy distance of Bath, far enough removed so as to be quite hidden from Society there, then I am sure it would not take much to persuade aunt E to spend longer periods with her ancient beaus. I should be able to visit you."

"You shall do no such thing," Rachel said, cutting into her sister's stream of thought. "You shall never marry, or even be allowed in the lowliest of village assemblies, if there is so much as a hint of a scandal surrounding you."

"But I wish to meet my niece or nephew."

"And you also wish to settle down with your Mr Worth. He will hardly look kindly on a woman whose sister hid her child from the church, the law and her husband." Rachel allowed the briefest of smiles to cross her face. "I am sure papa would not be surprised at such an end for me."

"Oh do not talk so. End indeed."

"It is true, Becky, and the sooner you come to terms with it, the sooner you will be able to leave me behind in the wilds of some county far removed from Bath and London."

"I will not talk to you about this anymore. We can arrange it all later."

Rachel agreed to end the conversation. She knew she would not be able to argue with her sister. But this road she had chosen had its sacrifices. One of the largest had been made. Another would be to cut ties with her family. It was the only way to protect them, to some extent herself, and most importantly the child. She knew she would need a new identity in some place she would not be recognised or known. She had been thinking about it last night. It would be easy enough to make up some story of widowhood.

But all connections to her past must be severed if it was to be upheld. She would have to leave the place where Arleigh installed her upon their separation with all the independence he bestowed on her.

"Will you wed Mr Worth?"

"I hardly know." Her sister's gaze was now following the same flint and stone wall as her. "He helped me to find out the truth of what you hid from me, but I have not heard from him since."

"A child scolded is hardly quick to run back for another brow-beating. Don't you remember that poor governess of ours? We were forever hiding in the creamery or milking parlour from her foul moods. I hardly think men are much different, my dear, or women for that matter. There is a protectiveness we feel towards our hearts which is unconsciously triggered when we feel pain. We run away from that pain and the person who has caused it may need to persuade us to come back again.

"Is that what you are doing—running from your pain, dear sister?"

"It's different."

"I am no fool, Rachel. I know what it is you plan and the magnitude of it. I know you are in pain. I cannot know the extent of it, and I know Caro's words at the ball hurt you, but she was right. You must be sure."

"Here we are." Rachel ignored her sister in

favour of the carriage which was stopping before the doors of the hunting lodge.

She barely waited for Dobbs to let down the steps before she was out and breathing in the fresh country air. It was a relief after such a long journey and the constant sick feeling in her stomach. But just as she turned her face skywards, a series of heavy raindrops fell upon her skin.

"Weather's been on the turn behind us, my lady. Seems it's finally caught up." Dobbs ran to the door and rapped upon its ancient oak to rouse the housekeeper to readiness.

It was opened and they were admitted to the dim, ancient corridors of the Elizabethan lodge. Oiled oak ran along the walls. Rachel had forgotten how dark it was here and in this light, it appeared gloomy. When she had last been here, the weather had been bright. The future had been bright.

She followed the surprised-looking housekeeper to the morning room.

"I am most sorry, my lady. Had I known you were arriving, I would have had the rooms made ready for you." The middle-aged woman was blushing furiously and had curtseyed thrice already.

"It's quite all right, Mrs Fesse. We were not expected and so I had no expectation of the rooms being ready. I apologise for our abrupt arrival. We will be fine in here while you prepare two bedrooms for myself and my sister, Lady Rebecca. If you would be so good as to bring us some tea?"

The way she fell into her old role of mistress so easily surprised her a little. She had been grieving so deeply over the last two days that she was shocked she could speak coherently. But it did come back to her easily. She had learned her role well over the past months.

She remembered this housekeeper's name because Mrs Fesse had been the one to order the picnic they had enjoyed when Arleigh had taught Rachel archery. The housekeeper had smiled indulgently at her new mistress when Rachel giggled at something Arleigh whispered in her ear. Mrs Fesse had bobbed away, the smile still on her face. That was now so long ago.

"Right away, my lady."

She left the sisters in the morning room. They were surrounded by a sea of white. Sheets had been spread over all the furniture to keep the dust at bay. It was like walking among ghosts, surrounded by what was no longer here. She touched gloved fingers to the chairs that were scattered about the empty fireplace. They had lain there, together, before the fire in each other's arms until the birds had begun their morning chorus.

The memory sent a lancing pain through Rachel's heart and she snatched her hand away as if the pain were physically transferring itself.

She had made it here. She had held it together. She had escaped to safety before the severing of her ties to the man she… to her husband.

With that realisation, the mask she wore fractured. Tears came in a flood, and a great soulful wail escaped her before she collapsed on the floor among the ghosts.

Chapter 29

Arleigh changed horses at another inn without stopping to rest. He had left London the day before and made a brief overnight stop when the light forced him off the road. Since dawn, he had ridden like the devil himself. The hired hacks he'd been on since switching from Sampson yesterday were hardly a match for his grey. The gelding he rode now was lighter in build and clearly struggling with Arleigh's height and weight. The slower pace was trying the Viscount's nerves and the renewed rainfall was doing nothing to improve his mood.

Arleigh's valet had been shocked when his master had said he would not be needed. It would only slow the Viscount down and this had gone on long enough. He needed to get to the hunting lodge and with every mile closer, his thoughts became more frantic and the need to arrive more urgent.

Water ran off the capes of his greatcoat in streams. He pulled the brim of his beaver lower in an effort to ward off the rain from his eyes as he finally managed to break the nag into a canter. His thighs were numb beneath the soaked buckskin breeches. The long skirts of his coat could not be persuaded to stay over his legs when he went at any pace above a walk and as such he had been soaked as soon as he had left London. He was used to riding in such weather on his estate and while a lesser man might have turned back or at least stopped at an inn, Arleigh was no lesser man today.

By the time he crested the hill which swept down towards the lodge, every muscle ached and throbbed, and to say that he was bruised from the gruelling ride was an understatement. But he had to do this, and soon. He had made a decision. The line of his mouth was as firm as ever and in spite of the weary shadows beneath his eyes where sleep had been stolen from him, the eyes themselves were bright with purpose.

He allowed the nag's canter to lull to a walk and gave him his head, holding the buckle of the reins and leaning back in the saddle to give his back some relief. Now that the lodge was in sight, he was reminded of why he was here. He was reminded that he had things to say—things that must be said. He had to act. And staring at the flint wall of the deer park, which was rising towards him, he felt bereft of words. How should he deal with this? What would he say, specifically? He knew what he wished to be done —

no, what needed to be done — in the name of duty and honour, but his heart and mind, though strong in their conviction, did little to yield useful words.

∞ ∞ ∞

To say that Rebecca was surprised by the sight of the Viscount Arleigh, dripping wet in the hallway of the hunting lodge, would be a gross understatement. She was shocked beyond belief as she came out of the morning room to find the origin of the commotion in the hall.

There he stood, towering above Mrs Fesse and one of the under footmen, a great ominous figure clad in an enormous dark and soaked coat. His hat was pulled low on his forehead, a scarf wrapped around his neck, and a whip in his hand. If the latter had been exchanged for a pistol, Rebecca was sure she would have thought him some highwayman.

"Mrs Fesse, never mind refreshment. Where is my wife?"

Rebecca had frozen on the threshold of the morning room and half of her was inclined to retreat before she was seen. It was too late. His frank gaze caught her.

He moved forward and she could see he

had left a pool of rainwater on the hall floor and was tracking a considerable amount more with his footsteps. Mud and grit were plastered up his leather boots and had splattered the buckskins she could see through the open front of his coat. He really did look like some vagabond rather than an aristocrat. If the situation had been different, she might have commented and even rebuked him for it. But the dirtily dressed Viscount had a look in his eye that she knew would be unwise to provoke.

"Lord Arleigh," she said, curtseying and waiting for him to speak. She needed to know why he was here before she gave anything away.

"Lady Rebecca." He removed his hat in a shower of raindrops, revealing unpowdered, wet and bedraggled hair, barely kept at bay by the black ribbon at its back.

He had a spot of mud high on one of his cheekbones. It was as if he wore a mocking patch on that unpowdered, undandyfied face.

"I trust you are well?" he asked, as if they had run into each other on the street. He must know that she knew all. That was the only reason Rachel would have asked her here. He must know.

"Yes, I thank you. We were not expecting you. Have you ridden through the night?"

"Alas no," he said, handing his hat and whip to the waiting footman and starting to peel the wet, shrunken leather gloves from his hands.

"There has been no moon to travel by the last few nights — as I'm sure you're aware."

It was a pointed statement. There was an edge to his voice.

"I have been riding for two days. If you would be good enough to tell me where your sister is, I must speak with her."

"She was not expecting you. I believe she thought you were to send a letter notifying her of any arrangements."

Rachel had not once mentioned the possibility of Arleigh coming here.

Why was he here? Had he really ridden all this way to give her the news of their impending separation in person? If so, what was the reason for it? It would not make the news any easier to hear. In fact, Rebecca was sure it would make it harder. Her sister had wept for much of the afternoon yesterday before retiring early to bed. Rebecca had heard her footsteps until she had drifted off to sleep in the small hours herself. And when she had risen this morning, Rachel was already up. She doubted her sister had slept at all.

"I'm going for a walk," Rachel had declared on seeing Rebecca in the breakfast room. She had already been dressed, with an old greatcoat about her shoulders.

"A walk? My dear, have you even breakfasted? Besides, the clouds are not looking kindly upon the country. It will surely rain soon."

"I don't care! I cannot be in here." Rachel had gestured around her and then she had left.

Now here was Lord Arleigh, demanding her whereabouts, and Rebecca was not sure it was wise to tell him.

"A letter would not suffice. Shall we adjourn to the morning room?"

Rebecca assented, though she needn't have bothered, for regardless of her answer, he strode so quickly towards her that she almost tripped over, scurrying back into the room she'd been reading in since Rachel had disappeared. A tray of spent tea things was resting on a table near the fire and the furniture had been released from its coverings making the old-fashioned room quite usable.

She could hear the Viscount refusing refreshment a second time and then the heavy thud of the oak door closing. She moved over to the fire, making a show of warming her hands, and then turning, with false innocence on her face, to Arleigh.

"How was your ride? I am not sure of many people who could ride from London to the Mendips in barely two days. You must be exhausted."

"It hardly has any bearing," he replied, eyes locked onto the carpet in front of the fire before they flicked up at her. "Am I to believe that you know the whole?"

The blunt words caused Rebecca to pause. Her hands stopped halfway through warming themselves and her brown eyes rested on the Viscount's unflappable face for several moments before she spoke.

"I am aware."

"Where is she? I have pressing business with her."

"Business? Yes, I believe this whole thing was a business deal was it not?" Rebecca couldn't help but let a little venom creep into her voice. She had been of no comfort to her brokenhearted sister yesterday. If she could be anything, she would be a barrier to further harm. "She was expecting a letter to confirm her independence. You had no need to ride like a madman across half the country to tell her as much."

She watched Lord Arleigh's lips purse.

"Am I to tell her that it is settled? You may tell me the particulars of the independence she is to receive, and *I* shall pass it on. I do not believe she will be available for your call. After that, you will see her no more." No one shall, thought Rebecca.

Arleigh did not immediately respond. He walked across the room to where large shutters were open to a vista of the deer park. He shrugged off the coat he had hitherto not relinquished, throwing it across a chair and taking its partner opposite. Crossing his legs, he took his chin in his fingers and stared out at the view for several minutes.

Rebecca wondered if she should order

fresh tea. He did not seem inclined to speak further. Perhaps she should just leave him here. He might wish to rest a little. Or perhaps he was angry. She started towards the door, but upon seeing movement, she turned and saw the Viscount rise quickly and come back to his uninvited guest. He clasped his hands behind his back and levelled her with his gaze.

"I shall not tell you the particulars of the settlement, for I have made none. Now, if you will be so good as to tell me the whereabouts of my wife, I wish to tell her as much myself." He spoke testily.

"You mean you will not give her the settlement you promised?" asked Rebecca in horror.

"I mean I have not arranged for her settlement or separate establishment," he replied, his eyes hard upon her own.

He looked like a man caught between the desire to strike out in frustration and the desire to be understood.

"Why?"

"That," he said with emphasis, "is something I wish to discuss with my wife and not her sister. I did not expect to have to explain myself to you before I could do so to her, and have had no pleasure in doing so. Please excuse me."

"But..." She watched as he turned towards the door and strode away. "You love her."

His step was arrested, just as his hand fell upon the door handle.

"I shall find her myself."

"She's not here."

He turned towards her.

"What do you mean she's not here. Her letter said…"

"She went for a walk this morning," Rebecca cut in, her voice suddenly betraying the worry she had been feeling ever since Rachel had left.

Arleigh's eyes flicked quickly to the rain-soaked country outside the window.

"Yes, I know. I told her not to go, but she would not listen. She left a little under an hour ago. I was just about to send Dobbs after her when you arrived. She will catch her death in this weather, especially…" Rebecca stopped abruptly, but thankfully the Viscount seemed not to notice. It was not her place to say anything. Rachel had made her swear not to speak of the child. She only hoped her sister would see sense when Arleigh found her. Rebecca could see the sincerity in his eyes. More than that, she hoped Rachel was well.

"Stubborn, headstrong woman!" Lord Arleigh snapped in an uncharacteristic loss of temper. He snatched up his greatcoat, swinging it high as he pushed his arms back into its soaked depths, and threw the door open. He paused only briefly, as he thought of something. "I shall find her. Order a hot bath to her room. She shall need it if she has been out in this infernal weather for as long as you say."

And then he left.

Arleigh's heart had not slowed since hearing of his wife's disappearance into the grounds. According to the gamekeeper, he had seen her enter the deer park and head towards the old stone bridge which spanned the stream that fed the lake. It would have been quicker on horseback, but the nag he had ridden in on was spent and the rest of the riding mounts were still in London.

His quick pace was hampered by the rugged terrain of the tufted grasses. The downpour was steady. He had replaced his hat and the rain ran in rivulets across its brim, onto his greatcoat, and cascaded down the capes. Was she really out in this?

His pace quickened again as he scanned the countryside in sweeping looks. Everywhere had been turned to a muted grey by the rain and even the few deer and other animals he caught sight of were taking refuge beneath canopies of trees and bushes.

He followed the faint path that wound through the wild grassland to the right until the lodge was out of sight. A little further and the bridge would come into view. When it did however, his heart dropped. He could not see her there. He continued regardless and got to the firm surface. He came to its heightened middle and scanned the parkland in a full circle.

If his senses hadn't been heightened by the thought of his wife's exposure, and that he might be the cause of any danger she faced, he might have missed it. There was the flash of a coat and that of a skirt between the trees which lay across the clearing beyond the bridge. He kept his eyes trained on the woods, and after a few moments, he saw it again. She came from the direction of the hill which lay behind the lake. Had she been up there?

He didn't linger any longer. He struck out from the bridge across the clearing and was thankful when he saw her emerge from the trees, making her way back towards the bridge. Towards him.

He slowed his pace. What was he to say to her? He wanted to shake her for coming out in this rainstorm. He wanted to embrace her to make up for all the pain he had caused her.

Her long strides that had at first appeared sure became laboured, and a few times she faltered. Her head was bowed, her wild hair loose and dripping about her shoulders. She had not seen him. She did not see him until she was within ten paces of him. He had stopped to watch her approach. When her eyes caught sight of his boots, she stopped in her tracks and looked up.

She did not say a word as her eyes looked into his. He could see the shock on her face, but she looked more exhausted than anything else. At first he wondered if she really saw him, if she knew he was here and not some phantom. When she did not move, her hands clenched on the skirts of the coat she wore, rain dripping from her eyelashes, he spoke.

"Rachel..."

"No!" She raised a hand and made to turn. "No, you are in London. You are not here. I made my peace with that. I am never to see you again."

"Wait, Rachel, wait!" He moved forward, his hand outstretched. "You must come back to the house. You'll catch your death."

She did not respond except to freeze where she was.

"Why are you here?" she said finally on a ragged breath.

"I have come..." The words failed him. They died where they had sprung up from his heart because of the pain which lay there. Pain at seeing her so hurt, so broken, and knowing he was the cause. All he wished to do was to wash it all away. "I have come for you, Rachel, my heart, my wife."

He saw the muscle in her jaw clench and her lips quiver against the incessant raindrops.

"Rachel, my love—it all belongs to you. How can I ever part with someone who is a part of myself? You are the only woman I have—will ever—love." He reached for her again, his hands falling on her arms, but they were listless, frozen to his touch.

"What are you doing?" She pulled violently out of his grasp and stepped back. "Why are you doing this to me? We had a deal, did we not? We promised and you upheld it. You need not feel guilty for treating me as every man has. For taking what you needed and leaving me. Why are you here?" she cried again, and he heard the first notes of a sob in her voice. Her shoulders shook and he wondered if it was now warm tears and not cold rain upon her cheeks.

"Rachel, I love you." He came to her again, and did more than take her shoulders, embracing her, pulling her close to him as she cried. "Please, I came here for you. I have been a fool. You are all that I want, and I was blinded by my fear. I could not bear to be the cause of pain to you and so I kept you away from me. I said things I did not mean. Forgive me." His cheek lay against the side of her head as he whispered the words. It was all coming out wrong, muddled, unclear, but it was coming out, nonetheless. He had never been able to articulate himself as he wished and declaring his love for the woman he could not live without was no different. "You are the woman I love and no matter what we face we can overcome it together. That is all that matters."

"I cannot. No," she whispered between tearful sighs. "I cannot." She pushed against him and reluctantly, he released her.

He saw the look of brokenness in her face. He had not been able to bind it together with his words. He cursed himself.

She shook her head gently and began to walk away through the wet grass.

There was a moment when everything stilled, as he watched her slipping so easily through his fingers. She was going to see their deal through regardless. Even though he knew her hurt, her heartbreak was because of the love she felt for him. He loved her, she loved him, he knew it, and yet still she walked away.

"Rachel!" he shouted, suddenly, loudly bellowing the name, sending a few stray deer that were hiding beneath an oak leaping away into the undergrowth. "No!" He set off at a dead run and caught up with her in a matter of moments.

He took hold of her arm and swung her round to face him firmly.

"You don't understand. I *love* you Rachel. I cannot... I cannot breathe without you." He felt the prick of tears behind his eyes. "I cannot let you leave, not when I know you feel the same way. This started as a deal, but it will end with this." He freed a hand and gestured between them. "With love." And with that, he kissed her.

His lips fell upon hers, as soft, as sweet as he remembered them. Raindrops ran between them and for the first time he felt her respond. It was as if she came alive to him again. At first it was in her lips, and then as much as she had resisted it within herself, she melted against him, her frame held within his arms, her hands coming up and running through his wet hair now loose about his shoulders.

"Oh, I love you," he murmured against her lips. "I love you, I love you, wife. Don't ever go away from me again." She was here. In his arms. Where she was supposed to be. Everything he had to say had been said. All he had resolved to do had been done.

"I feel," she said, pulling back and swaying a little, her weight falling onto his left arm. "I feel…" she repeated again, trailing off, her eyes struggling to focus on him. "I feel faint."

As soon as the words had left her lips, she crumpled in his arms.

Arleigh called her name, immediately taking the weight of her shoulders in one arm and picking up her legs with the other.

"Rachel." He spoke her name into her rain-covered face, but she was unconscious. He pushed his cheeks against hers. She was frozen. Her skirts were soaking along with the coat.

He didn't wait any longer. He set off, as fast as his legs would carry him, his wife's unconscious body in his arms.

Chapter 30

I t was the second time that day that Rebecca had been brought into the hall by a commotion. But nothing quite prepared her for the sight of her sister, fainted in Lord Arleigh's arms.

"It's exposure," Arleigh shouted, his eyes alight with fear, and his voice hoarse from running. "The bath, did you order it?"

"Yes, yes, it's ready in the dressing room. Quickly!" Rebecca knew what needed to be done as well as the Viscount. She snatched up her skirts and ran up the stairs, her brother-in-law not far behind with his precious burden. She threw open the door to the dressing room, ringing the bell immediately for hot bricks to be put in the bed and a doctor to be called.

"How long has she been like that."

"A short time. She was conscious when I found her." The Viscount was already stripping the coat and outer layers from his wife's body. "She fainted in my arms. We must get her warm."

"Heaven's above! Thank God you found

her. But the child." Rebecca wrung her hands, pacing feverishly, before she dropped to her knees to help the Viscount with the fastenings of Rachel's stomacher.

The Viscount only paused for a moment. "Child?"

Tears had filled Rebecca's eyes and they spilled down her cheeks as she answered. "She is with child, my lord."

She saw something intangible flicker across the Viscount's face before he turned back to his work and set to it more quickly than before. They had her released from her dress, stockings and stays in barely any time at all. On a knock at the door, Rebecca left the Viscount to give the servant their orders.

All Rachel wore now was her thin chemise. Arleigh put a tender arm beneath her back and another beneath her legs and lifted her. He bit against his cheek, blinked twice, and then gently placed her in the water.

"Tell them to bring more water up!" he barked towards the half-open door. He kept an arm around his wife's back to prevent her slipping and found her hand with the other. He squeezed it tightly and whispered against her hair, begging her to wake.

Rebecca came back into the room a few moments later and took up position on the other side of the copper bathtub.

"I have ordered extra blankets for her bed

and as many hot bricks as can be managed, and Dobbs has gone for the nearest doctor." She relayed her activities, not expecting an answer from the man who stared unremittingly at his wife's sleeping face. "Can I help to hold her?"

The nod of his head was barely perceptible. He pulled his soaked arm out slightly so Rebecca could hold her sister's other side. Water that had saturated the woollen arm of his jacket poured all over the floor and re-wetted his buckskin breeches.

"If she does not recover... I will never forgive myself. I did this."

Rebecca saw a tear fall from the Viscount's eye into the steaming water, then another from that strong face. She reached across the tub and touched his arm. "She *will* recover." She held his gaze briefly, but in that moment she imparted all the hope she could.

"Rub her hands and feet to warm them," said the Viscount. "Once she is warm to the touch, we will move her into the bed." He paused before he spoke again. "She did not tell me."

"I know." Rebecca felt suddenly guilty at her knowledge of the child. "She... she did not wish you to choose her for that reason alone. She found out after she thought you would give her up."

"I have been the cruellest of men."

"Please, don't be so hard on yourself. She is one of the most stubborn women. Trust me, it runs in the family." She managed a small smile.

A knock on the door heralded fresh water. Arleigh handed over his wife's weight to his sister-in-law and poured the two jugs of water into the tub. He rubbed Rachel's feet and hands and after a while the heat returned to them. He lifted her from the bathtub and carried her through to the bed.

"Julius."

He stopped, quickly looking down to Rachel whose eyelids fluttered.

"Rachel? My love. Rachel?" he whispered.

Rebecca swept into the room. "Is she awake?"

"Not anymore. Quick, let's get her under the covers."

"That's a good sign, isn't it?"

Arleigh didn't answer. He laid her gently on the bed on which a fresh chemise was laid along with towels. They towelled off her body as well and quickly as possible and changed her chemise. Swaddling her in blankets and removing the bricks from the bed, they bundled her into it.

"Will she be well?" Rebecca asked, a tremble in her voice as she looked at her unconscious sister, her certainty faltering.

She felt a gentle hand cover her own and squeeze it.

"The doctor will be here soon," said Arleigh.

∞ ∞ ∞

Rachel opened her eyes to a room flooded with sunlight. Her eyelids fluttered against the brightness at first. She felt someone take her hand. They squeezed her fingers. She turned her head a little, opening her eyes again, seeing the face of her husband.

"You scared me," said Arleigh.

She made to speak his name, but her throat was too dry to do anything but rasp.

"Here."

She closed her eyes against the light. She felt so tired. She could hear the clink of a bottle. Then she felt a hand beneath her head, lifting her a little and the cold, thin feel of a glass being pushed against her lips.

"Drink this," Arleigh said gently.

It was sweet and herbal. It soothed.

After a few moments, she pushed against the covers and felt Julius' hands helping her to sit up. He gave her a pillow to rest against and she pulled the banyan she was wearing tighter around her, unconsciously resting a hand upon her stomach.

"I must let your sister know you are awake. She only went to bed an hour ago when I threatened to carry her from the room."

"Wait." Rachel stretched out a hand to waylay him. He came back and sat upon the covers beside her. He was ill-dressed, in a dirty, open shirt and filthy buckskin breeches. His hair was loose about his shoulders and he clearly hadn't slept. She remembered those clothes from the deer park. At least, she thought she did.

"What happened?"

"You don't remember?" His hand wouldn't leave hers. It was warm and comforting.

"I remember us fighting."

He raised a brow at that, his mouth pursed mockingly. "*You* were fighting. *I* was telling you that I love you."

She felt heat rush into her cheeks at the blunt words.

"At least you are getting your colour back," he said, picking up her hand and kissing the back of it. Lingering, his breath warm against her skin. He was smiling. He was smiling like a mad person. "I thought for a moment… but the doctor examined you and told us you had no fever, and it was just exhaustion from carrying the child through a rainstorm and barely eating the last few weeks."

He kissed her hand again when her fingers involuntarily gripped his.

"Your sister told me last night, when I brought you in from the rainstorm. You fainted in my arms. She was worried not only for you, but for the child." He looked at the hand she had laid protectively over her stomach. "We are to have a child," he whispered. And then he laughed. The sound was filled with such joy that tears started in Rachel's eyes.

"Yes," she whispered, her feelings indescribable.

He smiled. "I came for you before I knew that."

She nodded slowly.

"And I loved you before I knew that."

She nodded again.

"Forgive me?"

She gave a third nod.

He moved closer to her on the bed, so they were only inches apart. "I do—you know—love you." He leant towards her, so his lips were moments from hers. "And you love me, do you not, Rachel, Viscountess Arleigh?"

"Yes."

"Good. Well, that's settled then." He smiled again, a glint in his eyes. "I have another deal for you. Be my wife, mother of my children, and do life with me." His smile grew broader. "I think we should seal this deal with a kiss."

"I'm not sure one kiss will be enough."

The End

About The Author

Philippa Jane Keyworth

Philippa Jane Keyworth, also known as P. J. Keyworth, writes historical romance and fantasy novels you'll want to escape into.

She loves strong heroines, challenging heroes and backdrops that read like you're watching a movie. She creates complex, believable characters you want to get to know and worlds that are as dramatic as they are beautiful.

Keyworth's historical romance novels include Regency and Georgian romances that trace the steps of indomitable heroes and heroines through historic British streets. From London's glittering ballrooms to its dark gaming hells, characters experience the hopes and joys of love while avoiding a coil or too! Travel with them through London, Bath, Cornwall and beyond and you'll find yourself falling in love.

Keyworth's fantasy series The She Trilogy unveils a world of nomadic warrior tribes and peaceful forest-dwelling folk. Explore the hills, deserts and cities of Emrilion and the history that is woven through them. With so many different races in the same kingdom it's become a melting pot of drama and intrigue where the ultimate struggle between good and evil will bring it all to the brink of destruction.

Ladies of Worth Series

From the gaming hells of 18th century London to Bath's fashionable Pump Room, the Ladies of Worth series opens up a world of romance, wit and scandal to its readers. With formidable heroines and honourable heroes who match each other wit for wit you'll find yourself falling in love with the Ladies of Worth.

Fool Me Twice

In the gaming hells of eighteenth century London, orphan Caro Worth is leading a double life.

By day she plays a proper gentlewoman on the lookout for a wealthy husband. By night she plays the infamous Angelica, her fictional half-sister with a talent for cards and an ability to finance the life her respectable self has built. An introduction to a rich Marquis brings marriage and security within Caro's grasp...until the arrival of the unpredictable and totally ineligible Mr. Tobias Felton. Dismayed by Felton's persistent appearances, shocking frankness, and enigmatic green eyes, Caro watches helplessly as he comes closer than anyone to guessing her secret, but when complete and utter ruin threatens, she finds that Felton's suspicions just might become her salvation.

As the walls she has built to protect herself crumble down around her, Caro learns that no matter how careful your plans, life and love have a habit of falling quite spectacularly out of control!

Books By This Author

The Widow's Redeemer

A penniless young widow with an indomitable spirit. A wealthy viscount with an unsavory reputation.

London, 1815: After her husband's untimely death, Letty Burton comes up from the country with her domineering mother-in-law. Hiding a past she wishes to forget and facing an uncertain future, all she wants is to navigate London Society as a silent companion. A chance meeting with London's most eligible bachelor sets in motion a series of events that will bring her quiet life under the unfriendly scrutiny of the ton. With the net of scandal, debts, and rivals closing in, will she let her dark past dictate her life forever? Will she learn to trust again? And most importantly, will she allow herself to love?

The Widow's Redeemer was a finalist in the 2012 RONE Awards (Reward of Novel Excellence) hosted by InD'Tale Magazine.

The Unexpected Earl

Six years after being jilted without a word of explanation, Julia Rotherham finds Lucius Wolversley standing before her once again–unexpected, unannounced, unwelcome.

With her heart still hurting and, more importantly, her pride, Julia must chaperone her younger sister, fend off fortune hunters, orchestrate a fake engagement, and halt an elopement–all whilst keeping the man who jilted her at arm's length. But what Julia doesn't know is that this time, the Earl has no intention of disappearing, and this time he has more than an explanation to offer…

The Edict

Amidst robberies, prison breaks, palace intrigues, and an oncoming war, the struggle for peace rests on the shoulders of unlikely allies…

The Reluwyn Empire of Emrilion spans from the Northern Moors to the Tao Desert. The Laowyn, a people chosen by the Spirit, are subject to the Regent's harsh rule on behalf of the Prince and a raft of oppressive Edicts is about to tip the scales toward rebellion. The Laowyn Resistance defend against persecution but the Regent Garesh's stranglehold on power is unrelenting. In a bid to solidify his position he arranges for the Edict of Maidens to gather all eligible brides for the Prince's choosing that the royal might ascend the throne as King with Garesh at his side as rightful power-wielder.

Kiara, a Laowyn woman whose race remains a secret, is chosen for the Prince but before she can be taken she escapes under the guise of a boy. Falling from one captor to another she eventually comes face-to-face with the man she loathes and suddenly two very different worlds collide.

The Edict is an epic fantasy and love story forming the basis of a trilogy that will see the fantasy world brought to the brink of destruction with only a chosen few capable of protecting it.

Printed in Great Britain
by Amazon